The Limbo Line

BOOKS BY

VICTOR CANNING

Mr Finchley Discovers his England
Mr Finchley Goes to Paris
Mr Finchley Takes the Road
Polycarp's Progress
Fly Away Paul
Matthew Silverman
Fountain Inn
Everyman's England (travel)
Green Battlefield
Panthers' Moon
The Chasm
The Golden Salamander
A Forest of Eyes
The House of the Seven Flies
Venetian Bird
The Man from the 'Turkish Slave'
Castle Minerva
His Bones are Coral
The Hidden Face
The Manasco Road
The Dragon Tree
Young Man on a Bicycle (and other stories)
The Burning Eye
A Delivery of Furies
Black Flamingo
Delay on Turtle (and other stories)
The Limbo Line
The Scorpio Letters
The Whip Hand
Doubled in Diamonds
The Python Project
The Melting Man
Queen's Pawn
The Great Affair
Firecrest
The Rainbird Pattern
The Finger of Saturn
The Runaways
Flight of the Grey Goose
The Painted Tent
The Mask of Memory
The Kingsford Mark
The Crimson Chalice
The Doomsday Carrier

The Limbo Line

VICTOR CANNING

HEINEMANN : LONDON

William Heinemann Ltd
15 Queen Street, Mayfair, London W1X 8BE

LONDON MELBOURNE TORONTO
JOHANNESBURG AUCKLAND

First published 1963
Reprinted before publication
Reissued 1972
Reprinted 1977

434 10751 4

Printed in Great Britain by
REDWOOD BURN LIMITED
Trowbridge & Esher

Spying might perhaps be tolerable if it were done by men of honour; but the infamy which inevitably attaches to the agent is a criterion of the infamy of the practices.

MONTESQUIEU

I

A HAND CAME over his shoulder and dropped a sheet of paper on the table before him. He did not look round, for he was day-dreaming.

'For London. Immediate.'

The familiar voice, edged with authority, with never an accent of kindness, dissipated the soft veils of his dreams. He nodded, still without turning, and heard the footsteps go out of the room. He did not look down at the paper. Everything was immediate here. It could wait a while.

He stared out at the August sunshine, over the busy strip of the Quai des Célestins, across the fork of the Seine to the Île St Louis. Two girls – they looked like tourists to him, American or English – leaned over the parapet; and the forward hunch of their shoulders drew their skirts up over their buttocks, so that he could see the back of their knees. The sight brought back his reverie, rosy, sensual, exciting. He luxuriated in it, seeing only Michèle lying back on the divan in her cheap room. He was a fool, he knew that. Through her he was walking straight into disaster. The oldest weakness in the world possessed him and he did not care. He might survive for a time, but in the end he would be destroyed. But did that matter? What was important was how the time, long or short, was spent.

He looked down at the paper. It read:

Agrip to Capa.
Give soonest date on Irina Tovskaya

Alexandre pulled the cipher books towards him and began

to encode the message. He worked automatically, and with ease. Ciphers and codes had been his life. That was the trouble, he told himself, there had been no other life. It was a wonder that he had not been given a Bazeries cylinder, instead of a rattle to play with as a baby. Transpositions, biliteral monoalphabetic substitutions, polyalphabetic systems; the whole of his life had become a cryptogram. Alexandre, the cryptogram. And, like every other cryptogram, he admitted to himself, it could be broken.

The clocks were striking twelve as he finished the enciphering. He dropped the message into the dispatch room on his way down to the canteen. He made a quick lunch, a cup of coffee and a sandwich, and walked out on to the Quai des Célestins, the AGRIP message clear in his head. Irina Tovskaya meant nothing to him. He could have looked her up, he supposed, but he felt no interest.

He paused outside the École Massilon in the Square Henri Galli, and waited for Yuri to catch him up. He was Yuri's responsibility outside. He was not supposed to know this, but he did. That was the trouble with any system, no matter how good; it had to be worked by human beings, and some of them were still sufficiently that, to resent the system. Yuri came up with a *Caporal* sticking out of the corner of his mouth, looking very French, and very fed-up. He was getting very tired of the heavy-handed astronaut jokes, which he had to shoulder because of his name. Alexandre had an arrangement with Yuri. Neither of them wanted to waste time during their lunch-hour.

Yuri said, 'The usual?'

Alexandre nodded. 'And you?'

'The usual.'

They walked across the square together and parted at the corner of the Rue de Sully. Yuri went off to play *belotte* in a café, and Alexandre went up past the barracks towards the Place de la Bastille. But, before he reached it, he turned right-handed into the Rue de la Cerisaie, where Michèle had her room. Some day, he thought, his love would not be rationed to these half-hours at the favour of Yuri. The decision had been made. He could telephone freely from Michèle's flat. A few months' grace to make enough money, and he would be free to buy the time which he felt was his due. Oh, he would pay for it eventually. One had to pay for everything. He began to think of Michèle, who would be waiting with no more than a dressing-gown over her nakedness.

*

All the way round Manston had been wondering when Sutcliffe was going to open up about his visit. There had been a few moments when he had been on the point of asking him frankly. There was no reason why he should not have done, now that he was out of it all. But the habit of years of service still stuck.

They stood on the elevated tee of the eighteenth with a light August breeze coming in from the channel; Richard Manston and Ronnie Sutcliffe, man and master, or so it had been until fairly recently. And that's the way it's going to stay, thought Manston.

Sutcliffe had telephoned at eight that morning from London, suggesting a round of golf. At ten he had arrived, golf-clubs in the back of his car, his plump face wreathed in a *bonhomie* which would have deceived most people.

The tide was in and a skein of blue-winged sailing dinghies was coming down the cut from Rye harbour. Everything was blue, green and white, and the air was full of the sound of larks. They were all square on the match so far, and there was a fiver on it.

Manston watched Sutcliffe drive; a humpty-dumpty figure, more muscle than fat, with his short, flat swing well in control. The ball whipped away, a nice combination of intelligence and power, heading for the buckthorn thickets on the right-hand of the fairway; and then drawing gently back to finish short of the deep, grassy pit beyond the thorns.

Manston took his driver, risking the Scylla of the deep pit on the left, and the Charybdis of the thorn on the right. He hit a sweet one, straight up the middle, through the neck of the fairway, well ahead of the other's ball.

Walking forward, Sutcliffe said, 'You've put on some weight in hibernation.'

'It comes from eating regularly.'

'No worries?'

'Not that keep me awake.'

'You're lucky.'

'You could be the same.'

Sutcliffe's head came round, and a pair of pale, almost too pale, blue eyes blinked at him sadly.

'Wish I could – sometimes.'

Manston smiled. The sadness in the eyes would last only as long as they were on him. Sutcliffe was pure design. From the day of his birth a blueprint had been pinned on the nursery wall. It was not only hangmen who kept their professions in the family.

They came up to Sutcliffe's ball.

'What do you do – intellectually?'

'*The Times* crossword puzzle.'

'Read?'

Manston nodded. The trouble with Sutcliffe was that you could never pick the right moment to be wary. But standing back, as Sutcliffe consulted his caddy and finally took his spoon, he knew that he was under examination. He would lay a hundred to one in fivers that there had already been a check of some kind . . . funny, he ought to have spotted it.

Sutcliffe thumped the ball hard up the middle. When it pitched it ran like a gazelle, and finished ten yards short of the green, on the left by the clubhouse.

Manston walked on to his ball and his caddy handed him his three iron without a word. Since his retirement he had played here three or four times a week, rain or shine, and the caddy knew him well.

He played the ball, well within himself, knowing he had plenty of club. He watched it through the latter part of its flight with a deep satisfaction. It hit the apron of the green, checked with the bite, and then rolled on to the green, finishing a couple of yards from the pin.

'Too bloody good,' said Sutcliffe. 'You've improved no end.'

'I get plenty of time to play now.'

Sutcliffe grinned. *The Times* crossword, and golf. No other distractions?'

'What else would there be in the Weald of Kent?'

'Women?'

Manston chuckled. 'Weren't they included in the report?'

'Really, Richard!'

It was genuine. He had been too frank. Sutcliffe wasn't ready for him and momentarily he had shown it.

A few moments later Sutcliffe played a bad approach shot to the green, leaving himself some twelve feet from the pin. Sutcliffe's mind was not really on the game, that was clear. He was usually deadly around the green. Sutcliffe missed his approach putt by an inch, leaving Manston two putts for a win. He sank his putt for an eagle three.

'Five quid,' said Manston. 'You want to lunch here, or come back to my place?'

'Your place.'

They paid off their caddies, changed, and drove off. Across the marsh meadows Rye was perched low on its sea-deserted island, French-looking under the sharp August sun. Beyond Rye, they took the Tenterden road and Manston drove without talking. He had no need to talk for Sutcliffe was doing that, an easy, light cover to what was to come. He had bought some new picture by an Australian artist whose values were increasing . . . Manston saw him sitting in his flat, staring at it; his thoughts full of a hundred other things, the picture no more than a focal point. Past Tenterden, they forked right and took the back road to Sissinghurst. A couple of miles before the village, Manston turned left down a rutted farm road, and the roof tiles of his house swam up through the heat haze, like a red raft in the green hollow of the valley.

On the far side of the house there was a terrace of Kent rag stone. The stream that fed the valley cascaded thinly over a fall at one end of the terrace, into the long, narrow swimming pool. He had bought the house for the stream and the pool. Under a table, shaded by a coloured umbrella, lunch and drinks were set out, the lunch protected from wasps by a gauze cloth.

Settling in a cane chair with a gin and tonic, Sutcliffe nodded at the table.

'You knew we were coming back for lunch?'

'It struck me we might.'

'Who looks after you?'

'My bailiff's wife, mostly.' He kept his voice deliberately flat, amused within. 'We're alone now, though,' he went on.

He sat down and put his feet up on a stool, feeling the glass ice-cold against his hand. A moorhen had invaded the far end of the pool, and was flirting its white butt amiably as it rushed the skating water-beetles. The pool was due for a clean-out.

Sutcliffe said suddenly, 'How long has it been?'

'Eighteen months.'

'No regrets?'

'None.'

He watched Sutcliffe pick the slice of lemon from his drink and suck it unexpectedly, suddenly a small plump boy, wrinkling his cheeks against the sharpness.

'Sure?' asked Sutcliffe.

'Absolutely.' Manston reached over and took Sutcliffe's glass, refilling it without looking at him. He handed the drink to Sutcliffe and began to deal with his own. He packed the bottom of the glass with ice and swirled it round, seeing the mist rise up the glass.

Almost in a tone of self-pity Sutcliffe said, 'It was a great loss for me when you left.'

As he talked, Sutcliffe lowered his fat chin, tight against the knot of his neck scarf, and idly flicked the rim of his glass with his finger, the pinging note sharp and clear in the hot, still air.

'Thirty-five. Record, excellent. You've got the languages. Nerve. No panic. No attachments that make a man hesitate that half-second too long. Self-contained.'

Manston lit a cigarette. His Gordon setter came round the corner of the terrace, bored with the heat; cocked a leg against a tub of geraniums and then came up to him. The black and tan pelt was shining, silvered by the slow muscle movement. The dog raised its muzzle to him, laughing against the heat, and then collapsed with an idle thud at his feet.

'Hear that, Joss?' He addressed the dog. 'That's me. Your master.' Then to Sutcliffe, he said, 'You're wasting your time if you want me back.'

'I wasn't even thinking of it.'

'Oh, no?'

Manston stood up and wandered to the edge of the pool. He had made his decision on good grounds eighteen months before. The decision stood. He did not want to go back, ever. He swung round. 'Look – lay off me. I'm fixed here nicely. A hundred and twenty acres of fruit and a good bailiff to handle it. I'm out, and I don't mean to go into the reasons again. I liked it once. At first. It was exciting. You get a feeling of power . . . Oh, you know it all. *Carte blanche* for so many things. Then, at last, it comes home to you that it's people you're dealing with, people you're screwing up. . . .'

Sutcliffe, benign, looking even a little hurt, shook his head. 'You're getting me wrong. I'm not asking you to come back.'

'Then what do you want?'

'A favour; just your professional opinion.'

'Snake!'

Sutcliffe smiled. 'I value your judgement of people. I just want you to have dinner with someone; then tell me what you think about them. That's not asking much, is it?'

'And no strings attached?'

'No strings. Just a simple favour. They're doing *Le Lac des Cygnes* at Covent Garden tomorrow. I've got a box. I'll leave the tickets for you at your club. Barry Dymen will be there, too. After the ballet, you go out to dinner with him and a couple of girls. I'm interested in one of them and would like to know what you think about her.'

'Why the ballet first?'

'This girl is dancing in it – only a small part. Just see me afterwards and tell me what you think. You'll do that?'

'I might. It happens that I'm going up to town anyway.'

'Good. Her name is Irina Tovskaya. You can pick her out from the programme.'

*

At eleven o'clock that evening the brooding heat of the past day built up into a thunderstorm.

Manston, in pyjamas and dressing-gown, sat at his desk, the bedroom windows open, the curtains flailing now and again in the sudden gusts of wind, and watched the torrential rain turn the surface of the pool into a curdy commotion. He reached out, flicked on the pool lights from his bedroom switch and sat enjoying the stage effects. Now and again, the lightning flashes illuminated the stretch of hop garden on the far side of the valley; and, at each flash, the geese down the valley stream set up a screaming protest.

He did not trust Sutcliffe and his simple favour. There was more behind it. Simple favour! Nothing was simple about Sutcliffe. He appeared on no Civil Service list. The only indisputable scrap of information about him was a London Telephone Directory entry which read: *Sutcliffe, R. M.,*

13 King St., Covent Garden . . . COVent Garden 2488. It must, thought Manston, be the only private flat left in the Covent Garden area. . . . Irina Tovskaya. Surely Sutcliffe hadn't, for one moment, thought that he could get at him through a woman? Not professionally, anyway.

The lightning smacked again at the far side of the valley and, wonderfully for a moment, he saw the whole run of wire stays and cross-strands alive with a trellising blue fire. Then the geese screamed to high heaven, and were silenced by a clap of thunder that shook the earth. In the silence that followed, a shocked silence as though Nature had gone too far and used a filthy word for the first time in front of the children, he heard Binky's car coming down the farm road, driving too fast as usual. He switched off the pool lights, closed the window; and went over to the table by the door and fixed two whiskies and sodas.

She came through from her bedroom twenty minutes later in dressing-gown and nightdress, took the whisky he held out to her and sat on the day couch by him, leaning back and lifting her legs across his lap, kicking off her slippers as she did so. He raised his glass and drank to her; and she responded silently, as he scratched gently at the sole of one of her feet.

Before he could say anything Joss came through from the other bedroom, flopped at his feet and licked half-heartedly at the little triangle of flesh showing between his pyjama leg and his slipper.

'He's pretending to be upset by the storm,' said Binky.

'Complicated dog.'

'Complicated you. How did it go?'

'What?'

'Sutcliffe.'

'Just a social visit.'

'How was Rye?'

'Burnt up.'

'Lunch all right?'

'Splendid.'

'No problems?'

'None.'

She ran a free hand up through her blonde hair, pushing it untidily forward over her eyes, grinning at him.

'Where've you been? London?' he said.

'Yes. I'm all fixed up to fly back.'

'I'll miss you.'

'I think you will; for a few days. But after that I won't exist; until I come back on another trip.' She winked at him. 'Don't worry, I'm not complaining.'

'You're wonderful.' He drained his whisky and put the glass on the floor. Joss sniffed at it and registered no emotion.

Binky gave Joss a gentle kick on the flank as she swung her feet free to the ground. 'Joss, be a gentleman.'

Joss got up slowly and walked back to the other bedroom. Manston followed and closed the door on him. When he turned round she was waiting for him. It was always a matter of marvel to him how she rid herself of clothes so quickly.

2

MANSTON CHANGED AT his club, and went into the bar for a drink before going off to Covent Garden. Barry Dymen had telephoned him to say that he would be late arriving at the ballet. A friend sitting in the window-seat overlooking Brook Street called him over. Manston sat for fifteen minutes over two whiskies and sodas and listened to an enthusiastic account of his discovery of an old Bugatti, type 49, in a farm barn in

Wales. Men with minor manias, Manston thought, always made the best company. All you had to do was to listen – he was good at that – and learn.

When Manston said he must be off to the ballet – interrupting a fascinating explanation of the peculiarity of Bugatti clutches in not disengaging fully at high speeds, thus enabling very rapid, single declutch downward changes to be made – his friend gave him a stricken look and said, 'Good God, must you? How awful for you.'

At the Royal Opera House, Covent Garden, he discovered that his box was on the left of the stage, next to Ninette de Valois's. There was no one else in the box, and he sat for a while looking round at the tiered red and gold splendour of the Opera House. It was a pity he hadn't been able to bring Binky; she would have enjoyed it. He sat there, thinking about her. Theirs was a warm, uncomplicated arrangement. Both he and Binky were the types who, by nature, found that there was always an emotional limit to their relationships with other men or women. In the past years the nature of his work had made that limit inflexible. It was better not to have deep feelings. Sutcliffe approved of that. And now, when he was free, the habit remained.

He flipped open the programme and began to read the synopsis of Act One of *Le Lac des Cygnes*. A paragraph caught his eye and made him smile:

> *The Princess reminds her son that he must choose his bride at the ball arranged for the following day. Siegfried is disconsolate; he enjoys his life of freedom ...*

Wasn't that like life, he thought. Somebody was always arranging a ball for you the next day, when you would have to make a decision. Sutcliffe was trying to do that for him. To hell with Sutcliffe.

He looked down the cast and found Irina Tovskaya

mentioned twice. She was one of the swans; she was also one of the two dancers in the Neapolitan Dance – very clearly not a very important member of the cast.

The house lights went down, the conductor entered and took his bow; and the overture of Piotr Ilich Tchaikovsky began.

It was not until Act Three that Manston was able to identify Irina Tovskaya. During the masquerade at the Castle, she came on with her partner for the Neapolitan Dance. He watched her through his opera-glasses. She was a dark-haired, slim girl of about medium height; and she danced as though she were not only giving a performance, but also thoroughly enjoying herself. Her smile, he noticed, was her own, natural and easy; not one of the fixed, rather strained affairs of some professionals.

As the curtain fell at the end of Act Three the door at the back of the box opened, and Barry Dymen came in.

'Evening, Richard – sorry I couldn't get here before. Been enjoying yourself, I hope?'

'Hullo, Barry. You're a bit late. Let's go and have a drink.'

'Ballet isn't exactly my cup of tea, as you know. We might stay in the bar and skip the last act.'

They walked through to the crush bar and Barry Dymen fought his way through the crowd to get a couple of drinks. Standing under the chandelier, a blazing pear-shaped brilliance above him, Manston watched Barry's lean shoulders and noted, with a grin, that the fair hair was still as untidy as ever, sticking up at the back in a small duck's tail. For a year they had worked together, liked each other, and never asked any questions. But, despite the self-imposed professional anonymity, they had become friends; and then were content to do no more about it. For all he knew, Barry might be married and the father of five children. He did know that he was utterly reliable, and that was the important thing.

Barry came back to him, carrying two glasses, his lean,

Scandinavian face concentrating with the effort of not spilling the drink in the crowd.

Until the warning bells went for the Fourth Act the bar remained crowded, and their conversation was polite and non-revelatory.

'How's the retirement, Richard?'

'Fine.'

'Lucky bastard. Lord, this place is hot. Wish I had private means – I'd retire, too.'

'You would?'

Barry cocked an eye at him and then winked. 'No; I'm the old man's type. Only just now and again it gets too much. That's when I get him to give me a holiday. He knows the warning signs in everyone, except himself.'

'He never has any.'

'Could be. Don't know how he stands it. The pressure gets bigger every year.'

When the crowd had cleared they found a table at the far end of the bar, near a window which had been opened against the August night heat of London. A couple of policemen were frog-marching an amiable but noisy drunk into Bow Street police station opposite. A few taxis cruised down the street, and there was a faintly sweet smell of vegetables in the air from the market.

He said, 'What's the score, Barry?'

'I don't know. I was told to meet you and take you out to supper. I know one of the girls in the Ballet. Nice little thing called Elsa Polani. She's bringing a friend.'

'Irina Tovskaya?'

'Yes, that's the name. Russian. One of the small ones who flew the coop. Her English is good.'

'Is that all you know about her?'

Barry raised his glass and smiled over the top of it. 'For publication at the moment; yes.'

*

Later they had supper at the Four Hundred. He liked both of the girls. Elsa Polani, he thought, was a little bit over-refined, but very friendly and obviously devoted to Irina. He guessed that Elsa had begun life as Elsa Pollard, or some such name, and had thought of nothing but a dancing career from the moment she started to go to ballet classes at Golders Green. Irina did not say much – Elsa made up for that – but when she did talk, her English was good, as Barry had said. Now and again he could catch the moment of hesitation, as she searched for the right word. Her accent was attractive, too. In fact, she was altogether an attractive girl, dark, with large brown eyes, typical high Slav cheek-bones, and the most splendid long legs and arms of any woman he had seen for a long time. Watching and listening to her, he wondered what Sutcliffe's interest in her could be. He knew from Barry that she had left her own country and had been granted British nationality. One of the branches of his old Department looked after the political asylum people; and he knew that she would have been well screened before being accepted. Whether these refugees were small people, or big names, they all went through the same process. Later, if it were felt necessary for their security, they were fixed up with false names and given a fresh start, sometimes in this country and sometimes abroad. That side of it was fascinating work, but he had never had much to do with it in his time with the service.

Now and again he caught her looking at him with a slightly puzzled air, and he wondered if she had any inkling why he was here. But only once did she show any curiosity, and that was while they were dancing.

She said, 'What does your friend Barry do?'

'I'm not sure. Something in the City.'

'And you?'

'I'm a farmer.'

She leaned back from him a little and he saw the little crease of surprise on her forehead. 'You don't look like it.'

He smiled. 'I've left my gum boots behind tonight. I farm in Kent.'

She danced beautifully, and he realized that she had been to the club before when, as they passed the band, the pianist winked at her and she smiled back. When the next number began she said, 'That is my favourite. The pianist always plays it for me.'

'You come here often?'

'Quite a lot. Elsa has many friends and she asks me to come.' She looked up quickly and smiled at him. 'Not all of them dance as well as you. Sometimes . . . my shoes!'

Elsa and Barry had to leave; but they stayed on for another hour at the club, and danced most of the time. One thing, at least, he could tell Sutcliffe; she was a stayer. She showed no signs of being tired. He was quite glad to flop back in the taxi on the way to her flat and take the weight off his feet. She had a small flat on the top floor of a block of solicitors' offices in Gloucester Place.

When they arrived she asked him if he would like to come in for a last drink.

'Thank you, I'd like that,' he said.

She went ahead of him up the dark stairway, finding the light switches. It was a small flat, a sitting-room, a bedroom, a bathroom and a tiny kitchen. He helped her off with her coat and fixed two drinks at the sideboard, while she went to a budgerigar, which was in a cage by the window, and gave it seed and fresh water.

'What do you call him?' he asked over his shoulder.

'Nijinsky.' She laughed. 'But he does not talk or dance. I am very fond of him.'

When he handed her her drink, she said, 'It is nice when the evenings are so warm to go up on my roof. Shall we take our drinks up?'

They went into the hallway and she showed him the fire-escape ladder up through the ceiling to the roof. A few moments later they were sitting on one of the inner parapets, a chimney-stack towering above them, and the smoking loom of West End lights to the south.

'You've got a wonderful view from here,' he said.

'You like it? Good. I love it. I've never been happier anywhere. I like London and I like the London people. So many people have been so good to me. Elsa says I should not live here all alone. She would like me to live with her. But I like being alone. I can sit here for hours. You know, although I was born in the country – deep in the country – I really like cities. I like to feel there are lots of people around me. Somehow, it makes me feel safe . . .' Her voice trailed away suddenly.

Manston said, 'What made you leave Russia?' Normally he would, out of tact, have foregone the question, but he had a report to make to Sutcliffe.

He saw her hesitating over his question and then she said, 'It is not easy to answer. It would be wrong to think I do not like my country. I do, very much. Until two years ago I never thought of leaving. You see, my mother and father died when I was very young. An aunt brought me and my brother up. He went into the army. We are very close to one another, my brother and I. Then three years ago, without saying anything to me, he left; deserted from the army in East Berlin and went over to the Americans. He is in America now.'

'Didn't that make it tough for you in Russia?'

'A little. At first. But I was with the Kirov Ballet and all dancers, you know,' she smiled, 'are very important people. For a year I was not allowed to go abroad on any tours. Then, I was allowed. Don't ask me why. Maybe they thought I was safe. And so I was. I mean inside myself. I had no thought to go. Then the Ballet went to Paris and it happened. It was my first visit. I can't tell you what Paris did to me. It was as though suddenly a great window was open and for the first time I was really seeing the world. The true world. And I wanted to be part of it.'

'So you skipped.'

'Skipped?'

'Left, ran away.'

'Yes. I went to the British Embassy.' She raised her eyebrows. 'I can't tell you the fuss that went on then. But in the end I was sent over here . . . You know, it is not possible now to be frank about how these things are arranged and what happens. I would like to tell you but I cannot. Anyway, in the end I was given British nationality and because I was from the Kirov – though not a very important dancer – Madame de Valois saw me, and I was given a job. It was all very strange at first; the language mostly, though I had learned a little English in Leningrad. And Elsa looked after me. She was wonderful.'

'Have you seen your brother?'

'No. Not yet. But next year I shall go to America to visit him. First it was necessary to remake my career here.' She paused and said, 'Forgive me; I talk about myself too much.'

'I'm interested. It takes courage to do what you did.'

She shrugged her shoulders, smiling. 'I did not think of that. It was just something I suddenly had to do. What do you call it? An impulse?'

'And one you haven't regretted?'

'Never. Oh, never. Not even right at the beginning, when sometimes I was lonely . . . you know, when you wake in the night and begin to think of what you have done?'

'I know.'

He moved away from her to the roof-edge and looked down. What the hell did Sutcliffe want with this girl? The more he stayed with her, the more he liked her and felt baffled. Surely Sutcliffe was not thinking that she still belonged to the other side, that her move to the West was a deliberate plant?

He came back to her side and said, 'It's late. I must go. You must be tired, too.' He took her by the arm and led her to the roof ladder. He went down ahead of her and then, as he stood at the bottom, he reached up and took her hand to help her. She jumped the last two steps and for a moment his hands went to her shoulders to steady her. She looked up at him, smiling, and, before he knew he was going to do it, he bent down and kissed her gently on the lips. She accepted the kiss without protest.

'Thank you,' he said, 'for a very pleasant evening. And say good night to Nijinsky for me.'

*

Irina lay in bed for half an hour before sleeping, thinking about him. Although she could not say why, she had the feeling that he was not just one of the usual party men that Elsa brought along. For one thing, most of them wanted to kiss her in the taxi coming home, and, for another, they did not have his air of quiet consideration. She liked him. He had quality. His face was masculine and firm and tanned, with nice, generous brown eyes. She liked, too, the way he moved when he danced. . . . She closed her eyes, seeing him standing at the foot of the ladder and, for a moment, she could almost feel the pressure of his hands on her shoulders and the brief warmth of his lips against hers. Tomorrow she must ask Elsa about him . . .

*

Before Manston opened the main door in the hallway to let himself out of the building he paused and, bending down, lifted the flap of the letter slit. Obliquely, and almost out of his vision across the street, he could see a man standing on the corner of Gloucester Place and the intersecting York Street. He had spotted him from the roof; and it amused him now to unravel some of the smaller routines of the game. He opened the door noisily, slammed it hard to lock it behind him and, as he went down the short run of steps, saw that the man had disappeared. Manston went south down Gloucester Place, crossed the Crawford Street intersection and, at the end of the block, turned right-handed into Montagu Place. A few yards along the pavement he stepped into a doorway and waited. Shortly afterwards, he heard the hurried shuffle of footsteps rounding the corner; then silence for a moment, as the follower found his quarry gone. Then the footsteps came slowly down towards him.

The man was illuminated clearly by a street light and Manston recognized him.

He said softly, ' 'Evening, Ritchie. Have a cigarette.'

The man turned, fast at first; then he slowed up, relaxing, and finished facing him, a low laugh floating away into the night.

'Well, I'm damned! You know, sir, I thought it was you. But they told me —'

'Eighteen months ago, Ritchie.' Manston closed his case and watched Ritchie snap a lighter to the cigarette he had taken. The yellow flame showed the familiar large, furrowed face, the dark overhang of bushy eyebrows and the drooping wing of a bow-tie which Ritchie always wore to hide the frayed edges of his collar. Ritchie was a free-lance; paid a small retainer and then so much an hour. There was no fortune in it and shirt collars got frayed.

'How many of you?' asked Manston.

'Four. Two on and two off. Not so bad this weather.'

'Any interesting visitors?'

'Not exactly visitors, sir. You're the first in a week to go inside. But there are some nibbles and —' He pulled up suddenly, aware of his indiscretion. 'You really are out of this, sir?'

'Yes. But it's all right. I'm on my way to the old man now.' Ritchie, he knew, had never met Sutcliffe, knew nothing about him, reporting through some intermediary, but he knew what the 'old man' meant. 'What kind of nibble?'

'There's a bloke pays off a taxi at the top of Gloucester Place, Marylebone Road, every night at half-past ten. Got a small Pekinese dog, and he walks it up and down for an hour, maybe longer, depends what time she gets in. Once in, he goes back to Marylebone Road and gets a taxi.'

'The taxi is someone else's job?'

'Yes, sir. But don't let on I told you any of this – if you're not on the job.'

'Don't worry.'

But when he had left Ritchie, he knew that had he been Sutcliffe and knew that Ritchie had spoken to him so freely, he would have been worried. Trust was the greatest hazard in this business. There were very few men who stuck literally to the letter of their contract. Ritchie knew him, knew he had retired; yet with a little prompting he opened up, basing his action on trust. This was the oldest and the most dangerous problem; one worked with human material, and human beings would insist on being fallible in their judgements. Trust no one, report only to X, a man like Ritchie could understand that. But Ritchie, like everyone else, could not live without trust. That every man had his price was obvious and to a very large extent this could be handled, but every man also had his friends. There was no sure guard against that.

He found a taxi in Montagu Square. It was half-past one and he knew that Sutcliffe would not be in bed. Bed, in fact, was not something one associated with Sutcliffe. Manston decided that he would have half an hour's decisive chat with Sutcliffe, pick up his car, and drive down to Kent.

At the top of St Martin's Lane he leaned forward, pushing the window back, and said to the driver, 'Drop me here.'

He walked the few hundred yards to Sutcliffe's flat. Never in his life had he taken a taxi right up to the place. He rang the bell and waited three minutes, watching the lorries move up into Covent Garden. From somewhere beyond the darkness of the doorway arch he knew that he would be scrutinized by Hackett, Sutcliffe's man servant, before he was admitted.

When the door did open he was greeted unceremoniously by Hackett.

'For a gent of leisure, you ought to keep more civilized hours now. Come in and go up. He's been expectin' you.' In the dark hallway, he went on, 'Tell him it'll have to be whisky and soda. I'm not making coffee at this hour.'

Manston said, 'Not even for me?'

'Not even for you. Coffee is only for emergencies, as you well know.'

Sutcliffe, in a green corduroy dressing-gown, was lying back in an arm-chair, his feet on a stool. His eyes came up from a contemplation of his bare toes. He nodded gently and said, 'Fix yourself a drink. None for me.'

The room was simply furnished. The floor was thickly carpeted and the walls were hung with paintings, each with a little scallop-shell of light above it. It was a comfortable, monkish room, with plenty of space to move, and little, except the paintings, to distract the mind.

Manston made his whisky a little longer than normal, then sat down in an arm-chair which was backed up against the drawn window curtains. Sutcliffe slewed round a little to keep him in full view.

'Pleasant evening?' he asked.

'Very. Nice to see Barry again.'

Sutcliffe nodded, pushing the tips of his fingers against his plump chin.

'What did you think of her?'

'I liked her very much.'

'I thought you would. I hear you went back to her flat.'

Manston nodded. It was no surprise to him that Sutcliffe should already know this. He said, 'She seems to have settled down to her new life quite happily. I take it she was one of our babies?'

'Yes. The Polani girl works for us sometimes. She took her under her wing. We didn't have to give her any special cover. She wasn't important enough. What kind of character would you say she was?'

'I don't know. Just a fairly ordinary girl. Plenty of spirit. Shows what she thinks. But she wouldn't make any Mata Hari if that's what you're thinking.'

'I'm not. Physically, how would she go?'

Manston laughed briefly. 'You sound as though you're talking about a horse. She's a dancer. They train hard. She practically danced me off my feet. She's in good trim. And she's got guts. You have to, to walk out of the Kirov and start a new life.'

'I know.' Sutcliffe leaned forward and fished in the pocket of his dressing-gown for a pipe, wallet and matches. Manston watched the slow ceremony of pipe-filling, wondering what all this was about. Sutcliffe finally lay back in his arm-chair and pipe smoke festooned the air above him.

'I need,' he said, 'someone to talk this over with. Hope you're not in a hurry.'

'No, but I've given you all I can about her.'

'It's enough. I rely on your judgement. You never did any work on these political asylum people, did you?'

'No.'

'Well, at the moment they're giving us a big headache. Not only us, either. Interpol, and the police in France, Belgium, Holland and Switzerland. In the last two years, these Iron Curtain refugees have been going back from all these countries at about the rate of ten a month. Nearly two hundred and fifty in two years. Not the big names, but the small ones, like this girl. Usually the pattern is the same. They go back to their lodgings or house one night and in the morning they aren't there. No trace of them.'

'And then?'

'Then – so our Moscow people report – they turn up in Russia about a month or two later. Right back in the small town or village they came from, doing the same job, just carrying on as usual. Since they are all small names we've managed to keep it out of the Press. Couldn't do this with a big name of course.'

'What's the angle? If a big name goes back I can see it's a feather in the cap for Russia. But why these tiddlers?'

'It's simple really. And it's effective. These people are taken back and they have to agree to toe the line. That means that, in a hundred small towns or so, they go around amongst the people they have known all their lives, saying that they were fools; that they escaped to the West because they wanted freedom, but that when they got there, they soon discovered it was no paradise – it was a capitalistic hell. That's the kind of propaganda that works in small towns amongst people you've known all your life. If I were an engine driver, wondering if I'd have a crack at going West, I'd think more than twice about it if my lorry-driver friend, who had taken the plunge, came back and said it wasn't worth it. Behind the Curtain they don't lose any chances for a psychological advantage. There's another angle, too. Can you imagine the advantage it would be to us in this department if we could have for interrogation a hundred people who had lived in different parts of Russia for two or three years?'

'Yes, I can. I can also see that, if they're going back at the rate you say, it must be a pretty big organization. You must surely have a lead on that?'

Sutcliffe heaved himself out of his chair and went over to the drink table. 'Interested, eh?'

'You said you wanted to talk. I'm always ready to help an old friend – so far.'

'I knew you would be. Yes . . .' Sutcliffe came back with his drink. 'We know who's running it. That's about all. It's run from AGRIP in Paris.'

'That doesn't surprise me.' Apart from being a genuine official trade organization, enjoying diplomatic immunity, AGRIP was a recognized cover for other activities, which the Russian Embassy in Paris knew better than to handle direct.

'Three weeks ago we got a break. We've at last got a chap working for us in AGRIP. You know what kind of break that is; and it isn't likely to last long. But as long as he lasts we're going to milk him hard.'

Sutcliffe stood above Manston and sipped at his drink, looking down at him, a pudgy, brooding figure.

Manston said, 'I think I can read the score now. He's tipped you off that she's next on the list to go back.'

'He has. He doesn't know much about the kidnapping network but he does know the names of the people who are going back as they are picked out. She's next from this country.'

Manston stood up. He was remembering Irina dancing in gay Neapolitan clothes, remembering the pianist at the night club playing her favourite tune.

He said, without any show of emotion, 'What's the problem? If you know she's next you can give her all the security she needs.'

'Of course. That would be easy. But what happens then? We save her. We save the next one, maybe, when our contact gives us the name. But then our contact goes. AGRIP will rumble him for sure. And then we have no more names tipped off . . . and back the rest will go at the same rate. No – we've got a break and we're going to use it.'

'What the hell do you mean?'

'We're going to let her be kidnapped; let her pass right through the organization, almost up to the point of no return; but we'll have been following all the time. Then we jump, free her, and wrap up this bloody outfit.'

For a moment Manston was silent. Then, his voice cold with anger, he said, 'You can't do that to a woman! It stinks!'

Sutcliffe eased himself back into his arm-chair and flicked the loose end of his dressing-gown over his legs. 'We're going to do it. Pity it's a woman, of course. But, if we by-passed her, the next might be a woman. And after that there wouldn't be any next because our man probably won't be alive. No, it's got to be her.'

'But, for God's sake, Sutcliffe. Think what a job like this means. You've no guarantee the scheme will work. It's the hardest thing in the world just to follow a man across London. Here, you're going to watch a girl be kidnapped and then try to keep tags on her possibly half-way across Europe. It can't be done!'

Sutcliffe shrugged his shoulders. Then he raised his face to Manston, his eyes blinking almost apologetically. 'It's got to be tried. It could be successful – if we've got the right man to handle it.'

'Oh, no! You don't get me like that!'

'Listen, Richard. This is going to be done. And you're going to do it. Just this one job, that's all.'

'I'm not coming back. You can't do this to her, or ask it of me.'

'I'm sorry for her. She just came up in the draw. That's the best way to look at it. But you're not going to refuse. You can't. Of all the men I've got, or had, you're the only one I'd give more than an even chance of pulling this off. And you'll accept it because you've got a special kind of vanity.'

'In God's name, what are you talking about?'

'Vanity. All the best people have it. The best people of their kind. Stop looking so bloody angry. You can do this.'

'I wish to heaven I hadn't come up here. You and your simple favours. You know how I feel about this kind of thing. I cleared out because of it.'

Unmoved, Sutcliffe said, 'I'm going to do it. It's my job. I'm sorry for her. But it's got to be done and I want the best man on the job.'

Sutcliffe dropped back into his chair and the plump, boyish face was owlish, bland. Yet, somewhere there, Manston saw the shadow of triumph, as though Sutcliffe were already seeing far ahead, through Botwinnik mazes of moves, to some checkmate. He liked this man, enjoyed his friendship, and had the highest admiration for his ability, so that it was hard now to censure him for becoming the creature of his profession; no man could have done his job for so many years without learning to live with the moments of infamy, so necessary for success.

Sutcliffe raised his eyes to Manston. 'Well?'

'No.'

'There's no need to say "yes" now. Give me a ring tomorrow sometime and we'll begin work.'

Anger, open and direct, welled up in Manston.

'Go to hell!' he cried, and made quickly for the door.

*

Alexandre slept in one of the five attics at the top of the building overlooking the Seine. He shared his room with an elderly man, Vadim, who acted as reception clerk at the small desk in the hall. Vadim's hours were regular, and he snored through the night with great gusto. Alexandre envied Vadim his regular hours and his phlegmatic acceptance of a life bounded by the simple movements of rising, going down to the hall, and, once every other day, taking a stroll as far as Notre-Dame and back. Vadim asked for no more. When the bell above Alexandre's bed rang – as it had just done – Vadim never moved, never faltered in the deep, ox-like enjoyment of his sleep.

Alexandre got up, pulled a dressing-gown over his rough pyjamas, fumbled into his sandals and went down to his room, combing his hair back with his hands. Urgency, always urgency, he told himself. Nothing was so unimportant in AGRIP that it could wait. Whereas the truth was that most of it could have waited, would have waited if there had been a different man at the head of affairs. If only Oleg would learn the pleasures of sleep . . . What pleasures did Oleg know, anyway, outside his work? None; he was sure of that. Oleg was the Model Man, the completely Vertical Man, always on his toes. To hell with him.

In his office, Alexandre switched on the desk-light and sat down and waited. Tipping the shade of the desk-light away from the window to clear the reflection from the glass, he saw that the morning was coming up faintly, away to the left. Just a trace of grey against the purple, bruised-looking, hot night sky. Around the street lights across the *quai* moths danced in and out of the cones of silver light.

The door opened behind him and the duty clerk from the main office came sleepily into the room. Without a word, he dropped two envelopes in front of Alexandre and went out. Alexandre recognized the official envelopes from the Embassy and the inscription on them, 'For immediate decoding and attention of AGRIP.' Alexandre had long ceased to try to work out why some stuff came and went via the Embassy and some went straight out, or came straight in, to AGRIP. He took a pencil, unlocked the drawer of his desk, and pulled out his code book.

The first message was short and he could almost decode it without reference to the book

Capa to Agrip
Next consignment. Delivery usual place time August thirty. Confirm.

Alexandre glanced at the wall calendar. It was now the twenty-fourth of August. No, it wasn't. This was another day. The twenty-fifth. He reached forward and tore off the old day. Five days. He must get round to Michèle at midday and telephone. That would mean more money for him. . . . Just for a moment he wondered whether he was wise in letting Michèle keep the money. Wise or not, he had to, anyway. He couldn't bring it back here. For all he knew, Michèle might have another lover; some *Julot* who sponged on her . . . No, no; he pushed the thought from him. Michèle he could trust. Their day was coming . . .

The second message was longer and he smiled to himself as he recognized the tone. It read:

Limbo to Agrip
Payment not received for last delivery, advised Geneva. Promptness essential. Also, future consignments must be smaller. Difficulty handling three cases. Two maximum, insist.

Alexandre took the originals and his decoded copies and went through to Oleg's room, waiting briefly when he knocked on the door for the voice within.

Oleg was at his table, dressed, shaved, neat, impersonal; looking as though neither night nor day made any difference to him. He ran a hand slowly over his short-cut, stiff hair, and the ring on his finger glittered sharply under the light.

Alexandre put the messages before him and waited. Just for a moment, Oleg's stone-cold eyes travelled down the length of Alexandre's body, disapproving of the dressing-gown and pyjamas; but he said nothing and began to read the messages. He read them slowly, deliberately, taking an age. Then, as slowly, he unlocked a drawer, pulled out a pink file, slipped the messages inside, then replaced the file and locked the drawer.

He looked up at Alexandre, then said evenly, 'Your record here is excellent, but you are getting careless in your dress. Yesterday your shoes were unpolished and it is not good to wear a collar for more than three days.'

Alexandre made a little movement of his head. He was not required to say anything. Oleg drew a thin grey tube of a cigarette from a box on the table and, lighting it, puffed a fine gauze of smoke between them. From behind it he said, 'We all get homesick. We must not let it affect us. Go back to bed.'

Alexandre went. He did not even debate Oleg's remarks in

his mind. He had given that up long ago. Oleg was a rock that spoke. It wasn't any good trying to understand him, unless he gave an order.

3

By the time Manston had got his car from the Lex Garage, picked up his bag from the club, and reached Westminster Bridge, Big Ben was striking three. The roads were free of traffic, so that there was no need to take any short cuts to avoid congestion. He went over the Elephant and Castle and straight down the Old Kent Road. After the roundabout at Foot's Cray, he had the A.20 almost to himself.

Manston drove fast, mechanically, letting the speed ease his thoughts and his still lingering anger with Sutcliffe. The warmish air came back over the screen, thick with the smell of earth, petrol and road dew. Beyond Swanley the dawn began to edge up to him and, his mind more settled now, he found himself imagining what was going to happen to Irina Tovskaya. Sutcliffe had made up his mind. Nothing could stop it. And if he, Manston, didn't do the job, who would? Someone like Barry Dymen, probably. Well, Barry was competent, and anyway there would be as many more behind him as he could want; the Special Branch, every service in the country. The thing would be organized to the last minute, but it still wouldn't be foolproof. Nothing ever was. Sutcliffe would think of everything that his own people might have to do, but there was always the unknown factor from outside which could throw the machinery out of gear. Somewhere along the line, someone would be faced with the moment not marked in the blueprint, the moment when a quick decision had to be made. And, by God, it would have to be the right one or Irina Tovskaya would find herself back where she did not want to be . . . and after her a lot of other people. Oh, damn, damn; what was it to do with him anyway? Sutcliffe could go to hell. He was out. He put his foot down hard on the accelerator, deliberately forcing himself not to think about Irina Tovskaya.

The sun was just up as he turned off the road into the farm lane. He cut the engine and coasted down the track, and on to the garage square, not wanting to wake Binky. A couple of white doves went up from the garage roof with a lazy clap of wings. As he went round to the front of the house Joss took a four-foot jump through an open window, and his soft muzzle was thrust hard into the palm of his right hand.

There was a thin layer of August mist over the surface of the long pool and, at the far end, he could see the frigate manœuvres of three moorhens around one of the tame mallards. The birds had their own pool but they preferred his, mucking it up.

He went into the small gazebo and stripped off. He dropped into the pool and the water fowl took off noisily from the far end. Joss came down the steps and waded in after him. Lazily he swam the length of the pool. It was too late now to go to bed. Joss paddled half-way with him, then turned and swam back towards the house end. A swallow dived low over the broken surface, taking early gnats. Everything, he thought, was utterly peaceful and restful here.

Then, thrusting in on the tranquillity of this moment came the thought of Irina Tovskaya, next on the list to go back. He remembered the way she had jumped down the last two steps of the roof ladder, coming into his steadying hands . . . and he saw her face lifted to him, her dark eyes shining, her lips close to him . . . smiling happily. He shook the memory from him, put his head down and began to swim quickly to the steps. So what? So what? Nobody was responsible for anybody else's happiness. Especially for people who meant nothing to one.

He came out of the water, and Joss whined and ran around him. As he did so, a window opened above him. Binky was looking out, blonde hair ruffled with sleep, a smile just waking on her lips.

'Catch!'

She threw down a towelled dressing-gown.

'I'll make some coffee and bring it up,' he said.

She nodded, blew him a kiss and disappeared. Manston put on the gown and went into the gazebo for his matches and cigarettes. Bare-footed, he walked around the pool, smoking and thinking. Joss, bored with his inattention, finally went off on his own.

He went into the kitchen and fixed the coffee percolator and laid a tray; and all the time he was telling himself that it was nothing to do with him. He'd been out of it for almost two years. There wasn't a reason on earth why he should go back just for this.

And all the time he was arguing with himself he knew that Sutcliffe was right.

The milk for the coffee boiled over on to the hot ring and filled the kitchen with a foul smell. He swore loudly.

*

During the morning, which was hot and airless, surly with the promise of thunder, Alexandre sent three messages of importance, apart from the usual routine commercial stuff. The first was to Capa:

Agrip to Capa.
Confirm thirtieth. Time, place same.

The second was to Limbo:

Agrip to Limbo
Payment instructed today Geneva. Apologies. Consignment quantities requested by you will be observed unless

emergency demand. One, repeat one, consignment arriving Taru thirtieth August. Taru will hold. Collect earliest. Inform when.

And the third:

Agrip to Taru.
Thirtieth August. One consignment. Usual arrangements.

As Alexandre went off during his lunch-hour to see Michèle he was wishing that he could put a real name to Limbo and Taru. For that information he could, in one deal, make all the money which he needed for himself and Michèle. As he parted from Yuri at the corner of the Rue de Sully, the first big drops of the storm began to fall; and, by the time he had reached the Rue de la Cerisaie, the rain was lashing down and thunder was rumbling heavily over the roofs. He was wet through by the time he reached Michèle's place. He stood in her room, the heavens shaking above them, his clothes drenched and the rain running down from his plastered hair, freshening the pallor of his cheeks. His woeful state suddenly touched a deep maternal spring in Michèle. *Pauvre bougre*, it was right that he should have a little happiness. She kissed him, putting her arms around his wet shoulders, and then, as he stood there, began to help him take his clothes off.

'These will never be dry for you to go back. Never. We must do something.'

'They'll be all right, Michèle. Take them into the kitchen and wring them out. I must telephone.'

In his underpants he went towards the telephone. Business before pleasure. From the kitchen door, as he began to dial a Balzac number, Michèle said stubbornly, 'No, no; these will never do. I have a suit of my brother's. It is the same colour almost and the size will do. No one will notice. Then you can collect the next time. No?'

'All right, all right . . .' Alexandre waved a hand at her for silence as his number began to ring.

But later, when he came to dress, Alexandre refused to take her brother's suit. It was true that it did look a bit like his and was almost the same fit, but he was certain that someone, Yuri, Vadim in the hall, or Oleg coming in with work to him, would notice the change. Somebody certainly would; and that could be dangerous, for it would lead to questions. Where had he been? How had he got the suit? Not even Yuri would stand by him. No, it was far too dangerous. The only concession he would allow Michèle was to borrow one of her brother's shirts, so that at least he had something dry next to his skin.

As he put it on and buttoned the front, Michèle stood by him, her dark hair free over her shoulders, hugging her arms across the loose front of her dressing-gown.

'You have never mentioned your brother before?' he said.

Michèle smiled. 'We have so little time together; there are other things to talk about.'

Alexandre nodded, and then smiled, reaching forward and kissing her lightly on the lips. 'Time, yes. Soon we will have time. We shall go away. Where is this brother of yours and what does he do?' The edge of suspicion was with him. He saw Michèle so seldom that she had all the time in the world to entertain other loves. Only one thing he knew for certain; she was, indeed, a cinema usherette and went off to work about four o'clock in the afternoon.

'He is a lorry driver and lives at Blois. He comes to Paris with his lorry. Sometimes he has to stay up here a day or a night, waiting for a return load. He likes to keep some good clothes here so that he can go out and enjoy himself.'

'He sleeps here?'

'Why not – jealous?' She laughed at him. 'Would you have him pay for a hotel when he has a sister to stay with? One day you will meet him. You will like him. He is very much a gentleman when he is dressed up . . . nothing but the best. His shirts cost thirty francs. Imagine that.'

Alexandre – the rain now stopped and the sun shining hotly – went back to AGRIP with his wet shirt, wrapped in newspaper, under his arm.

Vadim, sitting at his hall desk, saw him come in. He raised his hand slightly and gave him a slow nod, watching him, noticing the damp suit.

*

They were having drinks on the terrace before dinner when Binky said, 'I've never known you like this before.'

'And what am I like?'

There was a shade of resentment in his voice and Binky laughed at it.

'You've always been the kind to make up your mind quickly and get on with whatever it is you have to do.'

Manston smiled. 'You're as good as a witch.'

Binky asked, 'Is it so unpleasant?'

'Damned unpleasant.'

'Then why do it?'

'Just because it is so damned unpleasant. I've got to do it.'

'Seems an odd reason to me.'

Manston smiled. He stood up and pulled her up to him. With his arm round her waist, he said, 'Don't let's bother with it. It's your last evening. I don't want it spoiled in any way.' Binky was going to London the next day, and he was to see her off at the airport late in the afternoon. 'You'd better come and say good-bye to the moorhens.' They began to stroll down the edge of the pool.

After dinner that evening Manston telephoned Sutcliffe's flat. Sutcliffe was out, but he left a message with Hackett; a message which he knew Sutcliffe would understand. Then for the rest of the evening he put the whole thing out of his mind.

Once, much later, waking in the night and hearing Binky's

quiet breathing at his side, he asked himself, 'Why the hell am I doing it?' He was free and had been enjoying his freedom. He could have refused Sutcliffe, could have taken off with Binky the next day . . . could have refused to put himself back in bondage.

The next morning he drove up to London with Binky. She was going to spend a morning doing some last-minute shopping, and they were to meet for lunch.

At ten o'clock he was back in his old room at the Department, from which, he guessed, someone had been hastily ejected. The people he still knew showed no surprise at his return. The secretary allotted to him was new.

She said, 'Mr Sutcliffe hasn't arrived yet. The morning papers are on your desk.'

Manston watched her leave the room, and there was something about the flick of her trim ankles that brought back to his memory the sharp movement of moorhens on his pool. He settled down with the papers and waited for Sutcliffe.

Just after the secretary had brought him coffee, Sutcliffe came into the room, trailing pipe-smoke and with a flat file tucked under his arm. He stood in front of the desk and beamed, not with triumph, but with real pleasure.

'I'm grateful, Richard. Very grateful,' he said.

'I'm here, but don't think I approve. It's a dirty business.'

'So long as you're here. That's all that matters.' Sutcliffe dropped the file on to the desk. 'This is the first time for months and months that this room has seemed properly furnished.' He tapped the file with a pudgy hand. 'This will give you all the dope. We've made a lot of progress. Barry's been running it so far. He will go on under you. It's in your hands now and you can have anything you want. The whole bloody Brigade of Guards if necessary.'

'A few good men will be better than that. I'll get stuck into this file, then I'll see you later. . . .' He paused, eyeing Sutcliffe.

'You knew I'd come back, didn't you? How could you be so sure?'

Sutcliffe shrugged his shoulders. 'I've been here a long time. I've had men as good as you leave before – and I've had them come back. Maybe only for a couple of jobs. But they come; if the jobs are right. This seemed to be your job.'

When Sutcliffe had left, Manston lit a cigarette and began on the file. There was a complete biography of Irina Tovskaya. *Born Volkhov, 23rd June, 1940. Height 5 feet 4 inches. Hair, dark brown. Eyes, brown. Distinguishing marks, mole on right thigh.* Who the hell had supplied that titbit, he wondered? Probably Elsa Polani. He read on. In brief, official jargon her whole history was laid out. Her father had been a schoolteacher, her mother a doctor, and neither of them had been members of the Communist Party. Her brother, Gregorovich, was three years older than Irina. Both parents had been killed in the later part of the war. Irina and her brother had been brought up by an aunt and uncle in Leningrad. Through the aunt, Irina had joined the Leningrad State Ballet School. Gregorovich had gone into the army, Engineer Corps. He had deserted from East Berlin two years before Irina had done the same thing in Paris. There was a complete dossier of his interrogation by the American authorities and a similar dossier for Irina, beginning at the British Embassy in Paris, then continued by the Department. They had both been cleared.

There was a clip of reports from Paris on the agent they had with AGRIP. His name was Alexandre Shernof, a cipher clerk. Their Paris agent was now someone new to Manston, a man called Robert Casalis. The last report from Casalis read: *I am milking Alexandre Shernof as hard and fast as possible. He doesn't impress me as the kind who will last long.* Manston saw that he had been enlisted through the agency of a French girl called Michèle Guichard, who had now and again worked for the Department. There were photographs of Shernof and Guichard, and a report on the organization of AGRIP, together with a photograph of the man who was running its clandestine operations. He looked a tough number, Manston thought. Georgi Oleg.

Slowly, Manston read through the transcripts of the messages which Alexandre Shernof had passed over. Capa, Taru, and Limbo. It was interesting, he thought, how unconsciously the people who played this dirty game – and that must include himself – couldn't resist the romantic touch in the choice of a code-name, as though, somehow, the music of a word might offset the sordidness of the operation. From the facts they had it was clear that there were three movement stages. Capa was the London end. They handed over to Taru and Taru to Limbo. Shernof could give no locations for Taru or Limbo. They might be anywhere.

He went through the details of the set-up for watching Irina Tovskaya, which had been made since her name had been passed to them. They were competent, and had Barry Dymen written all over them. There was nothing he could add to them. In addition, there was a report on the possible identity of Capa. The man with the Pekinese, who was in the habit of taking a stroll down Gloucester Place each evening, was Charles Hardwick, aged fifty-four; originally a Pole, now a naturalized British subject. He had changed his name, on naturalization, from Horvic. He lived in St John's Wood, was a bachelor, and owned a garage near Regent's Park. The garage was also the business headquarters of a small continental coach touring company – Hardwick Tours – which Hardwick ran in partnership with a Miss Pauline Rylands, aged forty-three. She had a thirty-five per cent share in the company. A brochure of the Hardwick Tours was attached to the reports on both these people.

Right at the end of the file was a complete list, covering the last two years, of all the people who had been kidnapped and taken back from England, and the other European countries concerned. Sutcliffe was right about their being small people; minor officials from trade delegations, airline pilots, Embassy chauffeurs and servants, athletes; there was not a big name amongst them.

When he had finished, Manston sent for Barry Dymen.

Coming in to him, Barry said, 'Welcome back. Couldn't resist it, eh?'

Manston smiled. 'I'm here. Let's leave it at that. Well . . .' he indicated the file, 'what do you think of all that?'

'So far as we can say at the moment, I'd presume that Hardwick was running Capa. He's taking an enormous interest in the girl. The continental coach tour business might be a lead.'

'I see you've got a man into the garage.'

'Yes, there was a vacancy for a petrol-pump attendant. Do you think they would ship her out in a coach?'

'Could do. But it means she would have to be packed away neatly, and kept unconscious for a few hours at least. What I'd like is a complete set of photographs of these coaches and detailed specifications of them from the manufacturers. Until we get any other lead we must watch this one. When does the next tour leave?'

'They do one a fortnight. The next – France and Italy – leaves on the thirtieth.'

'That's the date that Capa have given AGRIP.'

'Yes. I've got a man booked to travel on it. I've a feeling it's going to be this way.'

'Twenty-sixth today. We've got four days. They can pick her up any time from now on.'

'That may be a bit awkward for them.'

'Why?'

'Because,' Barry said, 'I've just learned from Elsa Polani – she doesn't know anything about this business, of course – that the Tovskaya girl isn't working, as from today. She's got a week off. No dancing, no rehearsals. For all Capa know she could be going away.'

'They'll know soon enough that she's not working and that her movements may be irregular. They must have met that situation before. I think I'll go up and have a look at this Hardwick Garage before lunch. We'll get together on this again later.'

Before leaving the Department, Manston went in to see Sutcliffe. He told him that, so far as he could see, the only likely lead they had at the moment was the Hardwick Tour one.

'It's pretty clear that AGRIP organize the whole thing, but I imagine are not active in it. This is a cash job done by other people. Limbo, certainly, from their messages are cash-minded. Stinks, doesn't it? You want the bodies delivered. We'll do it, so much a nob. I'd like to have a talk with this Robert Casalis in Paris. He'll have to arrange things the French side for me.'

'I'll get him over first thing tomorrow.'

'Good. Now, I'm going to have a look at this Hardwick place. One advantage, at least, we've got: so long as this Shernof bloke keeps clear of trouble, AGRIP have no idea we're beginning to sit on their tail.'

*

Before lunch, Manston took his car and went up to Regent's Park. On the north side, short of Lords, he pulled into the Hardwick Garage and filled up with Esso Super. There was a big yard at the rear of the garage, full of cars under repair; and, in a couple of bays to the right of the yard, he saw two long-distance coaches painted yellow and black. The coach tour offices were above the garage offices. All he could see of them was a run of glass window, half-frosted at the bottom and surmounted with a long notice in yellow neon strip, HARDWICK CONTINENTAL TOURS. BOOK HERE.

He drove back to his club in Brook Street, by way of Gloucester Place. Barry Dymen had taken over an empty flat in one of the houses obliquely facing Irina's building.

Manston found Ritchie in the sitting-room which overlooked the street. He was making a lunch of corned-beef sandwiches and bottled beer. Another man sat just back from the window, watching the street and the building.

Ritchie straightened his bow-tie and let a slow smile escape from under his bushy eyebrows. 'So you was kiddin' me all the time, sir.'

'Something like that, Ritchie. How are things?'

'We've got a comfortable pitch here. We keep two out and two in.' He tapped a telephone which stood on the table. 'Direct line. Couldn't be more comfortable. That's Williams.'

The man at the window turned briefly and nodded.

'New, but promisin',' said Ritchie.

'Is she in?' Manston nodded through the window.

'No, sir. Gone out. Looked real nice, too. But then any girl does these days in a summer frock. Special Branch have got a bloke in the bedroom. They take over once she moves out of our area. Must be important, as well as a pretty piece?' Although it was a question, it was never intended to be answered. Ritchie knew better than that.

Williams at the window said without excitement, 'That's funny. Here he is, about ten hours too early. Got a woman with him, too. And the dog.'

Manston moved closer to the window. On the far pavement a man and a woman had halted by the steps leading up to the house. The man was tallish, elderly, neatly dressed in a dark suit and bowler hat. The woman was dumpy, plain; wearing a grey dress, and a little black hat with the edge of a purple feather showing in it. As Manston watched, the woman reached out and took a dog's lead from the man's hand. A Pekinese appeared from behind his legs. The woman, with a faint wave of her hand, walked on down the street. The man turned and went up the steps. He needed no key to open the door; for during the office hours of the firms that occupied all the floors, except the Tovskaya flat, it was held back with a large door-stopper.

'Having a quiet look round,' said Ritchie.

'And he knows that it's safe,' said Manston almost to himself. 'When did the girl go out, Ritchie?'

'About fifteen minutes ago, sir.'

'Then there was someone hanging about waiting to spot her. He's now had time to phone and get his boss down. Check with your other two when they come in and see if you can spot him. He'll probably be here again.'

'Yes, sir. But what about him?' Ritchie nodded across the room.

Manston shrugged his shoulders. 'Just report it.'

Five minutes later he was standing at the bar in his club, having a glass of sherry while he waited for Binky. By this evening, he thought, he would have seen her off; she'd be on her way to Africa. Just for a moment he wished that she were not going, that nothing was to change, that Sutcliffe had never come down to play golf, that . . . Oh, hell, that so many things had not happened.

Out of the window he saw her getting out of a taxi. He finished his sherry and went down to meet her.

4

ROBERT CASALIS ARRIVED from Paris the next morning. It was the twenty-seventh of August and the day was already building up to one of scorching heat. Manston and Casalis sat in the office with their jackets off, and Manston went through a quick briefing of the situation. He found, very soon, that Casalis was not the kind who needed to linger over detail. He had a quick, ranging mind, almost photographic, which enabled him to look at a page of notes and take it all in without appearing to read it. He was a man of about forty, youthful-looking still, but a shade overblown with muscular fat, in the way rowing men sometimes go when they give up their sport. He was fair-haired and honest-looking, his friendly face made more friendly by soft, brown eyes.

'The odds are, at the moment,' said Manston, 'that they are going to use a coach. We've got a man booked on that. I shall come over on the same boat from Dover. From Calais we've got to have cast-iron cover, and it must be the kind of cover that can go on for days, if necessary, and move quickly.'

'Shouldn't be too difficult. We can have three cars in radio communication. One out ahead of the coach, one close behind – we can be in that – and the third can be left, swinging, to move as we want it, say along a parallel road. They won't be official-looking cars; and, with reliefs, we can keep them running for a month, if you want.'

'I hope not. You can fix all that, can you?'

'Sure. The Sûreté will make an awful stink about it, but they'll do it. Their instinct is that, once something comes on to their territory, they want to take it over.'

'They can't. There isn't going to be time for any nice hand-over. We've got to be right behind this girl all the way. If you want any big priorities, or to put the pressure on in Paris, then you'd better have a word with Sutcliffe. All I want is to come ashore at Calais, and be behind that coach, and know that we can call up help in a few minutes. O.K.?'

'O.K.'

'And, above all, nobody is to do any jumping. This is just a watch-and-follow job.'

Casalis smiled. 'The hardest. Watch-and-jump any day for me.'

After Casalis had gone, Manston called his secretary and said, 'Get hold of the lab. people and tell them I want a complete list of normally procurable drugs, which can be hypodermically injected and knock a person out cold for twenty-four hours. I want to know all about them. How quick they work, characteristics of behaviour as the person recovers, and possible after-effects.'

He spent the half-hour before lunch going through the coach photographs and specifications which had come from Barry Dymen. All the Hardwick Tour coaches were thirty-two seaters, eight double seats on each side, and two more seats up front for the driver and someone they described as the tour manager. All luggage was carried in an enormous boot at the rear of the coach. Using the Leyland Motors detailed drawings and specifications Manston spent some time with a ruler and pencil, making modifications of his own to the scale drawings. He had a moment of vicarious claustrophobia as he realized into how small a space a human body – deprived of any power to struggle or shout – could be packed.

He called Barry Dymen and gave him some instructions for the man who was working as a pump attendant at the garage. He finished, 'but get it into his head that he mustn't force any opportunity to do this. No initiative whatever. Just take the chance if it comes.'

He left the office, and the heat from the pavement came up into his face. The red buses swam by, their tyres singing on the soft tarmac; and the sky over Trafalgar Square was leaden with heat. Seeing the fountains playing, and a bunch of children, police-defying, shouting with pleasure, romping in the waters of the fountain basins, he had a quick picture of his own pool.

He got a taxi and told the driver to go to Gloucester Place, by way of Berkeley Square. In the Square he stopped the taxi for a few minutes, and went into Moyses Stevens and bought a dozen yellow roses. He paid off the taxi at Irina's house and stood casually for a moment or two on the steps before going in. Ritchie, or one of his men, would be watching and he wanted them to know it was him.

The main door was open, propped back by a wrought-iron porpoise. He went up the stairs, and rang the doorbell of the flat. There was no sound of movement from within and, for a while, he thought that Irina might be out. Then, when he was about to give up, he heard someone moving inside.

The door opened and she was standing there, blinking at him a little in the gloom of the tiny hall. She was wearing a loose house-coat, and her legs were bare, her feet thrust into tiny golden slippers. He told himself that she had probably been sun-bathing on her roof.

'Oh, it's you.' Her voice, surprised and pleased, was a little husky with the sun, too.

He smiled. 'I had to come up to town for a few days, and I've brought you a bribe.'

He held out the roses. She took them, lowering her face to them, and watching him over the yellow blooms.

'How lovely. What for?'

'I want you to have supper with me tonight.'

She laid the roses against her breast, and said, 'I'd love to.'

'What time will you be free?'

'Well, actually I'm not working for a few days.'

'Good. In that case I'll call for you about six.'

'Six – isn't that early?'

'I thought we'd go out into the country and eat. It will be cooler. Bring a swimsuit – I know a place where we can swim. Six?'

She nodded.

He had a glass of Chablis and two crab sandwiches for lunch, in a pub in Dover Street, and went back to the office.

Barry Dymen came in after about an hour.

'I hear you called on her at lunch-time. Stayed ten minutes.'

'Correct.'

'With a bunch of yellow roses?' Barry raised an eyebrow.

'Part of the service. I'm taking her out to dinner tonight.'

'Is that wise?'

'Nobody except Capa is supposed to know what is going to happen to her. They must fit in with whatever she does. We don't have to make anything easy for the bastards. So, she gets taken out to dinner in the country.'

'Very nice, too.'

Manston ignored this, and said, 'I'll give you our timetable and route and I'll phone twice during the evening.'

When Barry had gone, Manston sat, wondering why he was taking Irina out. It was a pleasant thing to do. He liked the girl very much; but there was more to it than that. In a way he felt guilty about her and wanted to do whatever he could for her. This service, of which he was part, was going to use her coldly and callously for its own purposes. If anything went wrong, it would be prepared to write her off; and be equally prepared to try again with someone else, if it got the chance. People didn't exist in their own right here. He was finding it hard to adopt that attitude . . . damned hard.

*

Oleg leaned back to escape the shaft of strong sunlight that streamed across his desk. On the desk lay a routine commercial message which Alexandre had brought in to him just before going off to lunch.

Sideways out of the window Oleg could see the stretch of the Quai des Célestins. He eyed the movement down there without any emotion. Except where work and duty were concerned, he had long learned the trick of putting a glaze over his eyes and thoughts, a kind of permanent refrigeration of part of himself, which he had no intention of allowing to thaw out, until he was back in Russia. Outside Russia, a man worked. He could only live when he got back.

There was a knock on the door and, in answer to his call, Vadim came in. The elderly man came forward, crablike, his left shoulder leading his right. He came right up to the edge of the desk and then made a slow movement of shoulders and arms which sketched a laboured attempt at standing to attention.

'Well?' Oleg put a little extra bark into the word to show that he was in no mood for long-windedness.

Vadim sniffed, and said, 'Two days ago Alexandre went out to lunch. It was the day of the big thunderstorm. When he came back, his suit was wet through and he was carrying a small parcel wrapped in newspaper under his arm. That evening he took a damp shirt from the parcel. He put it in his dirty laundry bag.'

'So?'

'The shirt he was wearing when he went to bed was quite dry.'

'He sleeps in his shirt?'

'These nights, sometimes, when it is so hot, yes. His pyjamas are very thick. This morning he changed the shirt when he got up.'

Oleg's blunt nose wrinkled a little in disgust at the hygienic habits of his clerk who wore a shirt for more than forty-eight hours.

'So?' The word cracked in the room like a sheet of ice going.

'At first I imagined, perhaps, that getting wet through he had bought himself a dry shirt at some store and, perhaps, changed in the lavatory. A man would do that, perhaps, to be comfortable.'

'Perhaps.'

'But this morning I examined the shirt. You have said so often that one should not overlook any detail.'

'Correct.'

'It was not a new shirt. It had been laundered many times and' – Vadim's right hand fumbled in his jacket pocket and he pulled out a piece of paper which he held close to his eyes to read – 'the tab at the back of the collar read, *Gerard Frères, Avenue Victor Hugo, Blois*. A shirt from Blois, not new.'

'Interesting. Thank you, Vadim.'

Vadim stood, hesitating by the desk, and then, his face

briefly and anxiously marked with a faded smile, said, 'I did right?'

'You did, Vadim. You may go.'

When Vadim had gone, Oleg sat for some time thinking. Alexandre was a first-class cipher clerk . . . in fact, as far as his work went he was almost brilliant. But he was dirty in his habits and, like all near-brilliant people, he was uncertain. Vadim's type would never give any trouble. And maybe forty-nine Alexandres out of fifty wouldn't, either. But there was always the fiftieth. Neglect nothing.

Oleg reached for the telephone and asked that Yuri be found and sent up to him.

An hour later Yuri stood in front of Oleg; and Yuri sensed at once that something was wrong. He was worried because he knew that he could not always produce answers as quickly as Oleg could put questions.

Oleg said, 'You followed Alexandre today?'

'As always.'

'What did he do?'

After a moment's hesitation Yuri said, 'The usual . . .' But he was thinking fast. 'After his canteen lunch here, he walks down the *quai* to the Square Henri Galli. He had a *bock* in the Bar d'Aubigne, as usual, and then walked right round the barracks. Some days, he goes one way and some days, another. Up the Henri Quatre to the Place de la Bastille, and back by the Rue de l'Arsenal. Sometimes he cuts off the top of the triangle by going across the Rue de la Cerisaie. He did today.'

'And what did he do two days ago, on the 25th?'

'The day of the big thunderstorm? He was in the Place de la Bastille when it started. He started back towards the Rue de l'Arsenal and I followed him. But it came down so heavily – we were both drenched – that he turned into the Rue de la Cerisaie and found shelter in a doorway. I sheltered too, in a doorway about twenty yards down the street. I stayed there about twenty minutes until the storm stopped. When it did, he left the doorway and I followed him back here.'

'Could you actually see him in this doorway?'

'No. There was no cover on the other side of the road which I could use. Short of going into the doorway with him I could do nothing.'

'Did anyone else use the doorway while he was there?'

Without hesitation, knowing that there was a limit to his loyalty to Alexandre, even, Yuri said, 'Yes. A girl wearing a mackintosh. She was not there when Alexandre left. She must live, or have been visiting, in the house.'

'Didn't this strike you as odd?'

'No. Alexandre shelters in a house doorway. If the owner or lodger returns and goes in that is not unusual.'

'He could have gone in?'

'For twenty minutes, yes. But it did not strike me as likely or worth reporting. But I can find out if he did go in.'

'How?'

Yuri smiled. 'If he went in for twenty minutes then it was at the girl's invitation. That makes her only one kind of girl. It should not be difficult.'

'I wish to know.'

'Very good.'

When Yuri had gone, Oleg sat thinking about him and about Alexandre. Alexandre was not supposed to know that Yuri had been assigned to him. Anyone who had access to secret files, codes or information was always covered. Alexandre was not supposed to know that Vadim watched him. But, Oleg acknowledged, Alexandre would be a fool to have assumed that he was not watched in some way, and, while it would be natural to assume that Vadim was one of the watchers, he ought not to have known about Yuri. Perhaps he didn't. The outside men were changed every four months and Yuri's term was about up. Even Oleg had moments of wondering whether all this surveillance was not, at times, so much overdone that the purpose behind it was defeated. Everybody watched everybody else, and the thing came full circle. For all he knew, Alexandre might be reporting on him. Though there was nothing to report. If he, Oleg, had been sheltering in that doorway and some tart with an eye to business had invited him in he would not have gone. But Alexandre might well have gone in; must have done to have been lent a shirt. That type of girl was commonly generous and compassionate, as well as shrewd. The shirt would have to be returned. Who knew, Alexandre might become a regular customer. Anyway, as soon as he heard from Yuri, he would make a full report to the Embassy. Yuri must be checked, too.

He had his report from Yuri by five o'clock that evening. The girl was Michèle Guichard, aged twenty-seven, a cinema usherette, and also, since her wages did not provide any luxuries in life, occasionally given to entertaining men. She had been born in Blois and had lived in Paris for eight years. She had a small flat on the third floor of the house in the Rue de la Cerisaie. She had entertained Alexandre for fifteen minutes and lent him one of her brother's shirts.

All this information Yuri had obtained from Alexandre himself. As he had left Oleg, he had met Alexandre on the first floor landing of the AGRIP building, and had jerked his head towards the lavatories. They had had a two-minute interview in which Yuri had reluctantly, but for the safety of them both, said that from now on he would be turning in the truth on Alexandre's movements, and had made quite clear to him, after he had heard about the shirt, what he was going to report to Oleg.

*

By six-thirty they were free of London and on the A.20. The evening was warm and he had put the hood down. Irina sat alongside him, a silk scarf over her hair, wearing a linen suit into the lapel of which, he noticed, she had fastened one of his yellow roses. She was the kind of girl, he thought, that any man would be flattered to have alongside him in a car. He drove fast and they did not talk much.

At Wrotham Heath he swung off the A.20 and took the road up by the golf-course, heading for Paddock Wood. It was a beautiful summer evening, the sun still burning the grass, everything wrapped in a green peace. Twenty minutes later they pulled up at the Rose and Crown in Brenchley for dinner. They had a drink in the Elephant bar and both decided to have melon and cold lobster, with a bottle of *Pouilly Fumé*.

Over dinner, at some point, he said to her, 'What is the greatest change in your life since leaving the Kirov?'

Irina thought for a moment and said, 'The fact that I am now an individual. You see, in the Ballet, I was one of a group. We weren't people, we were a group, a collective. You never did anything on your own. I lived with three other girls. When we travelled, we travelled together. We never had individual tickets, always group tickets, always altogether in the same bus. It was a bad thing to be different.'

'That's why you don't mind living alone now?'

'I love it. You can't imagine what it is to have a room, a flat, all to yourself. It's heaven.'

Before they left the Rose and Crown, Manston called the office. Barry Dymen was not yet on duty, but his assistant answered. There was nothing to report from the London end. Manston said he was going on to his house, and would ring Barry before he started the return trip to London.

They drove on through Horsmonden, Goudhurst and Sissinghurst to his house. Bumping down the narrow farm lane Irina said, 'This is where you live?'

'Yes. I thought we might have a swim and a drink before we started back for London.'

The sky was turning a purply smoke-grey, now that the sun had set, and the air above them was cut by the erratic passage of bats.

As they walked round the terrace, Irina cried, 'Oh, what a lovely pool. And look at the ducks!'

'Not ducks – moorhens. And they shouldn't be here. They've got their own stream. Shall we swim now?'

'Please, yes.'

He showed her the gazebo where she could change. She had a large white summer bag over her arm in which she had brought her swimsuit.

'I'll change in the house. Be with you in a moment.'

He left her and went into the house. He fixed a tray of drinks and left them on a table just inside the sitting-room door. Then he went up to his room and changed. He switched on the pool lights and, as he came down, he heard the splash of a dive. On the terrace he saw Irina swimming lazily down the length of the pool. He dived in after her.

The low-level flood-lights silvered the trails of summer evening mist over the water, which was so warm that their bodies seemed to float in a vacuum. Irina had her hair screwed back, and tied with a length of ribbon. Her shoulders and arms were brown; and he guessed that she did a lot of sunbathing on her rooftop. She turned and laughed at him and then abandoned herself to the water, rolling and diving like some slim, lithe sea-animal. She lay on her back and kicked her feet hard; churning the water into a white froth, sending great spouts into the air where the bright light reflections were shattered and silvered by the spray.

When he helped her out of the pool, he saw that she was wearing a white swimsuit. With her dark hair clinging damply to her forehead, her slim tanned body and the pleasure shining in her eyes, she was beautiful, vital, full of happiness. For a moment she was just a lovely girl; a gorgeous girl with whom he was happy to be spending an evening. Then, as his eyes travelled over her, he saw on her right thigh the brown mole mark, which had been noted in her dossier. Reality, the bitter knowledge of the future which lay close ahead for her, struck at him. Something of his feelings must have shown in his face, for she said, 'You frown. Is something wrong?'

He smiled. 'Wrong? Of course not. What could be wrong on an evening like this? A beautiful evening, a beautiful girl – and a large drink waiting for us as soon as we've changed.'

When they had both changed, they lay in deep wicker chairs on the terrace, and had drinks.

Irina said, 'You live here all alone?'

'I have a daily housekeeper. My bailiff's wife – they live in a cottage at the other end of the farm. She comes in and looks after me. Then there's Joss, my dog. He stays with the bailiff when I'm away. He doesn't really approve of my going away at all, though.'

'Neither does Nijinsky. He gets jealous and then he . . . he sculks.'

Manston laughed. 'Not sculks. Sulks.'

'Sulks. That's right.'

As she spoke, the telephone in the house began to ring. Manston excused himself, and got up and went through to his study.

It was Barry Dymen on the telephone. The moment he recognized his voice, Manston reached out with his foot and kicked the study-door shut.

'Barry here.'

'Yes. What moves?'

'Quite a bit. You've got her there?'

'Yes.'

'Nice evening?'

'Yes.'

'I'm glad.'

'Why?' Manston asked sharply, moved by the tone of Barry's voice.

'Because I think it's the last she's likely to have for some time.'

'What's happened?'

'Mr H. and another man went in about ten minutes ago. They've obviously settled there to wait. They had a key to the main door. There's a small green van parked around the corner with another man in it.'

As Barry spoke, Manston looked at his watch. It was now ten minutes to ten. He could be back in London with Irina before midnight.

At the other end of the line, Barry said, 'What's the form? You'll be bringing her back and they'll be waiting. If you go into the flat you'll run straight into them and they'll have to deal with you.'

Manston considered this. Any man who took a girl out for the evening would see her home. He would have to go up to the door of her flat. He did not have to go inside. He would have to let her walk straight into trouble. His lips tightened with disgust.

His voice hard, he said to Barry, 'Don't worry, I'll keep clear. The moment I leave her I'll park the car somewhere and go up to Ritchie.'

'I'll be there. We'll have the whole place covered. Nothing can go wrong. What time will you be back?'

'Just before midnight.'

After he had rung off he stood in the room, lighting a cigarette. She was waiting out on the terrace for him, relaxed with the pleasure of a pleasant evening. Not an idea in her head that anything could happen to her. It was then, in that moment, that he realized just how strong the feeling in him had been almost two years ago when he had resigned. He just didn't have the kind of lead-lined stomach which could take this kind of thing.

He went out and stood over her.

'We ought to be going,' he said.

She reached up a hand and he took it, pulling her from the long chair. For a moment, as she found her feet, she stood close to him, the flood-lights making her dark eyes shine, the fragrant warmth of her breath just touching his face for a moment. The compassion in him for her suddenly made him feel angry.

He shut up the house, and they drove off. He drove fast and was glad that she seemed in no mood to talk. She just lay back in her seat, the wind teasing at her head scarf.

There was little traffic about as he turned into Gloucester Place. Ten minutes to twelve his watch showed. He drew up outside her place, and he knew that many eyes were watching them. Not the least attentive would be the eyes from the flat windows on the top floor.

'Well, here we are . . .' he flopped back into his seat.

'Will you come in and have a drink?'

Manston shook his head.

'I'll see you up to your door, but I won't stay. I've got a heavy day tomorrow.'

They went up the steps together and then, flicking on the lights as they went, made the long climb to the top flat. At the door she halted, picking about in her bag for her key. He took it from her as she brought it out and reached towards the Yale lock. The door opened a shade as he turned the key.

'It was a lovely evening,' she said. 'Thank you very, very much.'

It was said simply, her voice low with pleasure. Her face was raised to him, as a woman does when, out of gratitude and friendship, she offers her lips to a man. For Manston it was a hard moment. All he had to do was take her by the arm and turn her away, take her down and out of the building. Instead he raised his hands and held her by the shoulders.. Then he put his lips on hers, and he felt her lips, feather-light, warm, caress his; move for a moment closer, promising; and then withdraw.

'Goodnight,' he said.

'Goodnight. And thank you.'

He stood, watching her. She made a little movement of her

right hand, then she pushed the door open and went in. The door closed and he heard the faint click of the light switch. There was no other sound. Slowly he turned away, and went down the stairs. He clamped down on his imagination, not wanting to know what might now be going on in the flat.

He slammed the outer door hard and then got into his car. He drove fast down Gloucester Place and into Montagu Place, and parked his car. Five minutes later, he was in the flat across the road from Irina's place.

The room was in darkness. Sutcliffe, Barry Dymen and Ritchie were there. They stood in a little group drawn back from the window. Barry had the telephone in his hand, talking to someone in a soft voice.

Sutcliffe said, 'Evening, Richard.'

'Evening.' Manston kept all feeling from his voice.

'Apparently they don't mind holding her for a couple of days. Must be sure of themselves. Light's still on.'

Manston looked up. The light showed from the windows of Irina's flat, where there was a gap in the drawn curtains.

Barry's voice said down the telephone, 'O.K. Well, keep two of them moving. It's a green Austin van. RMK 452.' Barry looked across at Manston. 'It's a van from the Hardwick Garage, but the number plates have been changed.'

Sutcliffe said, 'They're taking their time about it. She's been up there over ten minutes now.'

Manston said nothing. Imagination could not be kept at bay. He could see her in the act of tossing the big summer bag on to her bed. Someone would move behind her, the arm would come out around her throat, firm but definite, stopping all cry; and the chloroform pad would suddenly block her face, sending panic winging through her. . . . He swore to himself.

Sutcliffe said, surprisingly, 'It's a bloody business.' But Manston was not deceived. Sutcliffe often paid lip-service to a situation. Inwardly he would be delighted that the job was going smoothly.

Ritchie said, 'Here's one of them.'

The main door of the house opposite opened and a small man, hatless, the jacket of his suit open, came easily down the steps and walked up and around into York Street.

'Getting the van,' said Barry into the telephone.

A few moments later the van came round the corner and drew up outside the house. The driver got out, went round the back and opened the doors of the van. Then, after a look up and down the road, he went up the steps. The door opened from within as he reached it. He went into the darkness.

It happened then, quickly and smoothly, and was over and finished without leaving a ripple on the night. They came down the steps, Irina between them, and it was impossible to say whether they carried her or she walked between them. She was just between them, obscured, and they took her to the back of the van and eased her in.

The back doors of the van were closed. Hardwick got in alongside the driver, and the van moved off. The hatless man watched it go down Gloucester Place, then turned and walked leisurely up towards Marylebone Road.

Barry said into the telephone. 'The van's left now. Going down Gloucester Place. Got it?' He paused, waiting, then said, 'Good.'

Sutcliffe stirred, turned from the window, and faced Manston. 'Barry can handle things here. No need for us to stay.'

Manston said, 'Has anyone got a key to that place?'

Ritchie's hand came out through the gloom. 'Outer door and her flat, sir.'

Manston took the keys. 'I'm just going to have a look round. Then I shall go back to the office. Barry, tie in all the reports there, will you?'

Barry nodded.

Without a word to Sutcliffe, Manston went out.

He let himself into the building and went up the stairs to the flat. He didn't need a key for her door. It was ajar and the light was still on. The sitting-room was tidy, untouched. In the window Nijinsky chirped once, sleepily. He went into the kitchen. A small saucepan of milk had been put on the gas ring. Someone had turned the gas out. The milk was faintly warm. He went back into the sitting-room and through to her bedroom. The light was on and the moment he entered he could smell the chloroform. The rug by the bed was scuffled. Her handbag lay on the bed and, near the dressing-table which held a vase of yellow roses, one yellow rose lay on the floor, brushed from her jacket lapel. It had been trodden on, and the bruised petals were scattered on the bare boards.

He stood there, looking round the room and his face was set with the look of a man who has a bitter taste in his mouth.

5

It was a curious dream in which time and place, while clearly disjointed, gave her no worry at all. Memory and desire seemed free to roam and collect what they wished, in order to arrange life pleasantly; a life of the past which was also, oddly, part of the future.

She was staying with an uncle, her mother's brother, who lived a few miles from the shores of Lake Ladoga. Her mother, of course, despised her brother for his lowliness and coarseness, but she, Irina, liked him. He was a big, mountainous man, always laughing, and he made a living cutting reeds in the summer and wild-fowling in the winter. They drove down to the lake in his old trap with the sorrel mare hanging her head against the mosquitoes which plagued the shores. She could feel the sand, coarse and hot against her bare feet; and then she was swimming, finally turning over on her back to look skywards, where the fishhawks were black pinheads against the blue. She was a child and yet she was grown up. Lowering her eyes shorewards she suddenly saw Richard Manston come down between the birches, get into a boat and row out. A long rod jutted, pencil thin, over the bow. He rowed out to her and rested on his oars, the water slap-slapping gently against the side of the boat. He was sturdily handsome, and the water reflections moved in his eyes and over the brown skin of his face; and she was thinking to herself, the young woman accommodated easily in the child's body, that, if she had to fall in love, it could only be with him. Before he spoke she knew how his voice would be.

He said, 'If I had a net I'd try for sturgeon. But today it must be trout. Dive down and see if there are any.'

Obedient, enthralled willingly by the easy, commanding voice, she dived, arrowing downwards through the clear, jade-striped waters; and saw the trout, and the schools of thin, silver-flanked elvers, stream away from her. She came up to find him gone, but her mother was shouting angrily to her from the shore and her uncle was laughing. She swam in reluctantly and her mother's hand gripped her shoulder, as she rose from the water, shaking at her.

She came to, briefly. A short, middle-aged woman was standing over her, one hand still shaking at her shoulder. She wore a loose green wrapper, like a kitchen coat, and her face was ordinary and not unkind.

'Drink this.'

The glass was at her lips and she drank, suddenly aware of her thirst, the woman's free arm now half supporting her. The arm left her, and she dropped back. Her eyes went round the room and there was nothing to see except unplastered brick wall and, over the woman's shoulder, part of a door.

She closed her eyes, hoping that if she did so she would return to the lake.

The woman dropped on one knee by the bed and, her mouth close to Irina's ear, she said, 'Can you hear me?'

Irina nodded slowly.

'Good girl. Now try to understand this. You are quite safe. If you behave yourself, no harm will come to you. Just behave. . . .'

The woman's voice became mixed up with the echo of her mother's voice on the lake beach, and she drifted away and then came back, momentarily, to hear the woman's voice say, 'You may be sick. It means nothing. There is something by the side of the bed if you are . . .'

Irina tried to nod but the effort was beyond her.

*

Manston lay on the camp-bed, which was set up in the ante-room to his office. He had spent many a night on this bed, and there had been a time quite recently when he had known, for certain, that he never would again. So much for certainty.

It had been three o'clock before all the reports on the Irina Tovskaya kidnapping were in. The green van had been driven some way up the Edgware Road and then back for a complete circle of Regent's Park before going into Hardwick's garage. Irina had been lifted out, and taken through a door at the back, which led into the small garden of the house occupied by Miss Pauline Rylands, Hardwick's partner. The petrol-pump attendant, whom Barry had got into the garage, had already furnished a complete layout of the house and its communications with the garage. Irina was now somewhere in the house and the house and garage were under observation from six different points.

He lit a cigarette and blew smoke at the ceiling, frowning. From now on nobody could let up for a second.

The door opened and Sutcliffe came in. He sat down on a chair, straddling it, resting his arms on the back and began to fill his pipe.

'I thought you'd gone,' said Manston.

'No.' He was silent for a while and then said, 'This is the bad moment, eh?'

'It always is – when a thing starts rolling. You only hope that you've got everything under control.'

Sutcliffe nodded. 'You don't have to worry about the Press. That's covered. As for her friends at Covent Garden . . . well, she's on a few days' holiday.'

Manston, with an ironical lift of his eyebrows, said 'Holiday's a good word.'

Sutcliffe stood up, making no comment. He stumped towards the door, a mandarin frown shadowing his eyes. At the door he paused, looking back at Manston.

Abruptly, he said, 'You like her, don't you?'

Manston nodded. 'Yes, very much. She's honest, she's natural – and she's easily hurt. And, if you want me to say it again, I think the whole business stinks.'

'It does – but it's necessary.'

*

Early the next morning – the twenty-eighth of August – Barry came in with a report from their man who worked at the Hardwick Garage. Following Manston's instructions he had found an opportunity to check the coaches, and had discovered that the boot of one had been modified with a false back, leaving a cavity behind it big enough to take a body.

'Clinches it, don't you think?' said Barry.

'Is it the coach that's due out on the thirtieth?'

'He's pretty sure it is. Hell of a way to travel, eh?'

Manston said nothing, but all that day the thought of it kept coming back to him.

Before dinner that evening he took a taxi to Regent's Park and walked through towards Lord's cricket ground. Ritchie was installed in a small bachelor flat some way from the garage but giving a good view of it. The Special Branch had got hold of the owner, a middle-aged bachelor, clerk in one of the City banking houses; and had arranged for him to spend a few nights at an hotel. It was easy to do. Manston had done it himself many times. Ritchie was very happy in his look-out.

'Lordy, sir – you want to see some of the books the old boy has about. Erotica – that the word?'

Manston grinned. 'It makes it sound nicer.' There was no need to ask Ritchie what went on at the garage. The reports had been coming in all day from six different observation points. Nothing went on. It was just a garage.

'That Pekinese,' said Ritchie. 'Never known a dog that wanted so much walkin'.'

Manston said, 'When I go down to Dover the day after tomorrow, Ritchie, I want you to come with me. You can drive my car back. Fresh air will do you good.'

'And very nice, too, sir. Could do with a change.'

Manston stared out at the garage, with its run of parking-bays behind the small house of Miss Pauline Rylands, backing up to the bays. Somewhere in that house now was Irina. He turned away from the window impatiently.

He got a taxi and went to his club for dinner.

*

On the morning of the twenty-ninth of August, Alexandre Shernof came to a decision. Ever since Yuri had talked to him about the shirt he had borrowed from Michèle he had been worried. He realized, now, that he should have been more careful, but it was too late to be regretful about that. He knew, too, that Oleg – not necessarily through Yuri – would have Michèle investigated. It was this that worried him. His first meeting with Michèle had been a casual lunch-time affair in the Place de la Bastille. They had met two or three times and then Michèle had invited him back to her room. They had made love; and gradually Alexandre had admitted his desire to break loose from AGRIP and from his own people. To do this they needed money, and Michèle had suggested to him how to make it. She knew a man who would pay for information.

Alexandre had never met him. He communicated by telephone from Michèle's flat, and the payment was made to Michèle at her flat. Thinking it over now, Alexandre was horrified at the simplicity with which he had committed himself to a dangerous position. His only consolation was that he trusted Michèle implicitly and was sure that she loved him, would do anything for him and go anywhere with him. If that weren't true, then there was no longer any truth in life for him. The greatest worry now was how obvious any connection between Michèle and the man he sold information to might be. Michèle had assured him that for four years she had had no personal contact with the man. She refused to tell him how she had first met him, but Alexandre could guess that probably they had been lovers. Never once had he imagined that he was the only lover Michèle had ever had.

Half-way through the morning he decided that he would be a fool to stay and risk his future happiness. He had not made as much money as he wanted, but he had enough. They could go away. He could get false papers and he could work . . . drop into obscurity in Spain or Portugal or somewhere.

A message came in from Capa at mid-morning:

Capa to Agrip
Consignment collected. Now ready for shipment thirtieth.

And there was one from Limbo:

Limbo to Agrip
Will collect Taru first September.

And from Taru:

Taru to Agrip
All arrangements made take-over from Capa.

Oleg, whenever he saw him that morning, was his usual monolithic self. Alexandre was impatient to see Michèle that lunchtime. These messages would mean more money. But the payment would have to be prompt; that day, by special messenger to Michèle's flat. It would have to be. He was not going to take any more risks.

Later, Alexandre hurried through his canteen lunch and went off to see Michèle. At the corner of the Rue Henri Quatre, Yuri joined him.

Yuri looked despondent and his voice was tinged with a note of weary bitterness. 'You're a fool, Alexandre. You shouldn't go on doing it, not just for a woman. What is a woman? I've got to report it, you know.'

'This is the last time. You must do what you must, Yuri.'

Yuri shrugged his shoulders. 'I no longer care. There will be nothing I can do to help you. You have put me in danger, too.'

'This is the last time.'

He left Yuri and went to the Rue de la Cerisaie. Michèle was waiting for him, dressed as she always was these hot days, a wrapper over her underclothes, her black hair loose over her shoulders. She saw at once that something had happened to him. He took her in his arms, kissed her, but said nothing.

Later, Alexandre telephone his man, gave him the text of that day's messages and insisted that the money should be sent round that day to Michèle, by messenger. Alexandre said that this would be the last time he would be in communication with him. The situation had become dangerous. At the other end of the line the man said calmly, making no effort to persuade him to continue, 'I understand. Thank you for your help.' Even Alexandre, beset by his emotions and thoughts to the exclusion of all else, marked the note of finality.

Michèle brought him a cup of coffee and they sat on the bed together.

Alexandre said, 'You are ready?'

Michèle nodded. 'Whatever you say, *chéri*.'

'The rest of the money will be here this afternoon. Take it all, pack a bag and go to the Gare de Lyon. Buy two tickets for the eight o'clock train to Marseilles. I will join you at the station at half-past seven.'

'It is for good?'

'For as long as it lasts. You understand that.'

'I understand, *chéri*.'

'In Marseilles I can get papers. We can move on and I can work.'

'They need never catch up with you.'

'They will. Oleg will see to that. We shall have a year, two years, maybe longer. . . .'

'Oh, Alexandre, *chéri*. . . .'

He put his arms around her and kissed her hair. There was no fear in him now, only a deep contented resignation, and a joy in anticipating the happiness of a future, no matter how brief it might be.

'I shall be at the station. We have enough money to keep us for a few months. You understand,' as he spoke he tilted her face up to his, smiling, optimism giving him courage, 'this will be the first time I shall be free to go, to look, to be myself. And we shall be together. . . .'

Michèle nodded, and she put her hand up, drawing the tips of her fingers down his cheek. There had been many men in her life, but Alexandre was the only one she had truly loved.

Alexandre had to hurry back to AGRIP for he had spent more time than usual with Michèle. Back at his desk he settled down to the routine translation of commercial letters, which formed the bulk of his work apart from the cipher duties. An hour later Oleg rang for him.

He went into Oleg's room. Oleg was sitting behind his desk, his hands on his knees; leaning forward slightly, examining his blotter, frowning as though he disapproved of the ink stains on it. A man stood by the window, and there was another man with his back to the filing cabinet, which stood against the far wall. Both men were dark grey-suited, both looked oddly the same, and they held themselves almost ruggedly at attention, watching Alexandre stonily. Seeing them, there was suddenly a great cold hollowness inside Alexandre.

Oleg said, 'You have been visiting a Michèle Guichard at her flat in the Rue de la Cerisaie.' It was not a question, but a hard, unaccented statement.

'Yes.'

'For what purpose?'

'I am in love with her.'

'How many times have you visited her?'

'Twice.'

'That is not true.'

'It is true.'

Oleg showed no emotion at the denial. The two men stood bulkily listening, but expressing no flicker of interest.

Oleg said, 'You know such relations are forbidden?'

'Yes.'

'What do you know about this woman?'

'Her parents are dead. She is a cinema usherette. She was born in Blois. She has a brother who is a lorry driver.'

'That is all?'

Alexandre's mind, thawing now, despair even fading a little because he knew the inevitable must happen, shrugged his shoulders and made no answer. His silence, he saw, affronted Oleg who cleared his throat with an impatient grunt.

'Until four years ago,' saia Oleg heavily, 'this Michèle Guichard was the mistress of a British M.I.5 agent in Paris. She has kept in touch with him. Through her you have been selling him information about this organization.'

'No.'

'You have been selling him information. I need a list of all such information.'

'I have not done this.'

'You are stubborn now, but you know that you cannot continue in this stubbornness. You know this.'

'I am in love with Michèle Guichard. That is all.'

Alexandre never saw what sign Oleg made. But the man by the window, his swiftness making a mockery of the bulkiness of his body, was at his side. His hand flashed up and something hard smacked brutally against the side of Alexandre's neck. Alexandre fell to the floor, panting with a sudden animal distress.

Oleg said, 'Get up.'

Slowly Alexandre pulled himself up.

'I want,' said Oleg evenly, 'a list of all the information you have supplied. It is known through Yuri that you have visited this woman many times.'

'I have gone to her because I love her. Just that,' said Alexandre.

The other man moved with the same surprising rapidity and he kicked at Alexandre's legs, knocking them from under him and then, almost before he had reached the ground, the other man's heavy boot thudded into his ribs. For a moment as he lay there in pain Alexandre knew that somewhere recently, maybe in this very room, Yuri had gone through all this.

'Stand up,' said Oleg.

Alexandre pulled himself up. There was nothing he could do now, he knew. Michèle would wait at the Gare de Lyon. The Marseilles train would go.

'I want a list of all the information you have passed.'

As though someone, a stranger inside him, had taken over his faculties, Alexandre heard himself say, 'Go to hell.'

He was struck on the side of the neck again and fell to the ground.

'Stand up,' said Oleg.

*

Five days later Alexandre's body was pulled from the Seine near the Pont d'Iéna. There was nothing about the clothes to identify him, and his face was unrecognizable. Yuri's body, equally unrecognizable, started from the same point just above the Quai des Célestins, but travelled farther; and was found seven days later near the railway bridge at Puteaux.

*

On the afternoon of the twenty-ninth of August, that is an hour after Oleg had finished interrogating Alexandre, a new cipher clerk, a woman loaned from the Embassy, took over his duties. Oleg, after a conference with his superiors, sent the following message:

Agrip to Taru
Report here immediately.

*

The grey-haired woman came in with a supper tray. Someone unseen closed the door on her and Irina heard the bolt go across. The woman, in a green cotton dress with white collar and cuffs, put the tray on the table and straightened up, smiling at Irina.

It was this pleasantness, this air of everything being normal in their relationship which in some way caused Irina more fear than anything else. She had the feeling all the time that the woman was some kind of nurse, being nice to her because she knew that she was in for a bad time.

On the tray was a glass of milk, and a plate of salad with some thinly sliced cold beef.

'I'm sorry it's so hot in here,' said the woman. 'It's the weather, of course. Heat wave. And then there's no real ventilation. We didn't think of it at the time.'

'What time?'

The woman looked surprised at the question.

'When we built it.' She nodded at the tray. 'It's a nice piece of beef. I do hope you eat it. You haven't had much since you've been here.'

Irina said, 'I'm going back, is that it?'

She had asked the question before and now she got the same reply as before.

'I don't know about that, dear.' For a moment the woman sighed, and then added, 'One is just told to do something. One does it. But what there is beyond one doesn't question. I gave up asking questions long ago. You never get the truth. Mind you, I didn't have to have any part in it. I just did it for him. Sometimes I wish I hadn't. But if you love a man . . . well, you have to share what comes, don't you?'

'I just want to know why I'm here and what is going to happen.'

The woman nodded. 'That's right. You would. But I can't help you. All I can say is that as far as we're concerned you won't get hurt. It's a bit unpleasant – but no more than, say, having your tonsils out. Everything's hygienic and he is a doctor. I shouldn't think about it if I were you. Have you finished the magazines I brought?'

Irina shook her head. A pile of magazines lay on the floor by the small wash-basin that had been fitted against the wall by the door. Everything had been thought of. There was a closet cut back into the wall by the basin and closed by a plywood door.

Irina said, 'Other people have been here?'

'But, of course. We wouldn't do all this for one, would we?' Her hand waved round the room.

'You're English, aren't you?'

'Yes.'

'How could you do this?' Irina's voice hardened, anger rising in her. 'You know what you're doing, don't you? I left my country of my own free will. One should always have that right. Now, you're helping to send me back. I'd heard that it happens sometimes. But I never thought of it for me. I'm nothing. I'm never even going to be a star dancer. Why should they want me back?'

The woman considered her sympathetically. 'Yes, I know. But it's no good asking questions, is it? How can you ever hope to understand the whys and wherefores of the things they do.'

She smiled encouragingly. 'Perhaps really, when you do get wherever it is, they'll be quite nice to you. Anyway, all we want you to know is that you don't have to be frightened while you're with us.'

'But I am frightened.'

'I know. They all are. And I'll tell you something interesting. Most of them aren't as calm about it as you. We've had a dreadful time with some. Not only women, either. The men. They go all to pieces. 'Course, when they're like that, I'd never come in here alone.'

Irina said, 'I've got some money. Not a lot. But about three hundred pounds. You could have it all if you let me go.'

The woman considered this sadly, then shook her head. 'Money's got nothing to do with it, dear. I mean in the first place he had to do it. He gets paid of course. But it's no good you offering me money. I mean, it just isn't to be considered. You know' – She looked around as though somebody might be listening – 'although he's really kind, he doesn't like me coming in and staying for a chat. He thinks it's dangerous, but I say to him if a person is frightened then it's the least you can do.' She moved towards the door and tapped on it. As she waited for it to open, she said, maternally, 'Now, you try and eat that. It's a lovely piece of beef. Best rib.'

She went out as the door opened, and there was nothing to be seen in its brief opening except a run of brick wall, just like the walls of the room.

Irina looked at the tray of food. Best rib of beef. So it might be, but she knew that she was not going to eat it. The most she could do would be to drink the milk. The woman's kindness touched her. She had enough imagination to realize that whoever these people were there was nothing personal in their treatment of her. In a way, she agreed they were as much victims as she herself. Indeed, the woman's manner seemed to be asking her for sympathy.

Suddenly, staring at the clinical whiteness of the hand-basin against the harsh red brick wall, she remembered her evening in the country with Manston. Richard Manston. All that evening, out of some shyness, she had avoided using his first name, and she had noticed that he had done the same with her. It had been nice that way. Particularly the swim in his pool. How much she had enjoyed that. She remembered how she had gone into her flat after he had left, standing for a moment inside the door, hearing his footsteps fade on the stairs . . . She had been full of happiness. And then. . . .

A swift turn of misery swept over her. Oh, no! Oh, no! she cried to herself. This can't be happening. It can't be.

Her misery stirred her to anger. She got up and went to the door and beat on it furiously with her fists.

*

While in London, Manston had been staying at his club. After dinner he made arrangements to leave early the next morning. He sat down and wrote a letter of instructions to his bailiff in Kent telling him that he was going abroad for a while, a week, maybe a month, he couldn't say. Writing, he had the feeling that his house and farm no longer existed. They belonged to another world. It did not altogether surprise him. This was what this kind of work did. You became absorbed and slowly true reality began to wane. You plunged into this Sutcliffe world and only the people in it remained true. Everything changed as you went under the surface and lost the sunlight. What a bloody game it was. Unlisted telephone numbers . . . even their offices were anonymous. No person outside their little world ever visited them or knew where they were, and when you wrote to the members of the outside world, you gave no address – just a box number at the top of the buff coloured letter paper.

Manston went along to the office at nine. He would be all night there. He might get a little sleep but not much. He and Barry Dymen had to be on call now right up until the Hardwick coach left the garage in the morning. The complement of tourists travelling with the coach was to be picked up at Eccleston Bridge in Victoria. Among the passengers would be one man from the department. Some of the coach tour people, most of them in fact, sent their clients by train to Dover and their coach waited for them at Calais. But Hardwick's Tours, with a few others, started from London and the tourists travelled with the coach across from Dover to Calais.

There were no fresh reports of any interest from the people covering the garage.

The telephone rang. It was Barry. 'I've got the lab chap here with the stuff you wanted about doping.'

'He's taken his time. Send him along.'

The lab man came in. He was new to Manston. He was tall, stoop-shouldered, smiling over half-lens glasses, and he looked too damn young to be able to speak with any authority. He stood with his hands thrust into the pockets of his white lab coat and said in a deep voice, 'I'm sorry I've been so long about this, sir. But it's not as easy as it seems and I wanted time to check it.'

'You mean you've carried out a test?'

'Had to. I was told this was important, not just to rely on theory. Despite what the average crime writer thinks and writes, it isn't easy to put anyone out cold for eight or twelve hours.'

'I didn't imagine it was. But it can be done?'

'Yes. If you know what you're doing.'

'These people will. Let's have it.'

'Well' – there was almost a note of relish in the deep voice – 'first you've got to give an intravenous injection of thiopentone sodium solution. That's 3 c.c. of five per cent solution, made by adding 10 c.c. of sterile distilled water to a half-gramme vial of sodium thiopentone powder. You give this over a period of ten seconds – in the elbow – and the patient will be unconscious before the injection is completed.'

'And that's it?'

'No, sir. Not by a long chalk. A couple of minutes later you've got to give the same dose of the same solution, but intramuscularly. And two rectal suppositories of chlorpromezathine, about a hundred grammes each. Then, if you want to get the full time limit, the patient must be kept cool we found —'

'We? Whom did you try this on?' Manston was forcing himself to think only of an anonymous patient, not Irina.

'I was the guinea-pig. They stretched me out on a rubber mattress full of iced water. You don't want too much jolting or vibration, that cuts down the time. And you need adequate ventilation, of course.'

'You sound as though you had a jolly time?'

'Well, sir, I was briefed on what you had in mind. I was driven around for eight hours and I was still out. Actually, I came round after ten and a half hours. But there was considerable disorientation for about three hours. I weigh over ten stone. With a woman, say eight to eight and a half stone, she should go the twelve-hour period easily.'

'Apart from the disorientation, no other after-effects?'

The lab man smiled. 'I didn't exactly feel like a million dollars for about eight hours. Hangover after a real binge would describe it.'

'This would need a doctor?' Manston was keeping his mind rigidly on the facts, forcing all personality from his thoughts.

'No, not if you were properly instructed. But it would, of course, be better to know exactly what you were doing. There was some bruising from the intramuscular injection. That was administered in the upper outer quadrant of the buttock —'

'Thanks. Now tell me something else. How long could this process go on? Say you wanted to have someone in an unconscious state for three or four days?'

The lab man pulled a face. 'Damned risky. A couple of times – that is, consecutively – maybe. But after that the old ticker might give up. No, you couldn't do it. You'd have a corpse on your hands.'

'I see. Well, thank you again. I'm grateful to you for testing it.'

'Not at all, sir. I was pretty sure it would work without carrying out the test. But there's never any harm in checking.'

When the man had left, Manston went over to his cupboard and fixed himself a large whisky and soda. It was no good now trying not to think of Irina. She was going to be put through the hoop. Intravenous, intramuscular . . . packed in ice, like a refrigerated salmon.

He drank his whisky quickly and went into Sutcliffe's room. Sutcliffe was not there. Manston could not make up his mind whether he was glad or sorry. He might have said something which he would have regretted. None of this was Sutcliffe's fault . . . or anybody's fault. It was just a thing that was happening; a dirty, disgusting thing which, for the sake of other people, had to be done. Irina Tovskaya was just unlucky.

6

At six o'clock, on the morning of the thirtieth of August, Manston had a telephone call from Sutcliffe asking him to go round to the flat in King Street for breakfast. He left instructions with Barry to tell Ritchie to pick him up at the flat with his car and his suitcase at seven. He took a quick shower at the office, shaved and changed; and then went out to find a taxi.

It was a fresh, clear morning and the air was cool. He walked down to the Embankment to stretch his legs. The tide was full in and a string of barges was coming down from Battersea Power Station. A police launch came upstream, one of the crew busy with a mop on the small fore-deck; and a couple of swans foraged in the river wrack, just off Cleopatra's Needle.

It was a fine London morning, the city slowly gathering itself to meet the rush of crowds that would be upon it in another couple of hours.

Hackett let him into the flat. Breakfast was set out in the dining-room which overlooked the forecourt of St. Paul's Church, Covent Garden. A tramp was sitting on one of the seats, slowly sorting a heap of rubbish from a sack.

Manston helped himself to coffee, and a plate of eggs and bacon. There had been a time long ago, when at a point like this he would have found it difficult to eat. But he had learned quickly to divorce his emotions from his stomach.

Sutcliffe came in, wearing a dressing-gown and already smoking a pipe. He helped himself to coffee.

He said, 'Sorry to drag you around here. But I wanted a word quietly with you before you went off. No snags so far?'

'No snags. We had a report from the garage observers just before I left. The coach was backed well into one of the bays. Hardwick, Miss Rylands and the driver were busy around the boot compartment and something was lifted in. Our watcher couldn't identify what. It's virtually certain it was the girl, though.'

'I see . . . Well, it's a beginning.' Sutcliffe moved to the window and looked out, deep in thought.

'What's on your mind?'

Sutcliffe faced him. 'Once things start moving over there, you might find yourself on your own, right up against it. I want it clear that I shall back any decision you make. If, at any time, you think the whole thing is out of hand, you can end it. You can pass the word and Casalis can get the French people to close in.'

Manston looked across at Sutcliffe.

'Somebody's been at you, Ronnie?' It was the first time he had used his Christian name for a long time.

Sutcliffe nodded. 'Frankly, yes. I had to clear the thing . . . you know how it is. And I've had a directive. The necessity for jeopardizing the girl is recognized; but on no account are things to be allowed to go wrong, so that they get her right away. If it begins to look like that, you've got *carte blanche* to pull the emergency cord.'

'I'll remember.'

'I hope to hell it won't be necessary. It's no good to end up with only the Hardwick outfit in the bag. The only way to wrap this thing up is for you to stick after her right up to Limbo. Have some more coffee.'

Sutcliffe stood up, the coffee-pot poised over Manston's cup.

'Thank you and' – Manston gave him a wry smile – 'don't worry. I'll go the limit. I know it's tough on her, and you may think I hate your guts for doing this, but I don't lose sight of the other people.'

Ritchie came for him at quarter-past seven and they drove down to Victoria. Manston, driving, went down Buckingham Palace Road and turned left over Eccleston Bridge. It was still only half-past seven and there was no sign of the coach. Near the bus shelters various people were assembled with suitcases, but he paid no attention to them. Somewhere amongst them was their man. He went on and turned into Eccleston Square. He left Ritchie with the car and walked to the corner of the square.,

A Special Branch car was parked just back from the corner. It was a small black van with the legend, REDFERN TILE COMPANY, in gold letters along its side. Two men in overalls sat in the front seats. Inside the van, Manston knew, would be another, a radio operator. One of the men, seeing Manston, wound down the window. He gave Manston a wink and said, 'Nice day for going abroad.'

Manston, who knew him, raised his eyes humorously, and said, 'I'm going to take a walk over the bridge. After that I shan't hang around. Nothing's likely to happen between here and Dover. Where's your other car?'

'Vauxhall Bridge. That's the way the coaches go out.' The man lit a cigarette. 'You're going straight down?'

'Yes.'

'You can pick up any interim report the other side of Maidstone. There's a police car there. Parked at the first layby past the Park Gate Inn. By Leeds Castle.'

'Yes, I know.'

He went back to the bridge. The coach had arrived and was drawn up almost at the far end of the bridge. Manston lit a cigarette and crossed the road. He came slowly down the pavement. The courier was standing by the entrance to the coach with a clip-board in his hand, checking names. The driver was at the back of the coach, the doors of the large luggage compartment open, and he was stowing away passengers' cases. Some of the passengers had already settled into the coach, others were grouped round the courier. He heard a woman say, 'My friend hasn't arrived yet. But she'll be here. Her train could be a little late. . . . Yes, yes, Darwin, that's the name.'

Manston didn't look for his own man. He was probably already inside. He walked past the coach, and details of the scene, scraps of conversation, floated past his mind.

'That's all right, ma'am. Don't you worry. Safe as houses it will be in there.'

An elderly woman, fussing about her case which had a soft top.

And again to the same woman, a born anxious traveller: 'No, ma'am, umbrellas and hand luggage inside the coach.'

The driver was a big man, his peaked cap pushed back a little to show a wide brow and a hint of fair hair, his face, morning fresh and shaved, brown eyes smiling at the woman; a big, burly, cheerful-looking man with a faint touch of some West Country accent in his voice. Which he should have, thought Manston, fighting now to keep Irina from his mind, for he was Albert Tadsbridge, born Plymouth 1914, living now in Camden Town, married, two children, and three convictions for breaking and entering. Maybe when he was driving and no one could see his face the shadow of anxiety came into the honest-looking brown eyes. The courier was Felix Oldstein, Polish in origin, naturalized. He had been a school-teacher in a secondary modern school for three years; but had been dismissed, after a conviction for interfering with one of the girl pupils, and employed since – that is for two years – by Hardwick. Somewhere he'd been caught, too. It was the same old pattern.

Manston stopped twenty yards past the coach and studied a bus timetable on the wall, watching the scene from the corner of his right eye. Oldstein – thirtyish, tall, vaguely elegant in a light summer suit with a muddy-brown cap on his head, like a thrush's nest turned inside out – came back to the driver, who was about to close the doors of the luggage compartment. A luggage compartment, thought Manston, normally eight feet deep, five feet six inches wide and four feet high. Only now it was only five feet six deep. The other two feet six inches by five feet six by four feet, belonged to Irina. There was no burking it now. She was there, not twenty yards from him, packed into her neat compartment, no doubt adequately ventilated; unconscious on a mattress filled with ice-water, neatly semi-refrigerated for twelve hours. Tadsbridge, the driver, slammed one door and left the other open. Oldstein gave him a cigarette and they stood there, waiting for some late arrival, and Tadsbridge said something that made Oldstein laugh. Seeing the blue skeins of cigarette-smoke between them, their easiness and normality when they knew so much, Manston bit his lower lip with a swift movement of sick anger. Sometime this morning it had happened.... He heard the lab man talking... 'There was some bruising from the intramuscular injection ...' Momentarily he had a vivid picture of Irina's face, the dark eyes full of fear, as they must have been when she was held and the hand with the hypodermic moved downwards ... 'an injection of thiopentone sodium solution.' Drug piled on drug, indignity and affront to human decency . . .

He turned away sharply and walked on over the bridge, lighting another cigarette as he went. He went round the station block, over Elizabeth Bridge and into Eccleston Square from the far side. The Special Branch van was still at the top corner.

Manston motioned Ritchie into the driving seat.

'You take her.'

'Everything all right, guv?'

Manston nodded.

Ritchie drove round the square and, as they came to the top, Hardwick's coach went by, yellow and black like a great hornet, the sun shining on its coachwork, garage-leathered, gleaming.

Ritchie said, 'Which way?'

'Over Lambeth Bridge.' The coach had disappeared and he was not anxious to see it again until they reached Dover.

Ritchie, recognizing his mood, drove in silence, his blue and white bow-tie drooping a little, a cigarette stuck in the corner of his mouth.

Ritchie drove fast and they made Maidstone in just over the hour. A few miles past Maidstone was the Park Gate Inn and, just beyond it, where the road rose to a small crest cut between pine trees, was the layby. A Kent County Constabulary patrol car, on special duty, was parked off the road. Ritchie drew in alongside it. As Manston got out, a police officer got out of the police car.

Manston gave him a code-word and identified himself. The faint air of disapproval the ordinary police had at such moments amused him. They didn't like code-words and the unorthodox identity procedure. What they would have been far happier with was a nice little wallet certificate, with a photograph stuck on it.

The officer said, 'The coach is approaching Maidstone now.

Everything so far has been entirely routine. . . .' There was a faint pause, and then he added, 'sir.'

'Good.'

'There's also this.'

Manston was handed a folded sheet of paper. He opened it. It was hand-written by the car's radio operator, a big, rather clumsy hand, and was from Barry:

> *Following received from Casalis. Quote. Paris AGRIP contact Alexandre Shernof after passing last information had arranged to leave evening twenty-ninth for Marseilles with mistress Michèle Guichard. Shernof never arrived station. No contact made by Shernof with Guichard since. Unquote.*

Manston pulled his lighter from his pocket and set fire to the message. The police officer watched, unmoved, as the black ashes fluttered away in the morning breeze.

Manston said, 'Thank you, officer,' and went back to Ritchie.

As they drove on Manston watched the road absently. So, the AGRIP contact had been broken. God knew what might have happened to Shernof. This could be serious. . . . He sat brooding about it, going over a dozen possibilities in his mind. Something always went wrong, damn it. He had to think this out carefully.

Ritchie, sensing his mood, made no attempt at conversation.

They were at Dover just after half-past nine. The car ferry did not pull out until ten-thirty. Manston went into the customs-shed and picked up his last report on the coach from the office there. It was proceeding, without any deviation from its normal routine. He did not stay with the customs people. They had been instructed to pass the coach through without trouble. As indeed, they would have passed it through.

He said good-bye to Ritchie.

Ritchie gave him a little nod, fingered the tip of his bow-tie, and said, 'Best of luck, sir. I hope you get all the bastards in the bag. She's a nice girl. I got quite fond of her, just watching.'

*

The trip across took an hour and a half. During that time Manston found his coach man on deck, and had a word with him.

He was a retired man from the C.I.D. and knew his job. Hair greying, blue blazer and dark grey trousers, he looked like some elderly bachelor off for a good time abroad.

He said, 'They're the usual crowd, sir. A couple of women teachers, sprinkling of North Country folk who've stopped overnight in London. I'd give them all a clean bill. Some of them have used Hardwick's Tours for several years.'

'Driver and courier?'

'Driver's a pleasant sort. Doesn't seem to have a worry in the world. He doesn't speak French. Some old girl asked him. The courier does, of course. He could be anything. But, I reckon, the girl's aboard all right.'

'We know that. But how do you?'

The man smiled. 'I've used coaches a lot for my holidays and day trips . . . Margate, Brighton. You can push these jobs along, you know, sir. Most long-distance chaps could give Stirling Moss a few tips. But this chap drove straight out of the Highway Code. Didn't want any trouble or accidents. Usually you get thrown about a bit, but he drove as though he had a case of eggs somewhere. That's the only thing.'

'There's been no alteration to the schedule?'

'No, sir. Calais at twelve and then about thirty miles out we stop for lunch. The courier already made an announcement about it. It's a roadside place that caters for this kind of trip.'

He stayed on deck all the way over. It was a fine morning with a slow, easy swell running. They docked at Calais five minutes late and Manston made his way with the rest of the passengers through the *douane*. He walked through the *gare maritime* and found Casalis with the car parked at the top end of the Bassin Carnot. The car was a black Citroën, showing no outward signs that it was radio equipped. The operator, not in uniform, sat in the back seat. He was a small, scraggy-looking man of about thirty, with a tiny piece of light-coloured, Charlie Chaplin moustache that underlined a blinking, rather solemn smile. He was Jean Belville.

Manston dumped his suitcase in the boot of the car and turned to Casalis.

'Any more dope on this Shernof bloke?'

Casalis, big, looking full of energy, the wind off the sea fretting at his fair hair, shook his head. 'Haven't been able to get anything. He's just disappeared. What do you make of it?'

'I don't like it. I've been thinking about it on the way over. There are two possibilities. Either he's gone off on his own and ditched this Michèle girl, in which case AGRIP must be wondering what the hell it's all about, or he's been rumbled by AGRIP, and they could know he's been passing stuff to us.'

'From what I know of the set-up he was pretty thick with Michèle Guichard. I don't think he would have ditched her.'

'It doesn't matter. We've got to work on the assumption that the worst has happened; that AGRIP have rumbled him, made him confess and then dealt with him. In that case, they must have asked themselves why we didn't stop Irina Tovskaya from being kidnapped. Agree?'

'Yes.'

'Which gives them the answer that we have other plans. The obvious deduction on their part is that we may be going to follow her through the line. We've got to assume this.'

'Why didn't they warn Capa or get them to change their plan?'

'Because there wasn't time, probably. And also because they must have realized nothing could save Capa – if we'd been keeping tabs on the girl. But there's a hell of a lot they can do to protect Taru and Limbo. They're not going to let us get a sniff at them.'

'So there will be a change in their normal routine this side?'

'We'd be fools not to expect it. The medical people say that it would be dangerous to try and keep anyone drugged for more than twenty hours. The usual routine was probably a change over to Taru somewhere between here and Amiens, or in Amiens. Since it would have to be done without exciting comment from the passengers, I'd say that it was done at Amiens. They stay the first night there at the Hôtel de L'Univers, and they get in early. The coach probably goes off to a garage to refuel. That could be the moment. But we can't expect the normal routine this time. And, if necessary, AGRIP won't care a damn about the passengers. We've got to be ready for any unexpected stop of that coach before it reaches Amiens.'

'You don't think they might give her a second shot and let Taru have her tomorrow, or later? They go from Amiens to Vézelay the second day, and the next on to Annecy.'

'They could. They could do any damn thing; except, I imagine, the thing they usually do. It's a good job we've got a bloke aboard. He might be very useful. We've just got to keep hard on the tail of that coach and be ready for anything. What about this place they stop for lunch? You've had a look at that?'

'Yesterday. It's a small place on the St Omer-Hesdin road, which caters for coaches. It's just short of Fauquembergues, and is called the Café de la Forêt. Nothing special about it. The main route to Amiens is down through Lillers and then on the N.16. But this way is through Abbeville.'

Manston smiled. 'Hardwick's Tours don't follow the beaten track. It's one of the slogans in their brochure.'

As he spoke, the yellow and black coach came slowly down towards them over the cobbles. He had a glimpse of Albert Tadsbridge's broad face, peak-cap pushed back a little, and he saw the courier standing in the body of the coach. And in the back . . . hidden behind the luggage compartment . . . Irina . . .

For a moment he remembered her face as she swam in his pool, the wet black hair, sleek to her head like a helmet.

Casalis put his head through the car door and said to Jean Belville, 'That's her, Jean.'

He turned back to Manston. 'I've got another car out ahead on the N.43. Because of this Shernof business, I pulled in another. That's going to take the side roads from Ardres down. We can switch it wherever we want it. We follow behind. We've got a radio link, too, with the Amiens police in case we need any help from there.'

'Good. Just let all your chaps know that the moment that coach starts any unexpected manœuvre they've got to be on their toes.'

They gave the coach a few minutes start, then they got into the car, Casalis driving. He reached into the dashboard pocket and handed an automatic back to Manston. It was a 6·35 mm. Browning automatic pistol.

'You didn't bring one through did you?'

'No.'

Sometimes one did, but mostly one didn't. It was always easier to pick up one this side. You could always run into an efficient *douanier* who had missed being instructed; and then you had a public fuss on your hands, with the wrong people – it could be – staring at you.

Manston opened the Michelin sheet – 51, Boulogne-Lille – folded it conveniently, and began to study it.

Behind him, Jean Belville began to give instructions to the two other cars. Manston, who spoke French well, listened with half his attention. Jean, his voice touched with a natural sadness that matched his solemn smile, crooned, 'Carlo, Carlo, approaching Les Attaques. Niki, Niki, come in . . .'

He was silent for a while, listening, and then he looked up and reported, 'Niki is at Guines and going down to Nabringhen on the N.42. He'll wait there for instructions. Carlo is the other side of Ardres on the N.43.'

'Niki is the swinger,' said Casalis. 'He could come in fast down N.42 and then D.191 to Fauquembergues. Carlo is up ahead.'

He speeded up before they got to Ardres, and they had a glimpse of the tail-end of the big, yellow and black coach; then he slowed, dropping back.

'Tell Carlo to move, Jean. Tell them the coach is doing about sixty-five to seventy kilometres an hour. They can adjust to that. Tell Niki to report at Nabringhen. Then call Amiens and tell them our positions.'

Behind, Jean went off into his sad little mumble. Manston lit a cigarette and relaxed.

Casalis said, 'Good crossing?'

'Yes.'

'Any sleep last night?'

'Not much.'

After a pause, Casalis said, 'It's a hell of a way to travel. I suppose they don't mind if the goods get knocked about a bit.'

For a moment Manston felt inclined to resent the callousness, but he killed the feeling. Casalis was doing a job and there was no reason why he should sentimentalize over any of its aspects. In fact, there was every reason why he shouldn't. Sentiment just got in the way.

Manston said, 'This Shernof type. He was going to do a bunk with the girl?'

'That was the idea. He wouldn't have got away with it for long. The girl was pretty cut up about him, so my man says. But, no doubt, she'll get over it. Far as I could make out she wasn't much more than a tart. Good-hearted, but quick to forget. Useful, though, while it lasted. She'd been tied up before with us; and we had to back-pedal on her for a few years, before it was safe to put her into circulation again.'

Following Casalis' instructions, Carlo waited in St Omer and reported the coach turning right-handed down the N.28 to Fauquembergues.

Casalis speeded up then, leap-frogging Carlo and going ahead of the coach, with Carlo following behind. Niki, at Nabringhen, was ordered to take the side roads down to Hucqueliers and wait there. Hucqueliers was slightly west and south of Fauquembergues and within easy striking distance of the N.28. When the coach stopped for lunch Carlo was to go on and wait just the other side of Fauquembergues.

Casalis drew into the parking space of the Café de la Forêt a few minutes ahead of the coach. They parked the car well up, close to the run out on to the road, and Jean stayed with it. Manston and Casalis went into the bar which adjoined a long dining-room.

The Café de la Forêt was oddly named, for there was no forest within sight of it. It stood off the road, a long, low, wooden building, faced with a run of verandah along which were strung hanging baskets of flowers; petunias and geraniums, dried up and shabby looking from the heat. To one side, under five or six tall poplar trees, stood a collection of umbrella-shaded tables. At the other end from the tables was an addition to the structure, with two doors marked *Hommes* and *Dames*. A collection of notices on short poles stuck into convex concrete blocks marked the roadside, announcing the usual tourist-trapping slogans . . . *Café, Vins, English Teas, English spoken, Un Bon Repas – Prix Fixe* . . .

The bar, which had a half-glass door that allowed one to look into the dining-room, was neat and plainly furnished. It was clean, and the glimpse of the dining-room, with its red and white chequered table-cloths, water-carafes and Cinzano ash-trays, was fresh and welcoming. A few other cars were parked outside and some people were eating in the dining-room.

There were three people in the bar; a man and a woman sitting near the dining-room door, and another man, sitting near the entrance door with a glass of beer, reading an old copy of *Paris-Match*.

Manston ordered beer from a girl who came through a door behind the bar, and looked over the other three people. They looked ordinary; the woman in a summer dress, hair dyed blonde with the parting showing darkly the original brunette; the man, jacket off, hitting the edge of the table with the side of his hand as he argued some point. The man reading *Paris-Match* looked as though he might be a local. He wore blue working trousers and thick boots; and his green shirt, under a well-worn corduroy jacket, was open at the neck. All his clothes looked a little tight on him, as though he had bought them years before and had grown in bulk since. He had a flat, undistinguished face which seemed to have been put together in a hurry by some amateur. As he read, he pursed his lips as though about to whistle.

As he turned back to his beer Manston saw the long length of the black and yellow coach slide by the windows, moving up to the parking place.

Manston said, 'When they're in the dining-room, you go in. Order for both of us. I want to look around outside.'

The woman at the far table suddenly laughed, shaking her head and the man reached over and smacked her jovially on the leg. The *Paris-Match* man gave them a glance, disapproving, and then buried his nose in his beer glass.

Outside, Manston could see the passengers descending from the coach, being shepherded by the courier. The driver was still in his seat, turned sideways, nodding and talking to the passengers as they got out. Already the holiday camaraderie was being established. 'Such a nice driver. Never had a qualm all the way. A real first-class driver.' 'And the courier – oh, dear, mustn't call him that must I? Tour manager. Such a help. No trouble too much.' 'And think of it, fourteen days for fifty-eight pounds. I mean. . . .'

The courier was ushering them into the dining-room by another entrance, beside the umbrella-shaded tables. The café manager was at the door, welcoming them. Manston saw the driver get down, stretch his arms, light a cigarette and then stroll towards the dining-room door. He stood there alongside the courier while their flock, chattering, came into the room.

The *Paris-Match* man stood up, nodded to the girl behind the bar, and went out. Manston saw him pass the bar window, heading as though for the lavatories. Every instinct awake now, Manston said to the girl, 'Is he a regular, the man who has just gone out?'

The girl shook her head. 'No, monsieur. I have never seen him before.'

Manston went over to the window. He was just in time to see the man go into the door marked *Hommes*. He went back to Casalis and said, 'I've got an uneasy feeling about that character. You go along and keep him company while he's in there. I can watch the coach from here.'

Casalis nodded and went out.

The girl behind the bar, coming back from a fresh order for the blonde and her friend, said, 'You will be eating here, monsieur?'

'Possibly.' Manston's eyes were on the window. The coach was empty. Jean Belville's car was parked ahead of it, obscured from him. Jean would be watching the far side of the coach.

Waiting there alone, Manston was acutely aware of the anxiety which had grown in him since he had received the news of Shernof. Following someone without their knowing it was hard enough, but to follow someone who knew; that was hell. The whole object of this operation had been to trail Irina secretly. The terms were different now. Sutcliffe had given him permission to crash-end the whole business if he felt it necessary. He had a feeling that it was necessary now. He ought to go out and grab Irina while he still had the chance. If AGRIP were wise to them how could they succeed?

He lit a cigarette, and saw the flame of the lighter steady as his hand held it. Somewhere – instinct suddenly backed by experience – little ice-cold jabs of awareness began to needle him. Already the intuition flashed into his mind, wordless for a second, and then formed; already something was wrong. And, with the message, he moved into action. The *Paris-Match* had been inside too long, and so had Casalis.

Manston went quickly to the door. He ran to the lavatory and went quickly through the door, taking his automatic from his pocket.

Casalis lay on the concrete floor, his head thrown back awkwardly, his eyes shut. Manston dropped on his knee beside him. There was a bruise and a ragged cut over his right temple and, in the moment of time as he knelt there, assuring himself that Casalis was only out cold, he saw a small pile of whitewash flakings on the floor alongside Casalis. The lavatory was open to the sky. The *Paris-Match* man had gone over the wall, dropping to the back of the café

Manston turned and ran to the front of the place. As he came out of the door he knew that he was too late. The coach was moving. He couldn't see the driver; but, as he ran forward, he saw the coach move away from the road exit, stop, and then suddenly reverse, roaring back in a narrow arc. The towering rear end of the coach rammed backwards at the Citroën. Manston shouted and Jean, standing by the Citroën, already aware of his danger, leapt to one side. Jean was not quick enough. Part of the rear end of the coach caught him on the shoulder and sent him sprawling. The next instant the back of the coach crashed into the Citroën, ramming it just forward of the driving door and forcing it over on its side into a small flower bed that edged the parking lot. The coach jerked out of reverse and came speeding down across the front of the café. Manston leapt out of its way. As it went by him he recognized the *Paris-Match* man at the wheel.

The coach swung out on to the road and at top speed began to head back along N.28 towards St Omer.

Manston ran up to Jean, who was picking himself up. The man was shocked and seemed incapable of doing anything except stare disbelievingly at the wrecked Citroën. At this moment Manston was joined by their man who had been on the coach. Jean stared at the two of them, bemused.

Manston turned to his man. 'The car's no good, but the radio may work. Get Jean, here, to raise the others and tell them what has happened. . . .' The map was clear in his memory. 'Get on to Amiens – ask for a general call. If anybody locally spots the coach they must let it go, just report it. Tell Niki to work the side roads to the West of N.28. We don't want it stopped. We just want to know where it goes. Call Carlo in here. Pick up Casalis in the lavatory and then follow me —'

He was gone, hoping that between them they had taken it all in, running through the crowd of tourists who had come out of the dining-room. He saw the driver and the courier forcing their way through their passengers, the café manager on the dining-room steps . . . everyone shouting.

Opposite the bar door was a small Citroën *deux-chevaux*, top down. He jumped into it, offered thanks for the ignition key left in the lock, and was away.

A turning came up on the right, running dead flat through beet fields, and corn plains already harvested and stacked. Manston could see half a mile along it. There was no sign of the coach. The next village back was Avroult and to the left of Avroult the land sloped down to the valley of the river Aa. Somewhere, tucked nicely away, people would be waiting for *Paris-Match*. It would take them five minutes to unload the suitcases and get Irina out.

A few minutes more and he was in Avroult. There was a turning to the left at the beginning of the village and a French workman in blue overalls was standing there by his bicycle. When Manston asked if a yellow and black coach had gone down the turning, he nodded and said briefly, 'Just, monsieur.'

Manston thanked him and turned off the main road, slackening his speed now. The road, metalled while it was in the village, became a rough track beyond it, and sloped, curving, down the valley side, bordered on one side by trees. Through the far end of the curve Manston suddenly saw a flash of yellow and black moving. He followed now cautiously, keeping his distance.

Ahead of him he saw the coach slow for a small stone bridge over the river. There was just enough clearance to take the vehicle. On the far side of the river was a belt of trees on the hillside, the road cut deeply through it. Manston drew up at the end of the curvc in the road, before the bridge. He watched the coach climb the slope slowly. *Paris-Match* was in no hurry now. Almost at the limit of the trees Manston saw the coach turn to the left off the road. It moved about fifty yards into the trees, its bright yellow bodywork flashing through their trunks, and then it stopped.

Manston got out of his car and walked down the road to the bridge. A man on a tractor was doing some early ploughing in a field to his right. Below the bridge a woman was driving some cows along the river path, black-shawled, and knitting as she went. The still summer surface of the river was stippled here and there by the rise of grayling; and a few martins whipped low over the water, hawking for gnats. Beyond the bridge Manston went left-handed into the trees and began to work his way up to the coach. Fifty yards up the slope, set amongst the trees, was an old quarry. He flanked it and on its crest found a rusty tin shed which had been used as a shelter for the workers. It had no doorway and in the far wall there was a window, hung now with rotting scraps of sacking. He went in and looked through. Twenty yards away, partly obscured by the intervening bushes and trees, he could see part of the coach. It was standing in a small clearing which ran through to the road.

Paris-Match was at the back of the coach with two other

men, dressed in working clothes like himself. They had the luggage compartment doors open and were tossing out suitcases on to the grass. Nearer the road stood a farm lorry, canvas-topped, its back end towards him. He could see that it was half full of cabbages in string net bags and a few crates which were crammed with poultry. He could not see the number plate from where he stood.

The three men worked without talking. When the compartment was empty one of them climbed in. While he worked inside, *Paris-Match* and the other man lit cigarettes and, although he could not hear what they were saying, they leaned forward now and again, giving advice or encouragement to the man inside. Once *Paris-Match*'s shoulders shook with laughter.

After a while, the man inside came crawling out backwards. As he stood up *Paris-Match* and the other man reached inside, and Manston guessed that they were easing out the false back of the compartment to free Irina.

So far, he had tried not to think of her too much. So far, it had been comparatively easy. But not now. In a few moments he knew that he would see her; for the first time since he had kissed her good-bye at her flat door.

He swore to himself silently as the three men lifted out the false back of the compartment. They dropped it carelessly on the grass and then turned back. For a moment they stood motionless, looking inside the compartment.

It was at this moment that, from the doorless entrance behind him, a voice said in French to Manston, whose interest was fully concentrated on the coach scene, 'Just stand back from the window and keep your hands well away from your sides.'

Manston turned fast, his hands dropping. Then, recognizing discretion, he raised them level with his shoulders.

Standing just outside the doorway was the jolly man from the Café de la Forêt, jacketless, his blue shirt stained below the armpits with sweat. One hand was raised, holding a heavy revolver, and the sunlight through the trees dappled his face with blotches of yellow light. Behind him stood the blonde woman, holding a large white handbag to her breast, wisps of her dyed hair falling forward over one cheek.

'Come out,' said the man. 'Slowly.'

The man backed away as Manston came into the sunlight; and then, when Manston was clear of the hut, he moved his gun hand, motioning him to halt.

'Turn round,' said the man.

Manston turned.

The man hit him hard and expertly. The last thing he saw as he fell was a scrawl of white paint on the hut side which read, *Non à De Gaulle.*

7

DURING THE MORNING of the thirtieth of August, Ludmilla Miachin, the woman cipher operator who had taken Alexandre Shernof's place, encoded and dispatched the following message:

Agrip to Capa
Dismantle. Repeat. Dismantle.

Oleg, standing at the window of the cipher room as the woman encoded it, stared down at the Quai des Célestins, watching the lunch-time clerks and secretaries strolling by the river. Capa now, he told himself dispassionately, was a rotten limb. It had to be cut away ruthlessly. It had happened before, and it would happen again. After a time Capa would be replaced.

*

At six o'oclock that evening Sutcliffe, in his office, was handed by Barry Dymen a report from Casalis, at Amiens, on the incident at the Café de la Forêt and the movements of Casalis and the French police since then.

The *deux-chevaux*, in which Manston had followed the coach, had been found close to a river bridge over the Aa, near Avroult. The coach had been found – two hours after its disappearance – abandoned in a small wood on the other side of the river. Manston was missing. The coach, its passengers, and the driver and courier were now in Amiens and, in view of the false compartment revealed in the luggage space of the coach, the driver and courier were being held. Casalis asked for instructions about them and the passengers. The French police had given full co-operation and had set up road checks throughout the area, but no trace or description had been found of the vehicle which must have taken off Irina Tovskaya and her abductors. It was presumed that Manston was either with them or following them; and, as yet, unable to get in touch.

After he had finished reading, Sutcliffe was silent for a while, thinking. He hunched forward, elbows on his desk, one hand cupped round his chin, staring at the lower waistcoat button of Barry Dymen. Then, as though talking to himself, he said:

'They must have Manston. He'd have got in touch by now otherwise.'

Barry nodded.

'Tell Casalis to hold the driver and courier. Get them back here. The passengers, too.'

'They'll be happy.'

'Who cares.'

'Hardwick and Rylands pulled out of their place by car an hour ago. We lost trace of them near Hampstead in a traffic jam. There's a call out for them. I've got all the port exits alerted. They'll be held on passport irregularities. You want them in?'

'Yes. But we won't get much from them. AGRIP have thrown them to the wolves. Damn that fellow Shernof.' Sutcliffe reached for his pipe and began to fill it with slow, deliberate movements of his thick fingers.

Through the ritual of lighting it, he went on, 'You'd better get over to Casalis. The stuff this side is routine. We can scare all hell out of that driver and get details of the normal change-over but I doubt if he can give us a positive lead to Taru. The real trouble is that AGRIP must know that we are on to them. Our only hope is Manston.'

'If he's alive.'

'I think he must be. They'd have found him with the coach otherwise.'

'There's no hope of getting the French boys to jump AGRIP?'

Sutcliffe gave Barry an old-fashioned look. 'You know there isn't. We know all about AGRIP. It's Taru and Limbo we want. You get over to Casalis right away.'

When Barry had gone Sutcliffe sat smoking, going over the affair in his mind. All they had wanted to do was to follow Irina Tovskaya quietly from point to point. That they had been able to plan to do this was due to the information they had received from Shernof. But in that information, in the very character of Shernof, had germinated the seeds of this set-back. Now, the whole picture was changed. There would be a private, high-level stink about that. That was the least of his worries.

He got up and stumped to his window, staring out absently at the lines of traffic, the crowded summer evening street. This kind of mess-up had always been possible. That's why he had wanted Manston. Thank God he hadn't been found with the coach, a neat bullet-hole through his head.

*

Irina was only vaguely aware that it was daylight. At least she imagined that it was daylight, but it was difficult to tell because her mind as well as her eyes seemed incapable of any settled focus. It was rather like one of those dreams where you know you are dreaming, can even stand aside for moments and smile or reassure yourself, and then are drawn back. She was ill, she knew that, but at the same time she knew that it was a sickness that would pass.

She lay on a bed and there was a woman leaning over her, and for a long time she wondered why she went on leaning. Then, in a flash of clarity, she understood that her clothes were being taken off. She made no protest beyond the mute words of protest in her mind. Her body seemed to be always lagging a few yards behind her thoughts.

Brief, clear scraps of detail and conversation stuck with her. When she vomited once, feeling the pressure of the woman's hand on the back of her neck, she heard her say in French, 'Poor kid.' She noticed, head down, nausea engulfing her, that the woman wore openwork sandals and that her big toes were ugly.

Stripped, she was cold, colder than she had been, and she shivered. The woman leaned over her and she saw the dark parting at the roots of her blonde hair. She shut her eyes, the lids so heavy she could support them no longer and her head whirled until she was the centre of a spinning nebula.

She felt herself lifted at shoulders and feet and heard a man say something. She tried to speak, protesting her nakedness in front of him, but her throat closed up on her.

They put her in a warm bath and she drifted away, vaguely conscious of the woman's hand moving, bathing her, the sweep of a sponge over her face like a soft palm.

After that it was darkness for a long time. Then there was a small light to her left and the woman was raising her by the shoulders and she knew she was in bed. She resented the disturbance and heard herself protesting now, her voice clear, angry. The woman laughed. Hot broth was fed to her, forced on her, and she went on resenting it, wanting only to relax into the darkness of sleep again.

She was dropped back gently against the pillow and let her mind and body slip, inviting sleep, but for a little while it held off, tantalizing her.

The man said, 'She'll be all right?'

'Yes. You should know. You've seen enough.'

'I know. But I am always worried. Especially with the women.'

A match scraped across a box, and the woman's hands moved at the bedclothes, drawing them closer round her shoulders.

The man said, 'She is beautiful, eh?'

The woman laughed then, saying, 'The bath, that is always the part you like, eh? Anyway, am I not beautiful?'

The man chuckled. 'Indeed you are – but you are fatter. Like a comfortable mattress.'

They both laughed, the room echoing with the sound.

Sharply, commandingly, Irina said, 'Go away. I wish to sleep.'

They laughed again, and the sound went on and on and she was asleep before it ended.

*

Manston watched the dawn come up, sitting on a small stool by the window. Except for the bed it was the only other furniture in the room. It was an attic room and the window was set in the embrasure of a small gable. There was a row of iron bars across it, about three inches apart, firmly set in a stout oak frame.

While he had been unconscious he had been handcuffed, with his hands in front of him. They were old-fashioned figure-of-eight cuffs, holding his wrists close together.

He looked out across a small stretch of lawn which was bordered by a shrubbery. Beyond the shrubs stood a row of tall pines, and through them he could see the river. There was a morning mist over the water channels which threaded their way through long, low sandbanks. Beyond the river the ground rose, lost in a thick barrier of woodland. Immediately below the window was a strip of gravelled drive, and a flight of steps that led down to the lawn. Two large stone urns flanked the steps and they were tidily planted with geraniums and lobelia. He could see something of the front of the house and it looked to him like a small country *château*. Some white doves flew round the corner of the building and settled on the stone steps. A small boat with an outboard motor came down the distant river, and he could see two men in it and fishing rods sticking out over the bow. The river had a familiar look to him. It could be the Loire. If so, from its size here, the house was probably between Orleans and the sea. The mist was lifting rapidly now.

He got up and went over to his bed, dropped on to it and awkwardly lit a cigarette. They had left him his watch and his matches and cigarettes; considerate of them. He had a thumping headache, dimming now. His right arm was slightly swollen. What had he been treated to when they had lifted him in among the cabbages and poultry? A simple 3 c.c. dose? Just enough to keep him quiet on the journey and carry him through to darkness, when he had awakened with a bumping head and a stiff neck.

He shut his eyes, figuring out the map. If this were somewhere on the Loire, the journey would have presented them no problems. It might have taken Casalis a couple of hours, maybe more, to find the coach. Then he would have to get some description of the vehicle, and get out road blocks. By the time all this had been done *Paris-Match* and his friends would have been well away southwards. Even if the coach had been quickly found and also a description of the vehicle, it would still take time to set up road checks; and, even then, there were a maze of small roads from Avroult down . . .

He sat up, suddenly angry with himself. It seemed so damned

obvious now that AGRIP would take the coach away. That was the trouble with these affairs. Afterwards, everything that happened seemed so obvious. Fancy letting himself be caught in that quarry hut. No matter how fast things had moved, he should have thought of being followed. *Paris-Match* would have to have had his rear covered. He only had himself to blame for overlooking the gentleman in the blue shirt and his blonde friend. He got up and went to the window again. The mist was almost gone now and, amongst the trees over the river, he could pick out gay blue and yellow patches of tents. France was still on holiday.

The door, which he had already tried, opened behind him after a preliminary protest of bolts. He turned.

A man came two steps into the room, carrying a tray. Behind him, blocking the doorway stood *Paris-Match,* hands in his corduroy jacket pockets, the flat, untidy face pouched to what was probably a smile. The man with the tray was the man with the blue shirt, only now he wore a neat grey flannel suit with a clean white shirt, topped by a small red bow-tie.

He put the tray on the floor and said, 'Breakfast' – and then with a wink, added – 'And my apologies for yesterday.' Then, as Manston made half a move towards the tray, he said sharply, 'No, stay where you are until we go. Sorry about the cuffs, but you'll have to manage.'

Paris-Match stepped back out of the room and the other man followed him. The door closed and the bolts were rasped into place.

On the tray were a pot of coffee, a jug of hot milk, some *croissants,* a boiled egg with a little green cover over it, salt, pepper, butter, sugar, and a tiny jar of peach preserve. Manston carried it to the window ledge, drew up his stool and began to eat hungrily. The coffee was delicious.

When he had finished eating, he sat with the last of the coffee, smoking a cigarette, and watching the river.

That they had preferred to have him alive rather than dead

was easily figured out. Dead men could not speak. But a live man could be made to speak. That was something he was going to have to face and, if they brought it to an issue, there was no quick way out for him. When his clothes had been searched they had known exactly where to look for the regulation phial. It was one of the first things he had checked.

And Irina? He could put the question to himself unemotionally because that was the only sensible way to put it. More than likely she was in this place, and by now she must be conscious. Her chances of being rescued anywhere along the line from now on were slim, and depended on him.

*

Later that morning, on the A.5 Holyhead road, a few miles north of Capel Curig in Caernarvonshire, an A.A. motor-cycle patrolman returning from Bangor noticed a black Jaguar car parked just off the road by the side of Lake Ogwen. He had seen the car parked there early in the morning on his run up from Bettws-y-coed. Now, he drew up beyond it, dismounted and walked back. On the far side of the lake the great grey and brown shoulders of Carnedd Llewelyn rose massively to the sky, and the lake waters lay unrippled in the windless, brilliant morning. Sheep moved on the high slopes, white, grub-like in the distance.

There were two people in the car, a man and a woman. They were both dead. The woman had a small automatic wound in the left temple and the man a similar wound in the right temple. The automatic lay on the floor close to the car brake. There was a large crocodile-skin bag on the woman's lap. Without disturbing the bodies, the patrolman took the handbag and opened it. Among other things it contained two passports, one for Miss Pauline Rylands and the other for a Mr Hardwick. There was also a long, brown foolscap manilla envelope addressed simply, *For the police.*

Capa was dismantled.

The patrolman walked back to his machine, wondering

what two people could have in their lives so black and hopeless that it could force them to forsake a morning so full of sunshine and promise.

8

MANSTON WAS KEPT in his room until eight o'clock that evening. He was given a midday meal, which he ate clumsily because of his handcuffs. He noticed that most of the time either *Paris-Match* or the other man was somewhere about in the garden, well within sight of his window. If they thought that he was going to try and attract outside attention by smashing the glass of his window, they were wasting their time. Apart from the fact that the few fishermen and holiday people he could see distantly down by the river would never hear the noise or his shouts, he was not anxious at the moment to start any action. He was content at the moment to let himself be taken along the line. He had a pretty shrewd idea what his ultimate destination was intended to be. His passport had been taken from him and the AGRIP organization would have been efficient enough to identify him and his profession.

At seven-thirty he heard a vehicle come to the house. From its motor note it seemed a heavier, more powerful type of engine than any private car would have. Half an hour later the bolts were drawn on the door and *Paris-Match*, gun in hand, and the other man came in.

The other man said, 'Come on – time to go.' He stood aside from the open door, and Manston moved through it. 'Walk between us,' said the man. 'And watch the stairs; the carpet is torn in places and you can trip. Don't want an accident.' He laughed.

Paris-Match said, 'You talk too much.'

They went down two flights of stairs to the ground floor. The man was right. The carpet was worn threadbare from years of hard use. The house smelt of soup, as though a stock-pot simmered eternally somewhere in the kitchen regions. In the narrow hallway, lit at one end by a door made of different coloured lozenges of glass, was an oak chest, a large earthenware drain-pipe full of sticks, fishing-nets and rods, and a small table covered with pots of ferns and tradescantia. Standing by the table was a youngish-looking man, whom he had never seen before, with sleek black hair and a tanned face. He wore a dinner-jacket and looked up pleasantly at Manston as he came down the last few steps. At his side was the blonde woman, pretty once, going plump now. Manston recognized her from the Café de la Forêt.

The young man said to Manston as the group halted, 'I don't usually speed parting guests. But you're special, no?'

He reached out his hand and slipped something into Manston's pocket.

'What's that?' asked Manston.

'A whisky flask. You can get at it on the journey. It's a long one.' He smiled pleasantly. 'Now, we're going to blindfold you. Don't try to take it off until you're aboard.'

The woman came forward, holding up a length of black silk. She dropped the silk over his eyes and knotted it at the back of his head.

His arm was taken and the pleasant voice said, 'Just follow me. Outside, there's a flight of six steps.'

Manston moved forward. He heard the front door open. A warm draught of evening air came flooding past him, and he caught the hot scent of pine needles.

'Steps.'

Manston went down them and on to the gravel of a drive. Guided, he walked about fifty yards and, then, was halted.

For a moment there was complete silence. Then Manston

heard a door slam. It sounded more like a heavy car door than the door of the house, and it was very close to him. Footsteps ground against the gravel, coming towards him.

Someone said, 'Hurry.'

There was a sound of metal moving across metal.

A strange voice, French, male, said, 'Don't forget the key for the cuffs.'

'Here.' Manston felt someone move close to him.

The unknown man said, 'Right.' And then, as though he might be nervous, he whistled a few notes to himself.

A hand took Manston's arm and he was urged forward.

The young man with the pleasant voice said, 'Put out your hands, then get your knee up and crawl forward.' His hand came down to his wrists and guided him. Manston felt cold metal under his fingers about waist high. He began to feel around but the young man said sharply, 'No need for that. Get up and crawl forward.'

Manston found a rest for his knee, moved his hands forward and lost the touch of metal now, feeling canvas, stretched tightly with something packed hard under it. He crawled forward blindly.

Behind him the young man said, 'That's far enough. *Bon voyage*.'

Metal clanged. Somewhere close ahead of him he heard very faintly a motor engine start and he could feel the vibration run through his hands and knees. Almost immediately the floor jolted under him and he was thrown forward, caught off his balance. He lay full stretch and knew that he was moving, feeling the sway and jolt of the vehicle over the ground. He began to twist round, awkward without the proper use of his hands.

There was a movement close to him.

A voice said, 'Wait.'

Fingers went to the back of his head and the black silk blindfold was unknotted. He screwed himself round into a sitting position and sat blinking at the sudden light. He was in a small, cell-like chamber, about ten feet long and five feet wide. The place was completely lined with rough, strong canvas, held in place by strips of thin steel. At the far end of the chamber a small electric light was set in a glass bowl, about the size of a car's headlamp, protected by thick wire. Along the floor on each side of the chamber were two long benches about eighteen inches wide. Sitting on one of these opposite him, her head clearing the roof by less than a foot, was Irina Tovskaya.

She just sat there, staring at him in amazement. She had one leg drawn up under her on the seat and her hands were in her lap holding his length of black silk. She still wore the linen suit, now rather rumpled, in which he had taken her to the country. Her face was pale, drawn with weariness, and there were dark shadows under her large brown eyes. The sight of it sent a sharp pang through Manston.

He put out his cuffed hands and took hold of one of her hands, his fingers pressing around hers, and he said gently, 'It's all right . . . it's all right. You're not dreaming; it's me.'

Her eyes closed for a moment and her head went back as though suddenly she had need for great draughts of air.

He said, his voice firm, 'Don't talk for a moment. . . . Reach in my pocket. You'll find cigarettes and a whisky flask.'

She shook her head and said suddenly, 'It can't be! Oh, it can't be! Richard —'

He held her hand tightly, giving it a little shake, and spoke quickly, knowing that she needed all the help he could give, 'It's me. I'm with you, and everything's going to be all right. Just don't rush at things for a moment, that's all. Now, come on, get the cigarettes and the whisky out and I'll explain.'

She leaned forward and got out the cigarettes and the flask. She lit the cigarettes for them both and then he nodded at the whisky.

'Unscrew it. You first. It'll do you good.'

As she unscrewed the cap, she said, 'Richard, please – tell

me what all this is about? Why are you here? I mean, I don't understand. I can't believe it. Why should you be here —'

'Steady. Take a swig.'

'Swig? Oh, of course....'

She drank and passed the flask to him and he took a sip and passed it back to her.

'Better?'

She nodded.

'Good. All you have to do is listen, and I'll explain things. You'll have to be patient because there's a hell of a lot to tell. However . . . we've got plenty of time. But let's get one thing clear at the start. I'm here to help you. I'm on your side. So long as we keep our heads everything is going to work out. These people —'

Suddenly she moved forward, dropping on to her knees in front of him, and her arms went round him and she pressed her head against his chest, holding herself there; and he silently cursed the handcuffs which stopped him from gathering her in his arms, and comforting her. She raised her face to his, and he leaned forward and kissed her on the forehead. Slowly she drew herself back and then sat on the bench beside him. She gave a small smile and he saw the return of spirit to her dark eyes.

'I'm all right now, Richard. I will be patient and listen.'

'Good girl.'

It was not an easy story to tell. He began by explaining about AGRIP, and the organization for kidnapping people from different countries and shipping them back to Russia.

'I knew this happened, of course,' she said. 'But I thought it was only for very important people. I never dreamt it could happen to me. I felt so safe.'

'Nobody's safe or unimportant. Over a hundred people like you are shipped back every year, and we couldn't find out how. It had us worried stiff?'

'Us?'

'I'll come to that later.' He went on, explaining to her why the small people weren't unimportant, and, then, how eventually the Department had got a break, by making a contact with the cipher clerk in AGRIP. 'From him we got the name of the next person on the list to be kidnapped from England.'

He paused and saw that she understood.

Quietly, she said, 'It was me?'

'Yes.'

'But if you knew —' There was a puzzled, questioning lift in her voice.

'We could have saved you? Yes.' He made no attempt now to avoid anything. 'But Sutcliffe, the man I worked for once, had a different plan in mind. Our contact with AGRIP wouldn't last long; hasn't lasted, in fact. There was just this one chance to find out about the organization and smash it once and for all. So, Sutcliffe's plan was to let you be taken, and for us, secretly, to follow you down the line, grabbing you back at the last moment.'

'Oh, no. . . .' She drew away from him, her face stony.

'You've got to try and understand,' he urged. 'This was his one hope of saving all the other people fated to be snatched back.'

She said nothing. He went on to tell her how Sutcliffe, although he had left the Service, had got him to come up to the Covent Garden ballet and go out to dinner with her . . . told her the whole story and saw in her the instant conflict between indignation, that anyone could treat another human being so callously, and the generous logic that accepted a sacrifice for the sake of others. When he told her how he had accepted the commission, she drew farther away from him.

His voice harsh, he said, 'I had to do it. Try and understand. It was hell, but I had to do it. It was going to happen to you anyway. I wanted you to have every chance. That was all I could think about.' He reached out for her hands, but she held them from him.

Coldly, she said, 'So, all the time . . . when you were so nice to me. . . . That lovely evening in the country . . . you were just sorry for me.'

Roused, angry himself at not being able to spare her, he said, 'Of course I was sorry for you. But I was trapped just as much as you were. For God's sake, why do you think I left the Service originally? Just because of this kind of thing. But, when I met you, I had to take it on.'

'And that night – as you took me back to London – you knew?' Her voice was little more than a whisper and the look on her face was unbearable.

'There was nothing I could do. Leaving you at your flat door was pure hell. . . . You've every right to feel as you do. But you were our one chance to stop this dirty racket. Irina . . . try and see it our way.' He reached out and caught her hand and she let him hold it this time, but she turned her face from him and, in profile, he could see the glint of tears at the corner of one eye.

'It's very hard . . . so very hard. I am trying.' She leaned her head back against the canvas wall and her eyes shut, the line of her throat tightening. 'It's like some bad dream. How can people do this to one another?' She opened her eyes and turned to him. 'Oh, no . . . not you, I don't mean that. I can see how you were caught. But this other thing, this kidnapping.'

'That's what we wanted to smash. And you were the one chance given to us.'

She was silent for a moment. Then quietly she said, 'I think I'd like another cigarette.'

He watched her light it and saw the blue trails slide up along the roof of the compartment, and then be sucked away through a small grating above the light.

Unexpectedly she said, 'And it was this kind of thing that made you leave the Service?'

'Yes.'

She nodded, and he saw that her face was calm now, her

mind accepting the facts. 'Yes, I can understand that.' She smiled faintly, 'It's all right. I'm not a fool. I can see how this Sutcliffe would think. It just is that I thought that evening you liked me . . . just that.'

'Of course I did. I wouldn't have done it for anyone else.'

'Is that true? You did it only for me?'

'That's why I'm here.'

She handed him the cigarette. 'You finish this. I do not really care for them.' As he took it, she said, 'But what now? What's going to happen?'

Manston moved closer to her. 'Things have gone wrong, but they're not hopeless. We're going to escape.'

Her hand came out and rested on his. 'You really think we can escape?'

'That's one thing you must never doubt. From now on, you and I are together in this. We'll find a way.'

'What way?'

Manston smiled. 'Well, it's early to say yet. We've got plenty of time on our hands. The chance will come as long as we never let up looking for it. All you have to do is to have confidence in me.'

For a moment she looked at him and then swiftly she came close to him, her head dropping to his shoulder, her arms going round his neck.

'Richard . . .'

'It's all right. . . . We'll pull through.' He cursed silently again his cuffed hands that denied him the ability to hold and comfort her. 'We're not anything like as helpless as they imagine.'

After a moment or two she drew back from him, her eyes still wet with tears, but her face smiling; and he knew that in her was a toughness of spirit which would help them both. When he thought of how some women would have reacted!

She said firmly. 'It's all right. I shall be sensible from now on.'

'That's the idea. And to hell with Sutcliffe, eh?'

'To hell with Sutcliffe, yes.'

'Good. Now, to show you that we've still got a few tricks up our sleeve, let's find out which way we're travelling.' He reached out his hands towards her, turning his left wrist up to her.

He said, smiling, 'Trick number one. Take hold of the winding knob of the watch and then give it half a turn and pull it out another notch.'

Puzzled, she did as he said. 'What is it for?' she asked.

He held the face of the watch to her. 'The second click frees the big travelling second hand. It's no longer revolving. It's a compass needle. It's useful to know in what direction we are travelling. From now on, we keep our eyes and ears open.'

He watched the second hand. It was flickering a little, but pointing straight to the wall opposite the one in which the light was fixed. Assuming they had entered through the back end of the vehicle – to which the needle pointed – they were travelling south.

'We were loaded on to this thing at eight o'clock. We're doing, say, an average speed of thirty-five miles an hour. So . . . we can work out the distance we travel roughly. You never know when some small piece of information isn't going to come in useful. My friend back at the house said it was going to be a long journey, anyway.'

Irina, for a moment her position and danger forgotten, said, 'You know, I can't think of you as a sort of secret agent. You don't look a bit like it.'

Manston shook his head. 'We never do. And now, I suggest you get some sleep. You look all in. Here—' He leaned forward and took a blanket from a pile of three that stood at the end of his bench. 'I'll tuck you in. Come on. You can have the extra two for a pillow.'

'But I shan't sleep.'

'Don't you believe it.'

She lay down and he tucked the blanket in around her and then sat on the bench opposite. For a moment she looked across at him and then, spontaneously, she slipped her hand free of the blanket and reached out to him. He took it in his own and held it. He said nothing, but inwardly he told himself that somehow, somewhere he would get her out of all this. . . .

*

Ludmilla Miachin, who had taken Alexandre Shernof's place at AGRIP, sat at his table in front of the window overlooking the Quai des Célestins. She was a well-built woman of about thirty, big-breasted, and with a large, soft, generous mouth. The clocks had just struck half-past ten and the summer darkness was shot with the soft blur of the riverside lights. In an angle of the embankment wall, faintly touched by the light from the nearest street lamp, a French sailor, the pom-pom on top of his white cap vivid scarlet, had a girl in his arms; he was kissing her and had been kissing her for the last two minutes . . . one long, dedicated embrace which had made a Laocoon statue out of them, given life, now and then, solely by the slow, ecstatic movement of the girl's left leg which, occasionally, was lifted behind her. Ludmilla watched, envying the girl. She liked being kissed and made love to. In fact, lovemaking was the only way she had of brightening the tedium of her life. When she had come here she had hoped that Oleg might help her to relieve the tedium of her work. Oleg, she had decided quickly and regretfully, was just a block of granite that walked, talked and thought, but did little else. Naturally ambitious, she preferred the head of a department, but here it looked as though she would have to make do with the clerk in the dispatching department. But she decided that she would give Oleg another couple of days. She had known granite come to life before this. . . .

She pulled towards her the message he had dropped in front of her five minutes ago and began to encipher it. It read:

Agrip to Limbo
Exceptional circumstances necessitated two consignments for you shipped this night from Taru. Your agent full details. But stress additional consignment must be treated with maximum care or could give trouble. Will inform onward movement arrangements two three days time.

When she had finished the message she saw through the window that the embrace had been broken. The sailor and his girl were now leaning over the parapet, smoking and talking.

The AGRIP girl left the room and went down to the dispatching department.

*

The journey lasted ten hours, and they were hours that seemed completely detached from life. Only once, after about five hours, was the journey broken. The vehicle stopped, the rear door was partly opened and Irina was called out, a voice explaining that the stop was purely for convenience. When Irina came back, she tied the blindfold on Manston and he was let out. He was led down a concrete path, a door opened, and the man with him said, 'Inside.'

Inside Manston pulled up his blindfold. The place was in pitch darkness, and smelt of urine. When he came out, the man grabbed his shoulders, swung him round and tightened his blindfold.

Back in the chamber, Irina took off his blindfold. She told him that she had been blindfolded, too, and had seen nothing.

As the hours went by Manston began to feel the beginning of a curious disorientation which made concentration doubly difficult. They might have been in some rocket capsule, being projected through space. The only thing that had an independent existence was the needle of his compass. As the vehicle bore round long curves, it would swing, faithfully homing on north.

There was no doubt that the general line of their journey was south by west and Manston was pretty sure that they must be heading down the western side of France. From the floor tilt it was quite clear that they had not entered any of the really hilly parts of France. If they had gone down anything like the Route Napoléon, for instance, it would have been very apparent. From his memory of the map he was pretty sure that they were not going down either the N.6 or the N.7 on the Paris, Avignon, Marseilles axis. The needle would have given them a south-by-east line for that. From the smoothness of their ride it was reasonably certain that they were sticking to the wide main roads. The chamber was so well insulated for noise that few sounds came through to them. They could have shouted and pounded on its sides and no one would have heard them.

After they had been in the vehicle nine and a half hours he felt it pull up and the engine stopped. Irina, who had been dozing, sat up.

They sat there waiting but nothing happened. Then, after a few minutes, Manston felt the vehicle vibrate as the ground close to it was shaken with a regular rhythm; and he heard the faint scream of a locomotive hooter, muted, seeming a mile away, but – he guessed – close at hand. A few seconds later the vehicle began to move again.

'We must remember that,' he said. 'They pulled up at a level-crossing and a train went by. Half-past five. Sounded like the hooter of an electric train.'

Thirty-five minutes later, the vehicle left the smooth main road, and they were jolted about as they struck some rougher side road. They held this track for three minutes and then the vehicle came to a stop.

Manston said, 'I think this is it. Thirty-odd minutes from a level-crossing. Three minutes down a rough side road.'

Irina said, 'All this will help us?'

He said, 'It might. When we are let out, don't miss anything.

They won't let us see much, if anything, but we have our ears and our noses.'

Behind them there was a sudden noise. Manston turned. The rear wall of the chamber had been opened an inch. A pale wash of daylight showed down the crack of the opening and through it he could see just a little of what looked like a wooden wall, the boards overlapping in clinker fashion.

From outside a heavy voice said, 'Don't make any move. Do as you are told. Monsieur will come first. Mademoiselle will tie the bandage round his eyes. It is understood?'

Manston looked at Irina. 'Do as they say,' he said aloud and, then, as she came across to him and her face was near his, he whispered, 'Tie it loosely.'

Irina put the silk bandage round his eyes, knotting it loosely and Manston raised his cuffed hands pulling it away from his eyes a little so that he could look down.

The voice outside said, 'Monsieur first – come out backwards.'

Stiff from the journey, Manston got down on to his knees and began to work his way backwards. He felt his feet touch the rear end of the compartment and stopped. Behind him the voice said, 'Now, mademoiselle, put your bandage on.'

Behind him the door of the compartment opened. The man said, 'Come out and stand up, and do not move.'

Manston crawled out backwards, groping for the ground with his feet. Looking downwards under his bandage he caught a glimpse of a tail-lamp and then the ground, hard-packed earth with a few strands of straw. As he stood up, he raised his cuffed hands, meaning to pull the bandage up free from his eyes. For a moment his hands were on the silk blindfold, tugging it upwards. He had a brief glimpse of feet and a pair of legs and beyond the feet a sight of a small dog looking upwards at him. It was a white mongrel, with a curly tail and a black patch on its side shaped like the map of Australia.

Then the movement to free his eyes was killed by two hands that pinioned his arms below the elbows, from behind.

'No, monsieur. It has been tried before.'

The hands held him and he heard the movement of another man. Suddenly the bandage over his eyes was tightened violently from behind. The man holding him moved, still pinioning him, and he felt the other man pass a rope round him, looping it through his wrists and then knotting it behind him.

'Good.'

The hands came off him and he stood there in blackness.

'Now you, mademoiselle.'

Manston stood there, hearing them dealing with Irina. He had a feeling that the place was some kind of farm building into which the vehicle had been backed. Although it was only six in the morning, the day was already warm. Somewhere, not very far away, he heard a soft chuckle from hens and there was a scolding of sparrows outside.

His arm was taken, and the talking man said, 'Come. You can walk freely. There are no obstructions.'

Manston began to move, counting his paces as he went. Twelve took them out of the building and he felt the sun strike against his right cheek. As you came out of the door, he noted, to your right was the east . . . no, at this time of day, a bit north of east. Ten more paces, bearing left across hard earth, and then the sun was shadowed intermittently. He could smell pines, and guessed they were going through the trees on a path broad enough to take the two of them. Twenty paces down the path, then the sound of rushing water and his feet striking, for three paces, boards that echoed under them.

The man halted him. 'Five steps,' he warned.

They went down five stone steps. Manston tried them with his feet cautiously, pretending to have difficulty and felt that their edges were without sharpness, worn smooth.

Another path, open to the sun now, and this time it was

hot on his left cheek. They had come round in a half circle. The path began to rise and there was no smell of pines. After fifteen paces they topped the rise and then descended for twenty paces, when the sun went altogether. They were in the shade completely now, but still not under cover. The path had gone and he was walking across turf broken now and then with tufts of some growth. There was a loud noise of bees and, to his right, the shrill call of a cicada.

Ten more paces and there was rock under his feet, hard, smooth rock, and he felt that he must be under cover somewhere for his footsteps had no longer the sound of being in the open, and the air was suddenly colder. The place smelt musty, dampish . . . a cave, he wondered? It was odd, but there was something very familiar in the musty, damp smell. They went forward over rock which was level.

The man said, 'Bend your head. Keep it down until I tell you.'

Manston did as he was told. The rock seemed to have a thin layer of sand on it which gritted under his feet. Behind him, he heard Irina and the other man.

'All right.'

Manston straightened up. The man left him. He heard a key turn in a lock and the clang of ironwork. The man came back and behind him. 'Go forward a few yards and then stop.'

Manston did as he was told. The sand was thicker on the floor now. Behind him he heard the man speak to Irina. There was the clang of iron again, the turn of a key in a lock and then the swift movement of the men's feet. Another door clanged and he heard bolts shoot home. There was no sound except the breathing of Irina close at hand.

Then Irina said, 'Richard; where are you?'

'Here.' He moved towards her.

He felt her hands come out and move behind him.

He said, 'You're not tied?'

'Not now. Wait.'

She freed the rope from his waist and hands and then he felt her fingers go up to the back of his head and tug at the knot of the bandage. As it came away from him he realized that the place was in complete darkness.

Irina said, 'Give me your wrists. They've let me have the key of the handcuffs.'

He raised his wrists and felt her warm hands mould round them for a moment. She was clumsy in the darkness with the key and she said, 'Oh, dear; I don't know how to do it. . . .'

'Take it easy. The lock's in the centre, it springs both bracelets.'

She did it at last, and the cuffs fell to the floor.

Manston said, 'What about you? Are you still blindfolded?' He raised his hands, feeling her shoulders and then her face and, finally, the silk over her eyes. He slipped his fingers into the knot at the back and freed the bandage from her. As he did so he felt a slow, relaxing movement run through her body. He slipped his arm round her shoulder and drew her to him, holding her comfortingly against him.

'The bastards,' he said. 'They might at least have given us a light.'

As though someone had heard him, the light at that moment came on, blazing down from a high, rock-vaulted ceiling above them.

9

THE HEAD OF the dispatching and receiving department brought the message up to the cipher room himself. Ludmilla Miachin gave him a quick look and then ignored him, opening the buff envelope and spreading the sheet of paper under her fingers. The man stood there, willing to loiter and talk, already attracted by the big, promising, peasant bust and the sturdiness of the firm body. The girl guessed what was in his mind, but she ignored him still, ready to slap vigorously at any movement of his hands towards her. The man hesitated, shuffled his feet, cleared his throat, and then went slowly out of the room.

Smiling to herself, the girl began to decipher the message. It read:

Limbo to Agrip.
Double consignment received safely in good condition. Note that additional consignment is of quite different standard and quality calling for exceptional handling, and clearly outside the terms of our contract. Can handle this but not within price schedule already agreed. Must request conference, usual place, to arrange new terms. Advise date and time.

After she had typed this, Ludmilla took it, with the original coded message, into Oleg's office.

He was sitting at his desk, going through a file, and for the moment did not look up. The morning sunlight, coming through the window behind him, cast his face in shadow and touched the edges of his brown hair with a faint rim of bright light. She put the messages on his desk and noticed, as he lifted his head, the slow movement of his wide shoulders and the hard passivity of his features as, for a second, his eyes fell on her. In that moment, the suggestion of brute strength in his body stirred her and challenged her. Standing in front of him, she willed him to look at her and to go on looking at her and, although she did not smile or make any movement of her features, her big firm body was before him, its strength and promise offered to him.

Oleg's eyes left her, the slight movement of his head as he looked down at the message full of indifference. She stood there, waiting.

She saw the crease of annoyance on his forehead as he read. Then, oblivious of her, he pulled a signal pad towards him and began to write. When he had finished he tore it slowly from its block and was about to push it across the desk to her when she put out her hand. He handed the message to her and, for a fraction of a second, her fingers touched his.

As her hand withdrew with the message, Oleg went on looking at her; and, for the first time since she had worked for him, she knew that he was really seeing her. His eyes held her face and then slowly travelled down the length of her body. Suddenly he gave a little nod, and said, 'Send this at once, Ludmilla Miachin.'

His eyes left her and he pulled the file he had been studying back to him.

Ludmilla nodded, and without pause turned and left the room.

As she sat down at the table in her own room to encode the message she was smiling to herself. There was warmth somewhere in the granite. It was the first time he had ever used her name and she knew Oleg well enough to realize that it had been done deliberately. She worked at the message automatically, thinking of the hard strength of his torso. The message read:

Agrip to Limbo
Third of September, usual place, usual arrangements.

The third of September was the next day. Ludmilla wondered where Oleg was going, but not because she was interested in this affair. She was only interested in Oleg.

*

At the moment when Oleg was writing a reply to the Limbo message, Sutcliffe was arriving at Le Bourget airport. He was met by Barry Dymen and Casalis.

Settling in the car which Barry Dymen was driving, Sutcliffe said, 'Faubourg St Honoré.'

Casalis cocked an eye at him, questioning.

Sutcliffe began to pack his pipe, awkwardly because of the jolting of the car over the cobbles; and not addressing either of them directly, but confiding his words without specific destination, talking with a rare touch of grimness which alone would have made the other two men conscious that his, at the moment, was a dangerous mood, said, 'Yes, the Embassy. This thing's gone right to the top level now. A celestial stink. The Embassy boys have got to help me with the French. The P.M. knows about the girl and Manston. I won't repeat his comments . . .' He smiled, on and off like a warning light, briefly, for their benefit. 'You are too young. The man has a command of the English language. And he gave one simple order. Those two don't leave this country. Something about the girl – frankly, the way we had to do it – has touched him, and, blast it, he was at Charterhouse with Manston's father. They don't leave. That's an order. Easy, isn't it?'

'Simple,' said Barry, concentrating on his driving.

Casalis said nothing, waiting.

Sutcliffe sucked at his pipe, got it drawing nicely, and went on, 'We've got to do it. The French will help, but won't accept responsibility. We can't ask them to do that, otherwise we could have an international rumpus on our hands.'

'Got to do what?' asked Barry, with an innocence that was not intended to deceive anyone.

Sutcliffe said, 'There's only one direct way, and there's no guarantee that we can even manage to do that. I told the P.M. this and he just said, "Damn well manage it." This thing is being run by AGRIP. Outwardly, they're perfectly respectable and we can't get at them. They've got diplomatic immunity. And the head boy in this affair, there, is this Oleg chap. We know all about him. I've got a nice surprise for you two. You've got to get your hands on him, quietly and where you won't be disturbed, and then he must talk —'

'What?' They both said it, and for a moment Barry's head came round.

'Watch the road,' said Sutcliffe calmly. 'You've got to get him. He isn't holed up in AGRIP twenty-four hours every day. Through the Embassy I'm going to arrange for you to have all the help you want this side. But it will only be limited help. When it comes to action, you do it.'

'They'll raise hell,' said Casalis.

'No they won't. They don't want a stink either; not if we get what we want. You get what we want and not a word comes out, or, at the most, a "Diplomat Beaten Up" headline. Robbery, a woman, anything. But you've got to get him – and quickly – and make him talk.'

Barry said, 'Does the P.M. know this?'

'He said, "Manage it." That's enough for me. This kind of thing has been done before by us, and by them, and you know as well as I do that it works only if it's successful. Casalis must get on with it right away. No time must be lost.'

Casalis leaned back against the leather and lit a cigarette. Slowly he shook his head and then said, 'This is a new one for me.'

'Not for me,' said Sutcliffe sharply. 'There's nothing new.'

Casalis, his voice suddenly grim as the full scope of the project opened before his eyes, said, 'You'd better drop me by the Opéra. It'll save time.'

*

The place they were in had obviously been deliberately fashioned and furnished for the purpose of holding people. It was a large rock chamber, the roof about eighteen feet above them and holding one powerful light. For the most part the walls were as nature had originally framed the cave, but in places they had been worked, or reshaped, with concrete to form a room about thirty feet long and twelve feet wide. The entrance to this chamber was in one corner and was closed by a stout wooden door. Eight feet from this door a grille of steel bars, set with a steel door, ran right across the cave from walls to roof. They were penned within this inner cell. The steel bars, running vertically and with six horizontal strengtheners, were about three inches apart. But in one place to the right of the steel door, which stood almost against the wall, the bars had been arranged in such a way that they formed a gap about a foot square. On the far side of this opening stood a rough table, and on their side of the opening was another similar table.

In their cell were three camp-beds, four cane chairs, their table and, against the back wall, a cupboard about the height of a man's head. On the top shelf of the cupboard was an assortment of crockery, some plastic forks and spoons, and pepper and salt containers. On the bottom shelf were blankets and sheets, neatly folded, some towels, and three old-fashioned, very long night-shirts made of a very cheap material. Everything was freshly laundered. The middle shelf held a few books and magazines, a couple of ash-trays, soap, a packet of matches, half a dozen cartons of American *Marlboro'* cigarettes and an electric razor. To the right of the cupboard and in the corner of the chamber, a large alcove had been hacked out of the rock and closed with a cheap three-ply door. This held a chemical closet, clean and ready for use, whose disinfectant odour faintly permeated the whole of the chamber. By this door was a tap, the pipe running back along the wall through the grille and disappearing into the ground by the main door. Under the tap was a bucket and a yellow plastic handbowl, also a small drain running clearly back towards the main door, its course marked by a concrete-covered channel let into the rock. The drain ended close to the point where the water pipe disappeared.

On the table by the steel bars was a large sheet of cardboard, with a white paper stuck on to it that contained the following instructions in three languages, French, English, and Russian:

INSTRUCTIONS TO OCCUPANTS

1. Meals will be served three times a day. These will be placed on the table outside the barrier and can be transferred through the aperture in the bars.
2. Bedding, crockery and other necessities will be found in the cupboard. All crockery and cutlery will be washed at the tap, but refuse must be placed in the paper bags (also in the cupboards), and passed through the barrier at the end of a meal.
3. The light will be switched off at nine o'clock at night, and will come on again at six in the morning.
4. Occupants are advised that the chamber is sound-proof to the outside world.
5. In the event of emergency, illness, fire, or such event, the attendant can be called by use of the bell in the wall just inside the barrier door. Irresponsible use of this bell will result in it being switched off. There is a plug point below the bell for the electric shaver.
6. The water in the tap is drinkable.
7. If bottles, flasks or other objects used for the serving of meals are not returned to the table on the other side of the barrier after each meal, no further meals will be served until such objects are returned.
8. Your stay here will not be long: it is for you to make it as comfortable as possible. Unruly behaviour will be disciplined strictly.

Irina read this over Manston's shoulder. He looked round at her and made a face.

'There's only one thing missing. Don't they usually put the price of the room on these things?'

Irina smiled. Then she said, 'What kind of person wrote all that, do you think?'

'It's someone who doesn't believe in unnecessary waste. Lights out at nine is a bit early.'

'It reminds me of the rules at the Kirov ballet school. This will be this, and that will be that, and unruly behaviour will be severely punished.' She laughed.

Manston studied the notice. It was typed and on an old machine, too. The line-spacing was inclined to wander and the 'n' on the machine had its legs worn so that there was little more than the arch of the letter showing. He handed the card to Irina.

'What's the Russian like?'

'I read it in Russian; it still comes easier to me, one does it naturally. It's perfect.'

'And done on a different machine. Had to be because of the characters. A nice new machine, too.'

The instructions in Russian had been done on slightly different paper, which had been stuck below the others on the board. Manston decided that when he left this place, he would rip off a piece of the card containing the English and French instructions. The typewriter would not be hard to identify.

The light in the chamber went out suddenly. He felt Irina move closer to him, instinctively, and he put his arm round her shoulders.

'What's happening?'

'It's all right,' he told her. 'My guess is that it is breakfast, rather late.'

They stood there in the darkness and waited. They would have to get used to darkness, he was thinking. Darkness of all kinds. They were living in a world of their own, their contacts with the real world restricted severely. But no man he knew could place others in complete darkness. So long as they existed, the real world, no matter how obscurely, made itself known in many small ways.

They heard the bolts of the far door drawn back and then the soft burring of the hinges. No light showed from the passageway. He stood there, listening, Irina close to him. Footsteps thudded slowly and deliberately on the loose sand of the chamber floor and he heard someone breathing heavily. As the steps came across to the grille, Manston took his arm from around Irina and slipped a hand into his pocket. He heard something being set down on the table outside the grille. There was a faint rattle of wood.

Manston stepped forward through the darkness towards the grille and, at the same moment, whipped his matches from his pocket. He struck one and held the light aloft, close to the bars. The spurt of flame in its first strong flare of ignition brought the chamber vividly to life. But if Manston had hoped to gain much by his ruse, he was disappointed. Outside the grille, just straightening up from placing a tray on the table was a man. He wore a pair of cotton trousers, blue, with a thin white stripe in them, and a loose corduroy jacket of some dark colour. He stood there while the match flared and then died, staring straight at Manston. Over his face, crude, bizarre, bringing a gasp of horror from Irina, was a carnival mask; bulging red cheeks a bulbous nose and a long, thin slit of a mouth from which projected tusk-like teeth. On his head the man wore an ordinary black beret which somehow added to the grotesque effect.

For a second or two he stood motionless, his hands half-raised and then, as darkness returned, they heard him turn and go back across the sandy floor to the door.

A few minutes later the light came on.

Manston shrugged his shoulders, smiling at Irina.

'They must have had that trick played on them before.'

'He looked ghastly.'

'A carnival mask. But we learned something anyway. From his hands, and the way he held himself, he was an elderly man.'

Irina said, 'What you did comes under the heading of "unruly behaviour".'

'Too bad.'

On the tray outside the grille was a jug of coffee, another of hot milk, a plate of rather stale bread, cut into thick slices, a dish of butter and another of plum *confiture*. There was also a screw-top glass jar full of soft sugar.

As they ate, Manston explained to Irina – ignoring the question of whether they would ever be able to use it – the considerable amount of small detail they already knew. They had a rough mileage of the journey they had taken, and, from the compass, he was pretty certain that they were somewhere down in the south-west corner of France. They knew that this place was about thirty-odd minutes run from a level-crossing; and it was certainly in the country. They were looked after by an elderly man with blue-and-white striped trousers.

'And this' – Manston held up the dish which had contained the bread – 'is some regional pottery. No mark on the bottom. But look at the design and remember it. Goat's milk, too. That could mean that we're not in good pasture country. The food may tell us a lot. We get whatever is going in the region. The beret the man was wearing was Basque-type. So you see, we know quite a lot. And the more we learn the quicker we can get at these people when we're free.'

'When we're free?' Despite herself Irina's voice had a doubtful note.

Manston lit a cigarette for her and shook his head.

'The trouble with you is you don't have faith in me.' He leaned forward and put his hands on the crooks of her elbows. 'Just keep clear in your head that we are going to have a break. It's going to come and, when it does, we're going to be ready. O.K.?'

For a moment she said nothing. She sat there, her face solemn, her dark eyes steady on him; then slowly she nodded, smiled for an instant, then turned her face away from him and stood up.

Her back to him, she said, 'I promise. And now' – her voice lightened, accepting his faith, discarding her own doubts finally – 'now, I'll do the washing-up.'

Manston stood up and put his hands affectionately on her shoulders.

'That's my girl,' he said.

10

LATE THAT AFTERNOON Ludmilla Miachin took a sheaf of routine signals into Oleg's room. He was standing at his window, looking out at the Seine. This, in itself, was an unusual occurrence, for Oleg was seldom caught just standing and staring. Ludmilla could not remember a time when she had come into the room and he was not sitting at his desk working.

He half turned as she came in, saw what she had in her hand and said, as his eyes went back to the river, 'Put them on the desk.'

Ludmilla dropped the signals on his desk, gave a little shrug of her shoulders behind his back, and turned to go.

His voice stopped her as she approached the door.

'Ludmilla Miachin.'

She turned to find that he was looking at her, his face in its usual expressionless cast.

'Yes?'

'I have been informed today that you are transferred permanently to my department.'

For a moment the beginning of a smile showed her surprise.

Oleg said, 'Does that please you?'

'Very much. I like it here.'

Oleg frowned a little, not approving of this too open pleasure. 'I do not have to stress to you the important and confidential nature of the work here. Nor, I imagine, are you unacquainted with the history of your predecessor.'

Ludmilla just nodded, but there was a fine edge of excitement inside her. There was only one reason why he should have had her work here confirmed as permanent.

Oleg came slowly back to his desk and sat down. Ludmilla waited for him to pick up the signals and dismiss her. But his hands stayed, poised sturdily on the edge of the desk, and she noticed that they were well kept, the nails scrupulously clean.

Looking directly at her, Oleg said, 'Tomorrow I have to go to Bordeaux on business. I shall take the 8.05 train and stay the night at the Hôtel Royal Gascogne, returning the next day . . .' He paused for a while, looking through her and yet making her aware that there was nothing about the splendid sturdiness of her body that, in imagination, lay unrevealed to him. Then he said without any change of voice, 'I am almost certain that I shall not have any need of your official services, but I have decided that you had better come with me. A room has already been booked for you under the name of your second passport. You will travel down later on the "Sud Express". Publicly, we shall not know one another. When I need you, I will get in touch with you. Is that clear?'

'It is.' Like him, Ludmilla kept her voice free of any emotion.

'That is all.'

She went out, and not until the door had closed behind her did she permit herself a full, satisfied smile. The pattern, she told herself, was a familiar one. With the heads of departments there was always an official reason. She stood behind her desk, looking out at the Seine, and she flexed her arms with a slow, deep excitement. After dinner in the hotel she would go to her room. He would ring through to her . . . How stupid she had been to imagine that he would be different from any of the others.

*

At eleven o'clock the next morning, the third of September, Casalis had a call over a closed Sûreté line from Barry Dymen.

'Cassy?'

'Yes.'

'Barry here. We've got a break with the boy we want.'

'How?'

'He bought a return ticket for Bordeaux and took the 8.05 train from the Gare d'Austerlitz. Alone. One overnight suitcase. Could be staying there. The lads here are arranging for him to be checked at the Bordeaux end and they've got two men on the train. Usual business; they'll watch-dog but nothing else. What do you say?'

'If he's for a night in Bordeaux let's get down there.'

'Thought so. I've laid on a flight to Merignac airport. We can get away as soon as we've had a check from the Bordeaux end.'

'If he stays there we shall need a car and a driver.'

'Not from the French boys. They're jumpy about the whole thing. So far, no farther. We'll hire, and you can bring one of your lads. O.K.?'

'O.K.'

'Ring you when we get something definite. His train doesn't get in until just before two o'clock. That gives us plenty of time to fly down. The old man knows about this and wants to see you.'

Half an hour later Casalis was at the flat, in the Avenue Foch, which Sutcliffe used when he was in Paris.

Sutcliffe, moving slowly up and down the room, was in what Casalis privately called one of his knifing moods. They usually arose when somebody, from whom he could have expected help, had disappointed him. When that happened the knife came out and he looked for a victim. Casalis was aware that it was a category into which he could, at the first mistake, slip.

'The French,' said Sutcliffe, 'are as sticky as hell about all this. They wouldn't normally be; but there's just the edge showing at this moment of some sort of political thaw and they don't want to – Oh, what the hell, you know what the hopes of politicians are like. Bloody straws in the wind . . .'

He stopped talking to relight his pipe, and Casalis tried to remember when he had last known him so openly moved.

'Anyway' – a spent match was jerked into the fireplace – 'they've no intention of getting their fingers burnt. Diplomatic immunity must be respected. They don't want to know anything about it. They'll give us all the information and routine service but not a pennyworth more than that. So . . .'

Sutcliffe swung round and looked at Casalis, lowering his large head a little and hunching his shoulders, as though about to charge.

'I get it,' said Casalis.

'You damned well better, Cassy.' The familiar nickname meant nothing. There was no subtlety now about Sutcliffe. Not a dozen people had ever seen this mood before, Casalis mused grimly, and not all of these still lived.

'This . . .' Sutcliffe sucked fiercely at his pipe which was refusing to draw and then dumped it angrily on to a small table. 'This is a solo job. You, Barry and our own people. You've got to get this Oleg away where you can work on him. You've got to do it clean, quick and without noise. The only thing the French will cover is "Diplomat Assaulted" junk when it's all over. When you've got what you want from him you can throw him back into the stream and he will swim home. He won't be getting any worse treatment than they've lined up for Manston.'

'Can I go the limit?'

'So long as he can breathe afterwards – yes. But if things do go wrong . . . well . . .'

He looked at Casalis and shook his head slowly.

'My head on a platter?' Casalis cocked an eyebrow.

'Not just yours. Mine. However' – Sutcliffe suddenly smiled – 'we've been in worse places before now. You can have one glass of sherry, tell me what you've fixed for Bordeaux, and then get moving. The French boys in Bordeaux know him. He's down about four times a year on trade trips – someone behind the Curtain apparently has a taste for claret – and he always stays at the Royal Gascogne. He's booked in there as usual, under his own name.'

'I wonder why he's making the trip?'

Casalis took the glass of sherry which Sutcliffe held out to him.

'He'll have an official appointment, don't worry. But the French are going to get us a list of everyone staying and full dossiers, and they'll watch his contacts. But nothing else. Maybe the trip's genuine and someone has run out of Château Margaux. Now then, what have you got lined up?'

Casalis sipped his sherry and was silent for a moment. Since Barry had telephoned he had had exactly half an hour to think about this; and now, with Sutcliffe's blunt statement that if it did not go like silk there was no hope of second chances, he knew that the last element time and circumstances allowed him was any kind of finesse. In some ways that was to the good. It kept the action simple and brutal; and it was surprising how often the method paid dividends over more elaborate schemes.

'We know how to make him talk,' he said quietly. 'The real problem is grabbing him, and it looks as though it will have to be in the hotel . . .'

He went on, outlining a preliminary scheme which he knew might have to be modified when he got to the hotel; and Sutcliffe listened, reaching for his cold pipe and beginning to light it, giving little nods of his head now and then.

*

At six o'clock that evening Oleg left the Hôtel Royal Gascogne. He went up the Rue Condé and into the Place des Quinconces. It was a fine, fresh evening, a slight breeze coming across the square from the Garonne and the air pungent with earthy smells, raised by a recent shower. Great snow-white dumplings of clouds bowled across the evening sky. Oleg walked along the bend of the river as far as the beginning of the Quai Bacalan, then turned back. He walked leisurely, content with life, and, for a while, almost forgetting his official self.

Just now and again he gave a thought to Ludmilla Miachin, but the thoughts were of no great duration.

He was back at his hotel within three-quarters of an hour. He collected his room key from the desk and went upstairs, but he did not go up to his room. He turned off down a corridor on the floor beneath his room, walked slowly down it, saw that there was no one else in the corridor and then stopped at the door of a room on the left. He knocked briefly and went in without waiting to be answered.

The room was almost a replica of his own on the floor above. There was a double bed, a large wardrobe that looked like a piece broken off the front of a cathedral, a dressing-table with a leather toilet case on it, a chair, and a bedside table with a water-carafe and, alongside it, a slim folded magazine with the postage band still on it. Oleg walked across the room and picked up the periodical, reading the name and address on the band. He frowned and dropped the packet on to the table.

To his left was an open doorway that led into the private bathroom. A faint wisp of steam crept over the top of the door and he could see part of the bath.

A voice said, 'Is that you?' in French.

'It is.'

It was a man's voice and, almost immediately, the man appeared at the open doorway. He nodded and smiled.

'Cleanliness is next to godliness,' he said. 'Though of course, not in your country. You can't be next to something that doesn't exist, eh?' He gave a deep chuckle.

'I do not understand the joke,' said Oleg.

'Never mind.'

'And I do not wish to waste time.'

'That is understood.'

The man stood there, a shabby dressing-gown thrown loosely over his shoulders, swinging open at the front to show a long pair of woollen drawers that went right down to his ankles. His chest, firm and broad, was matted with dark hairs. He was an elderly man, not tall, but solidly built; and on his lined face there was the suggestion of a smile, which was permanent, as though he had been born opening his eyes to see some splendid joke in life. He drew the gown about him moving, at the same time, to the bed where his clothes were laid out.

'Let us do business,' said Oleg.

'Indeed, let us.' He slipped off his gown and began to pull on a shirt. 'This new man is not the normal kind of charge we have. Compared with the others he is a thoroughbred against cattle. He could be dangerous.'

'It was necessary for security to handle him this way. I do not see why he should be more difficult to deal with or the reason for demanding more money.'

'Demanding? Nobody demands. This is business. We all want the business to continue – we must protect it. For the others the scale is fixed, fifteen thousand new francs.'

'And for this one?'

'Twenty-five thousand. One slip and he could ruin us.'

'It is too much. Twenty thousand, perhaps, since the circumstances are unusual.'

The other shook his head and began to knot a crumpled grey tie round his neck. 'Twenty-five. The price has been considered and there is no argument. . . .' For a moment there was a twinkle in the grey eyes, 'You think there is no other market for him? His own people would buy him back.'

Stiffly, curtly, Oleg said, 'Do not talk like that.'

'Then do not haggle. What is money to your people? Are they to sink millions in backward countries, knowing they'll never see it again, and then haggle over the price of a cup of coffee, the fee for a discreet service? By the way' – he stood up and began to draw on his trousers – 'though the food here is good, I would recommend you to the Chapon Fin in the Rue Montesquieu. Oddly enough, one of their specialities is *tournedos diplomate.*' He gave a surprisingly youthful chuckle and then went on lightly, 'Twenty-five thousand it is, no?'

Momentarily Oleg hesitated, then he said, 'It is agreed.'

'Good. And there must be no delay in moving him. His people are not sitting still. Each day increases the risk.'

Oleg said, 'Arrangements are being made. The details are the same as usual, but I will send you a signal giving the time and the place. Now I must go.'

The other nodded, and then, as an afterthought, said, 'Why is he with us? Has there been trouble somewhere?'

'There has not,' Oleg sounded almost indignant, and to avoid discussion on this point he moved across to the bedside table and took up the periodical. He held it up as though it were a torch. 'It was unwise of you to bring this. You are registered here as Edouard Cadillet. Your real name and address are plainly on the postal wrapper.'

Undisturbed, the other answered, 'It has been in my pocket until I took my bath. Before I leave this room the wrapper would have been burned. Oh, yes, I admit an element of carelessness. I am so used to stuffing that kind of thing in my pocket when it arrives, and I wished to have it here to read over my dinner. Yes, yes, detail, detail – that is the important aspect. Also' – he smiled broadly – 'it is the one which makes this affair tedious at times. However . . . for the money and what it buys we endure the tedium.'

He sat with the periodical in his hand as Oleg left the room. Then he pulled off the wrapper, walked into the bathroom and flushed it down the toilet. He stood, as the cistern filled musically, looking at the publication, which was no periodical, but a catalogue from a Paris bookseller of first and rare editions.

*

Although Oleg was wide awake, it happened so quickly that there was nothing he could do. The shaded bedside lamp was on and he was lying back in bed with his hands behind his head, staring at the ceiling. He was relaxed, full of a physical contentment which washed all thought from his mind. Below his window a car went rapidly down the Rue Condé and, distantly, he heard the city's clocks begin to strike twelve.

It was the combination of the car passing and the striking clocks, which made him miss the faint sound of the quick fitting of a pass key to the outer lock of the room door. The door opened rapidly. He had a glimpse of subdued corridor lighting rapidly blocked by the bulk of moving figures; and then the door was closed and two men had crossed the room, and he was pinioned to the bed. A hand came up and clamped a pad over his face and he felt his head jerked savagely first one way and then the other, as sticky tapes from the pad were wrapped round the back of his head. He had no time to cry out, but he lashed out with his legs and arms, thrusting his powerful body into an arc, fighting to escape. The two men, scarves over their faces, held him. The clothes were ripped back and he felt hands go round his ankles, felt the bite of cord into his bare flesh. He got a hand free as this was done and smashed his fist upwards towards the face of the man who leaned over him, fighting to control his arms. The man jerked his head sideways to avoid the blow and then grabbed his wrist as the other one came to his help. They held him down and bound his wrists, and it was then that he lay on the bed, making no more effort to resist.

The two men stood back.

They looked down at him and he saw the lamplight reflected in their eyes. Inside him there began to work a slow, deep anger that he should have been trapped so easily. There was no doubt in his mind of the reason, though he was surprised that it should have been attempted. Every man in his position was well warned against it, but it seldom happened.

The taller of the two men said in a French that was clearly not his mother tongue, 'He's a big brute.'

The other nodded. 'It'll have to be the service lift. I'll go and get it up and make sure the corridor is clear. Get a sheet or something round him. . . .' He paused, looking directly at

Oleg. 'My apologies, monsieur, for treating you like dirty washing.' He turned and went to the door. He opened it quietly and slipped out.

The other man went to the end of the bed and leaned over the rail, watching Oleg. Outside in the street a motor scooter went by, its exhaust chattering away like a machine-gun firing. Oleg's eyes left the man's face; cold, expressionless eyes. Beyond the man's shoulder the closed bathroom door slowly started to open. It came apart an inch and remained like that.

Suddenly the door was drawn wide open and Ludmilla came through. She was naked, her sunbrowned body rippling with muscle. Her face was frowning like some angry goddess; and Oleg saw the upraising of her right arm draw up her large, generous breasts, and then the flash high up of the water-carafe in her hand.

The man at the end of the bed heard her and half-turned, but as he did so she was upon him and the carafe crashed down upon the side of his head. He staggered, losing his grip on the rail of the bed and Ludmilla leapt sideways, turning, so that Oleg now saw only the swift movement of her back muscles as the carafe flashed up and crashed down again. He heard the man thud against the floor and then the sudden noise of glass breaking as Ludmilla struck again.

His body trembled with impatience. Now, now, every second was precious. He tried to call to her against his gag, and he struggled to a sitting position.

She turned, panting, her dark hair loose over his cheeks, and Oleg raised his bound hands and motioned violently towards the door. She understood at once. She ran to the door and shot the bolt across, and then came back to him. He raised his hands to her and, without a word, she began to undo the cord around them. He saw her hands shaking with the aftermath of her violence, and the run of lamplight along the length of her bare flanks gilded her skin. His hands came free and, while she unbound his ankles, he reached round and carefully pulled the plaster from the back of his head, freeing himself from the pad.

As it came away he heard the handle of the door being tried. He stood up, putting his hand on Ludmilla's arm, and moved her away from the line of the door and the bed. As they moved he raised a warning hand for her to be silent. The door handle moved protestingly again and then movement and noise ceased.

Oleg, ignoring Ludmilla now, went to the end of the bed. The man was unconscious, one side of his face covered in blood, the scarf torn away and lying on the ground beneath his head. Oleg took it and wrapped it round his face so that the blood would not touch the carpet. He took an automatic from his case and for the first time spoke to Ludmilla.

'Go through his clothes. Take everything.'

Ludmilla bent down and began to go through the man's clothes. Oleg watched her as she laid the things out on the chair at the end of the bed. There was loose money, cigarettes, matches, a folding flick knife and a torch.

'That is all,' said Ludmilla, her voice still breathless.

Oleg went to the door; he listened, then slid the bolt back and whipped the door open, his automatic held ready. He looked out. Down the far end of the corridor a man was standing. He was unmasked, but he held a face scarf in his hand. At the sight of Oleg he stepped to one side, his body covered by the corner of the corridor, only his head showing.

Over his shoulder, Oleg said quietly to Ludmilla, 'Come here.'

Oleg handed the automatic to her as she came to the door. He nodded down the corridor. 'Fire, if he makes one move towards us.'

Oleg went back into the room and took the man by the heels, dragging him out into the corridor. He straightened up, took the automatic from Ludmilla and motioned her back into the room.

Oleg looked at the man at the far end of the corridor for a

moment; then he turned his head towards the unconscious man at his feet and suddenly spat down at the body, the sound sharp, almost explosive in the midnight stillness of the corridor.

Oleg came back into the room and bolted the door. He stood behind it listening. After a time there was the sound of soft footsteps outside, then the subdued scuffle of something being lifted. Then silence. Oleg still waited, watching the door for a while. Behind him he could hear Ludmilla's breathing, evened-out now.

He turned slowly and smiled at her. She was standing by the bed, her eyes bright, her naked body, splendid with strength, held sturdily towards him. He moved towards her and as he came, she said, 'There will be no more trouble?'

He shook his head. 'We shall have to pay for a broken water-carafe. That is all.' He put his automatic on the bedside table and then reached out and let his hand rest on the length of her right arm. He felt her shiver at the touch. His hands moved to her breasts and she shut her eyes, her head going back at his touch. His arms went round her and his mouth came down to the smooth, strong line of her throat, as she fell back on the bed, taking him with her.

*

In his room on the floor below, the man known as Edouard Cadillet, whom Oleg had visited, lay contentedly in bed, reading a first edition of a work by the Dutch physician Regnier de Graaf entitled *De mulierum organis in generatione inservientibus*, printed in Delft in 1669. He had brought it with him because he liked to have in a hotel at least one small treasure, which made him feel at home. Now and again his attention wandered to the pleasant dinner he had had at the Chapon Fin. He smiled, as he recalled how he had almost been tempted to have *tornedos diplomate*, but in the end had preferred his favourite dish, *coq au vin de Sauternes*. One's wants should be few, he told himself, but they should be always the best of their kind.

11

By the morning of their third day in the rock chamber both Irina and Manston were beginning to feel as though they were a couple of guests isolated in some *pension*, bound to the house by bad weather, their worst enemy boredom. Except, as Irina found, boredom had no place with Richard. Now she had come to know him much better; and she began to see something of the real man and to admire the professional skill which had made Sutcliffe anxious for his return. She began to build an enormous confidence in him. He was convinced that they would be able to escape; and nothing that might help now or in the future was too small for him to notice; in this she became his willing pupil.

Their light went out regularly at nine o'clock and they slept on their camp-beds. Their meals came to them, heralded always by the turning-off of their light, but Richard never tried his match trick again. The change of food provided a great deal of their interest. Richard pointed out that their evening salads were absolutely crisp, garden fresh, not tired stuff from some market stall. Their wine came in unlabelled litre bottles and was sometimes red, sometimes white. She saw him tasting it, knowing that he was seeing ahead to some future point when he would maybe have the chance to identify it. The wine was local, he guessed, and so was the goats' cheese and milk. The food was sufficient, but not generous, tuna fish, *pâté de campagne*, cheese, and always a salad of some kind, potatoes, endives and green peppers. Nothing hot was ever served except the morning coffee, which was brought in a large earthenware jug.

Together they went through everything in the cell, magazines, cigarette cartons, the bed linen, the crockery . . .

looking for something, anything that might later serve to identify Limbo; laundry marks, makers' names, the pencil scrawl on the corner of a magazine made by a shop sorter . . . but there had been nothing. The electric shaver worked off a hundred and twenty volts, the black silk squares used to blindfold them had been cut from a larger piece of material and were unhemmed, the whisky flask which had been given to him was just a small flat, unlabelled bottle . . . nothing escaped their scrutiny.

Sometimes at night before she slept scraps of his conversation would float in her mind.

'This place is run like a Blackpool boarding-house. Someone has an eye to the pennies.'

'Why are French and Italian tomatoes always this cock-eyed shape?'

'In these night-shirts we look like a couple of penitents.'

Always before she slept he came over and kissed her good night. During the day he was always quick to notice when the sudden realization of where they were and what might lie ahead became a black thought for her. He talked to her, carried her through her mood, and always his great confidence was there to calm and encourage her. Sometimes, when they grew tired of playing cards, or the paper and pencils games he brought out, she would stand with one hand on the iron grille as though it were a *barre* and go through her *battements*. The first time she did this, he had said, 'Pity there isn't a golf club here. I could practise my swing.'

She was doing her *battements* on this morning when the incongruity of the exercise in this place suddenly swept over her. She stopped and turned away from him, looking through the iron bars.

Behind her he said quietly, 'What's the matter? A touch of the miseries?'

She looked round at him, nodded, and then with a passion that surprised herself said, 'I still find it all very hard to believe.

That people – my people – should go to such lengths. How can it be worth it for someone like me? I'm nothing.'

He smiled. 'I value you much higher than that. But it's a good question. Nations are touchy like individuals. They don't like losing face and they have to go on supporting a legend, "the West is decadent". So it's a great boost for the legend if you come back, supposedly off your own bat —'

'Bat?'

'Of your own free will. That makes an impression which is worth a lot. And don't run away with the idea that it's a one-sided affair. We don't like it when our people go over to Russia. We lose face, too.'

'But you would never go to this length to get them back?'

He looked at her, one eye dropping quizzically.

'You would?'

'If we really wanted a man or woman, yes, we'd do it. That's the kind of world we live in. That's why I left the Service, because I didn't like to see people pushed around.'

Irina nodded. 'Neither do I. You know' – she moved across to him – 'at first I could only think about myself. But since I've understood things . . . about all the other people who have gone back and the others who might, it makes me mad.'

He smiled. 'It's a good way to feel sometimes.'

'Well, that's how I feel,' she said vigorously. 'I'd do anything to stop it. That people should be treated like cattle! I'd take any risk to put an end to it.'

He looked straight at her, his face serious. 'You may have to, you know. The moment's going to come and, when it does, you're going to have to be with me. I may not be able to give you any more warning than, perhaps, a quick look and then, when I move, you've got to be moving with me.'

He stood up and put his arm round her, holding her to him. He went on, 'I've been thinking about it. These people are very careful and our only chance to escape will come when they move us. They'll probably do that at night. We've got to have a trick up our sleeve and I think I've found the thing we want. You'll have to use it. Now listen . . .'

He began to explain to her and, as he talked, excitement and hope rose in her.

He finished. 'There's only one thing you've got to remember. Not to jump the gun. That is, not to think we can try anything in here. Whatever they tell you to do, you do. But the moment we're outside, you watch me and be ready. O.K.?'

'O.K.'

When the light finally went out that night, they undressed and went to bed, but in the darkness they lay for a while talking.

Manston knew that this was always the worst period for Irina . . . the waiting in the darkness for sleep to come. This night he sensed that she was not ready for sleep, so he encouraged her to talk. She told him about her aunt who had coached her for her scholarship to the Kirov ballet school.

'Only she never called it that. To her the Kirov was always the Imperial Maryinsky Theatre, and Leningrad was St Petersburg. She taught me the first five positions, my *pliés* and *port de bras*, and started me off with French and the history of music and art. And at the school it was even harder work. She used to walk with me to the theatre every day and, as we went down Rossi Street – that's where the theatre is – she would remember all the great names she'd known and seen walking down the street . . . Pavlova, Karsavina, Nijinsky, Fokine . . . Oh dear – I wonder what's happened to my Nijinsky?'

'He's all right. I saw to that. He'll be waiting for you.' He went on quickly, 'Now tell me about your first part, your first real part . . .'

She went on, talking and answering his questions, and he had a vivid picture of a dedicated girl and of a profession as demanding as his own. Finally, tired by her talk, Irina slept.

Later that night, waking from sleep, he sensed that Irina was awake. He said nothing, but he heard her turn restlessly on her bed. Once there was the deep sigh of someone who fights wakefulness and its thoughts, and he knew that she was having a bad time.

After a moment's hesitation, he rolled off his bed and went across to her. He sat down on the edge of her bed and, as she pulled herself up a little, he put his arms round her shoulders and felt her head press against his side.

She did not say anything. He sat there, holding her, knowing her need for comfort. Gradually he felt the fear going from her until with a slow movement she sat up, and he felt her hands touch him and slide softly up to find his face. His head came forward and, briefly, her lips touched his and then there was no more contact between them.

She said, 'Thank you . . . It's all right now. Just for a moment it was bad . . . but not now.'

He heard her lie back on the bed and he reached down and pulled the blanket up, his hand brushing her bare arm lightly.

'Good night . . .'

He went back to his bed and lay there, knowing she was still awake, but calm. He lay for a long time thinking about her before sleep came to him.

*

Sutcliffe, staring down at the traffic moving up and down the Avenue Foch, said, 'How is Barry?'

'They made a mess of the back of his head and part of his face.' Casalis lifted his glass of sherry and squinted through it at the sunlight outside. 'Bloody balls-up I made of that.'

Sutcliffe shrugged his shoulders and, without turning, said, 'It's happened. Now that door is closed for good. What did Barry say?'

'He was pretty wobbly still. Couldn't remember a great deal. This girl came naked out of the bathroom at him. She'd been there all the time. We know about her now. Clerk in AGRIP. Travelled down alone to Bordeaux. Usual business. They both came back together yesterday by plane, after two men from their Embassy had flown down to travel with them. Damn her.'

'What about the other guests at the hotel? Oleg isn't the kind of man to go all the way to Bordeaux for a piece of skirt from his own office.'

'The French have given us a quick check. They're going over it again. No one there they would have any reason to consider fishy. But they may turn something up if we're lucky.'

Sutcliffe turned at that. He stood against the sunlight, bulky, looming, his plump face twisted with the distaste of his thoughts.

'Lucky; we want more than that. We want a miracle now. We've got nothing. Absolutely nothing. The whole thing's been messed up – and you know why, don't you?'

In the last phrase there came a sudden change of voice, accusation backed with cold anger.

Casalis put his glass of sherry down. He was for it and he knew it. And he knew, too, that he had no defence. In this service a man who relied on luck didn't last long, a man who strayed from efficiency could end up incapable of any movement. He knew it, they all knew it, and they all accepted it.

Sutcliffe had the bowl of his pipe in his right hand, the stem pointed at Casalis, jabbing at him as he spoke. 'You go into a room. You grab a man in bed. You know the room has a private bathroom. And you don't look in it. Why should you, you say, at that time of night? Because men sleep with women. You know that. And women go into bathrooms afterwards. You know that. And where were your bloody eyes? A double bed which has had two tumbling about in it looks different from a bed which has only had one in it. You had five seconds to realize it all as you went into that room – and you failed. You and Barry, you made a complete and utter. . . .' He turned away breathing hard with anger.

Casalis said nothing. There was nothing he could say.

Sutcliffe turned suddenly and Casalis, expecting another

outburst, was surprised to hear him say, 'Give me a glass of sherry.' He came over and sat down heavily and went on speaking, mumbling through his pipe stem, looking at the sunlight reflections on the ceiling from the sherry decanter. 'Capa is out. Taru is a blank for us. And so is Limbo. One big blank. From this moment, Manston is on his own. . . .'

*

Oleg's bell rang and Ludmilla rose without hurry from her window table and went into his room. He was sitting, grey-suited, solid, against the sunlight, and he raised his eyes briefly to her as she came up to him. But there was nothing in his look which betrayed even the shadow of any personal interest. He handed her a message form and said, 'Immediate.'

She took it, gave a faint nod, and then went back to her room. She was not at all disturbed by the correctness of his manner. In the office one worked and a strictly business-like relationship was necessary for efficiency. At night, when she was off duty, things were different. The moment she walked into his bedroom and heard him stir in the darkness, their natures changed.

She pulled the code book towards her, looked up the new code which had been adopted since yesterday and began to encipher the message. It read:

Agrip to Limbo
Shipment both consignments 2200 hours tomorrow. Usual arrangements and signals. Weather report favourable, but in event unfavourable change cancellation will be passed direct line before 2000 hours. Acknowledge.

*

At twenty minutes to nine o'clock in the evening of the next day the light in the chamber went out. Manston was sitting at the small table with Irina playing cards.

He put his hand out on to hers. 'Nearly half an hour early. This could be it.'

She was silent for a moment. Then she said quietly, 'I'm ready.'

'Good. Remember, watch me and wait for it. And, whatever you do, don't make any trouble in here. Leave that to me. Here they come —'

Through the darkness came the sound of the far door being opened. He stood up with Irina close to him. Feet scuffled for a while on the sandy floor and the door closed. At the same moment a thin pencil beam from a torch cut across the darkness, wavered for a second or two and then steadied on them. Vaguely behind the torch, just touched by the backwash of light from the walls, Manston made out the forms of three men.

A voice, flat, expressionless, all character deliberately withheld from it, said, 'We are moving you. You will do exactly as you are told. Mademoiselle first.'

Manston's hand tightened encouragingly on Irina's arm as the torch went out.

'What do you want her to do?' he asked.

From the darkness the voice replied, 'She will come to the barred door and stand with her back to it, close up against the bars, and put her hands behind her. We are not going to harm her, merely to tie her hands and then gag her. Please . . .' just for the fraction of a second the voice took character, was even sympathetic . . . 'Please do not be alarmed, mademoiselle. The gag will not be uncomfortable. It is necessary. When this has been done, you, monsieur, will be dealt with in the same way.'

The torch came on, and moved from them towards the door of the chamber. Irina hesitated for a moment and then went towards the door and stood with her back against the bars, her hands behind her.

Manston heard the men move, and in the backwash of the torch light he saw now that there were three of them, all carnival-masked. One was taller than the others. None of them seemed to have the build of their attendant.

Manston stirred and immediately the torch swung round on him. 'Stay where you are, monsieur.'

The torch went off. Manston heard the men working as they reached through the bars and tied Irina's hands and gagged her. He stood there, listening, a confused impression in his mind of the grotesque masks; and because he knew their hands were on her, that she had to stand there and suffer all this indignity, he felt his anger rise slowly. For the first time he found it hard to control himself, to force himself back into the cold detachment which he knew would serve her and him better than any other mood. These people worked without passion because they made money out of this human traffic. And he had to work in the same way – cold, hard and dedicated – unless he wanted to consign them both to a limbo from which imagination shrank. For a split second he saw himself, thousands of miles away, being interrogated, knowing the pressures to come . . . saw Irina broken, acquiescent, all the dark, flashing spirit gone from her.

The torch came on again, clear on Irina.

'Move to one side, mademoiselle. To your left.'

Irina moved, and Manston saw her hands bound behind her and over her mouth a gag tied.

'Now, monsieur. Your turn.'

The torch beam swung, rested on Manston's face and clung to him, as he moved his head instinctively to escape it.

Manston said, 'If you want me you must come and get me.'

'Monsieur?' There was genuine surprise in the voice.

'If you want me come and get me.'

'You will regret this, monsieur.'

Manston made no reply.

The torch moved with the men and Manston heard a key turn in the grilled door. The door opened and the three men came through. They were less careful now and the torchlight let him pick out details which burned into his mind, of the masks, and of their clothes; rough peasant trousers, a jacket one-buttoned over a woollen pullover, a workman's blouse, and a pair of open-work leather sandals, the bare toes showing. He knew he had no chance against the three of them and he wanted no chance, not here.

They were through the door and he heard it locked behind them.

The men paused and the torch shot up into Manston's face, holding him. He narrowed his eyes against it and waited for them to move. They would come altogether and he would have no chance against them, but he wanted one, just one of them for a few seconds before he was overwhelmed. He decided to take the man on the right facing him. He was a shade nearer and might be ahead of the others, a man who wore a rough working blouse, his head swollen with the paunchy cheeks and imbecile stare of his carnival mask. Manston's hand dropped slowly to his sides and he just touched the material of his trousers, flexing his fingers gently.

The torch went out and they jumped for him. As they did so he moved himself swiftly, forward and to the right, his hands reaching through the darkness. The man bore down on him and Manston got his right hand on the upper part of the man's right arm. As he felt his fingers grip the blouse sleeve a moment of real pleasure sweetened the darkness for him. He let the man's forward rush take him, made no opposition to it, and fell backwards so that the man was taken off balance by the lack of resistance. Manston reached up and tore off the man's mask. Then, as they both fell, he threw the man over his shoulder, somersaulting him so that he smacked into the rock wall behind. His body thudded against the hard rock and he lay groaning.

At once the other two were upon Manston. They smothered him and he had little chance to fight back. They overpowered him and finally, holding him, began to drag him upright.

The torch flashed on and, immediately, one of the men holding Manston shouted, 'Put your mask on!'

Manston tried to turn but he was jerked around and held away from the man. They tied his hands and gagged him and not until this was done did they go to the man who lay on the ground.

Manston, turning, saw him sit up and then be helped to his feet. He was silent now, fighting his pain, and his mask had been put back a little to one side. One of the others straightened it.

The man, pulling himself up stiffly, said viciously, 'The swine . . . he might have broken my back.' He put his hands behind him, pressing them into his back and gave a small groan.

The others said nothing, but they came back to Manston. The torch changed hands and the figure of the taller man moved closer to him.

The cold, flat voice said, 'This is forbidden. But you have demanded it.'

A fist crashed out, took Manston on the side of the face and sent him reeling back against the rock wall. Manston lay there and a voice from somewhere in the blackness behind the torch said, 'Get the blindfolds on them.'

A small, sack-like affair was pulled over Manston's head and tied around his neck.

12

WHEN THEY GOT outside Manston realized that it was raining. Shut away in their chamber, the weather was something they had forgotten. He could hear the soft beat of the rain against his enveloping head cover and could feel it on his hands.

They followed the same route as the one which had brought

them to the chamber, across heather and wet grass, the stone steps, and then the echo of feet across the boards of the small bridge. He knew when they were under cover, for he suddenly missed the beat of rain against his hood, and the ground under his feet was hard and dry. They halted, then he heard a door slam and the movement of men about him.

Without warning, he was taken by either arm and pushed forward and then someone kicked his feet from under him and he was briefly lifted off the ground. He was thrown forward and he felt himself slide across smooth boards. A door slammed behind him and he guessed that he had been slung into the back of a van of some kind. He rolled over and sat up awkwardly. A voice he had not heard before said, 'Just stay where you are.'

A car engine started and he felt the boards behind him jolt.

For a while the vehicle bumped and swayed over rough ground and then he heard the gear change and they were rolling smoothly.

At some period they went through a town or large village, for he heard the hoot of car horns and felt them stop and start and then the long, gear-whining drag up a hill. They must have stayed on a main road for some time because he could sense the car speeding and hear the scream of the wheels against the wet tarmac.

Later, the speed slackened and they were twisting and turning, probably along some side road. Then came a jolting and bumping and eventually the car stopped.

The doors at the back opened and the voice close to Manston said briefly, 'Out.'

Hands reached in for him and he was pulled across the floor and set on his feet, feeling at once that the rain beating against his hood was now backed with a strong wind. Distantly he could hear the roar of the sea.

He heard the movement of the men about him and from the sound knew that they were helping someone else from the car. It could only be Irina. He moved and a hand held him by the arm, the fingers biting into his flesh, forcing him forwards. He walked, wind and rain now beating at him, and the sound of breaking surf growing louder. Somewhere, high above him, he heard the long-drawn cry of a gull.

Concrete rang under his feet and then the hand on his arm held him back. A voice said, 'Steps.'

They began to go down the steps, which were awkward and wide-treaded. Manston counted them to himself. At one point they were broken by a flat level, about five paces long. The wind and the rain were gone and there was a damp, musty smell.

The steps ended. He was halted. The hand left his arm. A door squealed and then clanged. The hand came back to him and he was urged forward. The wind and the rain came back and now the sound of breaking surf was much closer. The ground was uneven, and he could feel the movement of loose stones, and then there was sand for a short stretch. The voice as its hand helped him said, 'Steps – up.'

They went up and now there was concrete again and, clear through the noise of wind, rain and surf, he heard the sweet, sharp call of a wading bird. He was halted on the concrete. Behind him, a pair of hands went under his arm-pits and, at the same moment, someone took his ankles from below; and he was lowered, steadied, and felt his feet on boards and then his body sway, only to be caught and steadied again. He was guided forward and sideways until he was pressed down and found himself sitting, aware now of the sturdy slap-slap of water running against the side of the boat which he knew he must be in.

He sat there and heard the process repeated for Irina. Then, for the first time, he had contact with her, because she was brought and sat alongside him. Nowhere along the line had any chance been given to him for action. Now they were sitting in this boat and the rest was not difficult to guess. They would be taken out to sea, and somewhere lying off this coast would be a ship . . . imagination flighted vividly, some cargo boat, carrying timber, machinery, grain, or maybe one of the long-range trawlers . . . and ahead of them the slow crawl through the Mediterranean, the Aegean and through the Bosphorus into the Black Sea.

A marine motor broke throatily into life. Manston heard the screw churn, then the boat was moving. A fierce scurry of rain beat back against Manston's hood and the motion of the boat increased. It lifted to a long length of swell and then dipped and he heard the smack of a wave against the bows up to his right. But after a while the long rise and fall of the boat evened out, and he knew that they were now out from the shallower coast water with its riding surf.

Nobody aboard the boat spoke. The motor beat away evenly. The hood over Manston's head, now soaked with rain, hung closely to his face and occasionally he had to shake his head to free it so that he could breathe more easily. Somebody must have noticed what he was doing for he felt Irina suddenly moved away from him.

A voice said, 'All right, mademoiselle. It is to make you more comfortable.'

He heard a man moving, breathing close to him, and then the voice said curtly, 'You.'

A hand began to undo the knot of his hood. It was lifted partly at the back and then the knot of the mouth gag was undone and the gag was whipped away. The hands re-tied the fastening of the hood at the back of his neck.

With his mouth free for the first time, Manston said, 'Are you all right, Irina?'

After a moment, she replied, 'I'm all right . . .'

The voice said, 'Don't talk.'

Manston said sharply, 'Go to hell.'

Later, and it was difficult to guess what time had passed, the motor eased up, beating now to a slow, idling note and

Manston felt that almost all the way had gone off the boat. They rested now, he guessed, with the motor just strong enough to keep the bows up to the sea and he heard the movement of feet across the boards. They stayed like that for some time. Then, distantly, growing louder, Manston heard a new noise. It was the steady thump, thump of screws, large screws, beating. It came closer and he heard the long hissing run of sea being cut by heavy bows and then, clear and unexpectedly, the triple ring of a telegraph bell. High above them a voice shouted, incomprehensible, and the thump, thump of the heavy screws was suddenly muted. There was activity all around him, but no more the sound of men's voices, only the sound of their movements and their breathing. He felt their boat rise and fall, the motion gentle now, and guessed that they were in the lee of the bigger boat.

The voice, familiar now, though offering no characteristics that would hold the imagination or stir memory, said, close to Manston, 'We are taking the blindfold off you. Mademoiselle will go first.'

There was an interval when he was aware of abrupt movements, the ring and thud of footsteps on the deck-boards, and the occasional grate and rub of their boat against the other.

Close to him the voice said, 'Stand up.'

Manston stood. Hands went round his waist, threading something under his arms. He felt the jerk of a knot being made fast. Then hands were at the back of his neck. His head cover came off.

He was standing in the forward deck well of a sea-going motor-boat. Close to his left rose the sheer, rusty side of a large steamer, down whose flank a companion ladder was lowered, its bottom platform a few feet from the bows of the motor-boat. From somewhere above, a light weakly illuminated the scene. Around his waist was a rope, and the free end trailed away from him and up the length of the steps. Looking up, he saw a man at the top of the steps holding the rope's end, which he had looped for security in a hitch around the ship's rail. At Manston's side stood another man wearing a singlet, arms and shoulders bare, and a pair of greasy trousers. He was a square, powerful-looking man, his face dark with stubble. Manston turned, looking aft. All he could see was a small, pillar-box sort of protection around the wheel and the shadowy figure of a man inside at the helm.

The man at his side motioned to the bows and put out an arm, helping Manston forward. At the same time the rope from his waist had the slack taken up. Irina, he guessed, had already made the journey to the deck, the man at the top steadying her, and his man coming along behind. The length of rope served a double purpose. In the past, he guessed, desperation had, at this moment, made someone jump for the sea, risking anything rather than be taken aboard. He looked back at the wheel-house, at the run of the boat's deck, swiftly cataloguing the details. There must be more men than the helmsman aboard, but he could see no one else.

His man gave his arm an impatient jerk and Manston went forward. When he reached the bows he heard the motor open up a little and the bows crept up to the bottom platform. The man at his side reached out with his free hand and caught the lower rail of the steps. He gave Manston a push and he was forced to jump to save his balance. His feet found the platform and slipped, but the rope from above tautened and held him steady as the man with him swung, cat-like, to the platform and held him against the sway of the steamer's motion. He climbed the steps awkwardly because of his hands behind him and when he was half-way up he heard the motor-boat's engine open up. He looked back, pausing, and saw it pulling away. He wanted to catch the name but there was a large piece of canvas stretched backwards from the bows. Manston went on. The stern, he knew, would have been treated in the same way.

By the time he reached the deck the motor-boat was lost in the sweeping veils of rain. The two men led him across the deck, aft of the bridge house. He heard the telegraph bell go, and then he was steered through a door, down a short flight of steps into a corridor. They halted him here and the long length of rope was taken from his waist. One of the men unlocked a door, gave him a push through it, and the door was locked behind him.

He was in a large, four-bunk cabin. The light was on and Irina was sitting on one of the lower bunks, her hands still tied behind her. Oddly, as he went forward to her, the first thing he noticed was that she was not wet through like himself. Then he saw on the ground at her side an old groundsheet. On the boat one of the men must have draped it over her.

He went forward and bent down and kissed her.

'Richard . . .'

She stood up.

'Turn round,' he said, 'your back to me, and give me your hands.'

She turned obediently and he felt for her wrist bonds with his fingers. The cords would be wet and difficult from the rain. Frowning with concentration he worked at them, talking to her as he did so.

'This could be our only chance. God knows when they'll be back. Do you think that stuff has stayed dry in your dress pocket?'

'I think so. Someone gave me a cape.'

'Mine's wet through. No damned good.'

She said, 'When you fought them in the rock chamber, one of the men's masks came off. I saw his face clearly. I think I'd recognize it again.'

'Good. I was working for something like that.'

He felt the first knot of her cords come free and then the next.

He turned. 'Now mine. Quickly.'

She bent down behind him and he heard her breath coming impatiently, anxiously, as she worked at his wet cords. As she did so he gave her instructions, forcing them home, knowing that so much depended on her, finishing, 'You know what to do. And remember this – they won't expect anything. That gives us a great advantage.'

She freed his hands. He whipped round, held her by the shoulders for a second, gave her an affectionate shake and then turned from her. Time, time, time – for all he knew they might have half-an-hour, but it could be only ten minutes. . . .

He worked now with a cold, swift competency. There was a wash-basin at one end of the cabin supported on an open framework of timber, two legs in front across which was a supporting piece of wood in which the basin rested. He gave one of the legs a couple of savage kicks and it came away at the bottom. He took hold of it and wrenched it free. The wash-basin held, still supported by the other leg and its fastening against the bulkhead. He had in his hand a two-foot length of stout timber.

He went to one of the lower bunks and pulled out the locker under it. There were three life-jackets in it. He took two and threw one to Irina.

'Stick it behind you on the bunk. Sit in front of it. And keep your hands behind you as though you were still tied.'

As she sat down he went over to her and sat beside her, putting his own life-jacket behind him. He put his hands behind him and thrust the length of timber under the jacket, his hands gripped round it.

For a moment he sat there, resting, letting his breathing even down. Then quietly, he said, 'From the deck I could just see shore lights now and again through the rain. When we've dealt with them we go straight up on deck, to the nearest rail, and over. Don't stop to put your jacket on. Do it in the water.'

She nodded and he saw the fear in her eyes. This was a hell of a thing for her to have to go through. . . .

He went on, 'Remember, when that door opens, you just sit here, looking as though you've reached the end of your tether. No matter who comes in we're going to go through with it. Just let them come across and, when I move, you move. Got it?'

Her head came up and her face turned towards him and he saw the ghost of a smile.

'You think it will succeed?'

'Yes – it's got to.'

Unexpectedly, she said, 'It's not a Russian boat. I heard the men speaking as they brought me down. It could have been Rumanian.'

'I'll get the name, with any luck, when we go over.'

They sat there, feeling the heavy throb of the engines, and sensing the slow rise and fall of the steamer. Manston stared at the door, his hands tight on the timber length behind him. He was looking forward to the moment the door opened. For the first time for days he was a free agent . . . no longer a parcel to be hauled around.

Without looking at Irina, his eyes on the door, he said, 'Remember, too; you don't stop for anything. Don't bother about me. You go straight ahead. Hell-for-leather. You know what that means?'

'Yes.'

'And if you make it and I don't—'

'Richard, please.'

'If you make it. Then ring the telephone number I've given you.'

They sat there, and the cabin light pulsed unevenly, shadowing the cheap, varnished woodwork of the cabin.

After what seemed an age, Manston heard sounds outside the door and his fingers tensed round his timber length. The same two men came into the cabin and the leading one, dark-stubbled, held in his hands long lengths of thin chain which chinked softly. Manston, watching him come forward, knew then that he had picked the right moment, the only moment to be offered to them. Here now came the full and final precaution against escape. . . . The man came forward and stopped a few feet from them. Over his shoulder Manston saw the other just inside the door. It was upon him that he concentrated. As the first man stopped, Manston – life-jacket in his left hand – jumped to his feet, and he felt Irina move alongside him. He saw the look of surprise on the men's faces and, as he swung sideways, he saw Irina's hands come from behind her to be lifted, cupped, towards the leading man's face as though in supplication. Then, with a sudden outward jerk of her wrists, she flung into his eyes the heap of pepper so jealously conserved in their rock chamber.

Manston went past the man, hearing him cry out, and his timber length smashed down at the far man. He hit without feeling, a machine striking, smashing the wood against his skull once, and then again, as the man reeled and fell. He spun round and saw the blinded man reaching forward, crying out in a language unknown to him, grabbing at Irina.

Manston hit him on the back of the head with the wood length, hit again and saw him crash forward, slamming into the support of the bunks, and slide to the ground.

He turned and saw Irina, life-jacket in hand, make for the door. As he followed, the man on the floor rolled over and half-raised himself, staring up at Manston.

The timber length crashed down again, killing any shout, and then Manston was in the corridor and running after Irina. She went up the steps a few yards ahead of him and disappeared. When he reached the deck he saw her running through the rain towards the rail. Somewhere above him a man shouted. He ran on, saw Irina poised for a moment awkwardly on the rails, saw her look back; and he shouted furiously, 'Jump!'

Her face flashed away from him and she pitched forward. He flung the timber length from him and, one hand free, reached for the rail top and vaulted over.

13

At five o'clock in the morning there was a knock on the door of Ludmilla Miachin's bedroom. She had been awake for the last half-hour. Sitting up in bed she reached for her dressing-gown, pulling it loosely over her shoulders. There was another knock and Vadim's head appeared around the door. He blinked at her, sleep still heavy in his eyes, and said, 'He wants you. Right away.' He looked for a moment at the open neck of her nightdress and then his head withdrew.

Ludmilla got out of bed, tightened the belt of her gown, and felt with her feet for her slippers. Going to the door she put up her hands, drew her hair back and tied it with a piece of ribbon.

Oleg, fully dressed, looked as though he had never been in bed that night, though she had good reason to know that he had. He was standing by the window in her office, staring out at the Quai des Célestins which stirred now and then with the rare passage of early morning traffic. He turned and gave her a nod.

'This must go at once.'

He dropped a message form on to her desk. Ludmilla sat down and pulled the message towards her. For a moment Oleg stood by her and she half expected his hand to come out and touch the back of her neck, a movement of affection which he sometimes allowed himself now, even in the cold routine of their official contacts. But, with a sudden, angry grunt, he turned away towards the door of his room. At the door he said over his shoulder, 'When you've done it, get dressed and come back. It will be a busy morning.'

Ludmilla nodded without turning. Day and night were

different worlds and she could pass between them as easily and unemotionally as Oleg. She pulled her code book towards her and began to work on the message.

It read:

Agrip to Limbo

Message received S.S. Lupka. *At 2215 hours both consignments lost overboard. Area searched for two hours unsuccessfully. Rain made visibility bad. Position S.S.* Lupka *at time 5 kilometres ENE Cap du Figuier. Tide running East, four hours to go to turn. Wind NNW. Safe landing on coast strong probability. S.S.* Lupka *estimates Hendaye-Corniche Basque-St Jean de Luz section, or, less probably, St Jean de Luz-Bidart section. Cover both areas. If contact made, take no action but report immediately and maintain contact. S.S.* Lupka *has proceeded on journey. Stand by on the hour every hour until further notice.*

As Ludmilla finished encoding this, Oleg came in and dropped two more messages on her desk and went out without a word. The two extra messages to be encoded read:

Agrip to Taru

Dismantle. Report here immediately.

Agrip to S.S. Lupka

Fullest report required. All details. Proceed direct home port.

When Ludmilla had encoded these, she handed them in to the dispatch office and went back to her bedroom to dress. While she was doing this, Vadim came in with her breakfast; coffee and two *croissants*.

He said, 'This place is beginning to buzz like a beehive where someone has stolen the honey.'

Ludmilla smiled. She was not concerned with anything that was going on. She just did her job. Even when she had been officially commended for the part she had played at Bordeaux, she had accepted it without elation. One had a job, one did it without getting involved. At any time one might be moved somewhere else to another job. The important thing was to find satisfaction in the hours when one was not working. She was beginning to feel that she was finding more than satisfaction, but she cautiously refused to let her imagination play with the full potential which the future might hold.

*

Fifteen kilometres south of St Jean-de-Luz a man on a motor-scooter, not his own, was making his way up a small D-class road towards the Franco-Spanish border. The road, narrow and twisting as it first followed the course of a small river, rose through oak and chestnut forests towards the frontier post at the Col de Marieta, five hundred and seven metres high and cradled between the north tip of the Pic d'Ormantelli and the south crest of the Pic Dassoa. It was eight o'clock in the morning, the sky, except for a wisp of thin cloud over the Pic d'Ormantelli, was a pale, washed-out blue that would fade more as the morning sun strengthened. To his left, in the long, sweeping valley bowl, the oak and chestnut foliage, not yet turned fully September colours, sparkled from the night's rain. Ahead of him he could hear the occasional outbreak of shotgun fire, filling the valley with staccato echoes. Now and again, at a turn in the road, he could see a flock of pigeons, fat from feeding on beech-mast and chestnuts, flighting towards the ridge of the pass. On a morning shoot like this, he told himself, they might get as many as five hundred birds.

The man himself was the one who had fought with Manston in the rock chamber the night before and, as he rode, he now and then flexed his back and shoulders, conscious of the bruising and cuts from the hard rock face when he had been thrown against it.

The road near the top of the pass shook itself free of the trees and the river; it snaked in sharp loops up the scrub-covered flank of the Pic d'Ormantelli and finally emerged on the flatness of the *col*. To the right of the road, across a stretch of goat and sheep-bitten grass, stood a small tourist restaurant and café. The grass was covered with parked cars. The road itself was blocked by a customs pole against which leaned a couple of Spanish guards.

The man, Pierre Salgazza, parked his scooter on the grass and turned left-handed away from the customs' hut, southwards towards the Pic Dassoa. He gave a wave of his hand to the guards, whom he knew, and took a small path through the bracken along the top lip of the valley bowl. Closing up to the top of the valley now, he could see the beaters working their way through the beech and chestnuts, and the skeins of pigeon coming up the slope towards the ridge crest. With the noise of the shotgun firing came the flash of the sun on the steel barrels from behind the bracken-fenced hides that lined the top of the valley. Here and there along the slope, wooden platforms on tall stilts had been built out and on each of these stood two men, bundles of flat, plate-sized slates at hand which they hurled out at the approaching pigeons that tried to break sideways from the drive, forcing them back to the narrow, tree-lined funnel of the valley top three hundred yards away. As the birds swept up the funnel the guns cracked, and Pierre watched with satisfaction the sudden feather-burst and fall of birds and the swift bracken-shouldering movement of the retrieving dogs. At the head of the funnel, strung between two enormous trees, was a great net fifty feet high, and twice as long, into which any of the birds that escaped the guns hurtled at speed and were picked off by guns behind the net. The smell of cordite in the air made Pierre breathe deeply. There was nothing he loved more than *la Chasse*, and above all the September *chasses des palombes*, the big, autumn-heavy birds. But this morning he knew that his luck was out. He had been waiting with a late party in the valley down below when he had been called to deliver a message up here, a message about which he knew nothing except that it was urgent, and about which he allowed himself no curiosity. He had learned in the last few years to be uncurious, to do as he was told, and to take his money. He tapped the right-hand pocket of his old jacket now to make sure he still had the envelope and continued to make his way along the rough track, accompanied by the sound of the guns, the whirr of the passing birds, calling now and then to people he knew in the various hides.

The best positioned hides were those close in on either side of the narrow funnel-top of the valley. As Pierre came along the path, the only man, except for the beaters below, to show any movement, he was at once noticed and recognized by five or six people.

The first of these was Amadeo Grandier. He was a man in his late thirties with a pleasant, sun-burnt face, square, and small-chinned and with a humorous look to the mouth. He had fair hair, closely cropped in American fashion and, surprisingly for the shoot, wore a flower-pattern Miami shirt and green linen trousers. With him in his hide was Comtesse Bernice Longeau-du-Quercy, the daughter-in-law of the owner of the shoot, of the Château Quercy in the valley far down towards Sare and also the land-owner of thousands of hectares in the upper Nivelle river valley, the river which eventually ran out to the sea at St Jean-de-Luz. Bernice was a tall, blonde woman, about thirty, with thin, almost haggard good looks, wearing a hundred-and-fifty-guinea Galitzine suit. She was a long-legged, poised woman, whose face, always a little withdrawn, almost sad in repose, sparked to life when Amadeo spoke to her. Alone in the hide they made no pretence to conceal the affection between them. Once, as Amadeo paused to reload, he leaned over and kissed her lightly on the cheek.

Thirty yards farther on nearer the edge of the funnel were Louis Saint-Amand and his daughter Claudine. Saint-Amand, a man closing on his sixties, was no sportsman. He was a scholar and a historian, but no recluse. He was a very sociable person, regretting only the long impoverishment of his family because it had stopped him from buying all the books he loved and giving his daughter the things she would have liked to have. He was not shooting, contenting himself with being a loader for his daughter. Between them there was a close physical resemblance. They both had round, short faces, unattractive in Claudine, but in both of them informed with a humorous, almost mischievous look. They both laughed a lot. Their affection for one another was clear, and Saint-Amand's pride in his daughter a well-known fact amongst his friends. That she was a first-class shot, a scratch golfer and a fine swimmer mitigated for Saint-Amand the fact that she was neither attractive physically, nor very intelligent. Nobody could have everything, happiness lay in making the most of what one had, was his philosophy.

On the other side of the valley funnel, in a hide below a great beech tree, were a married couple in their forties, Franz and Lottie Aspender, who had appeared from nowhere four years before, bought an old house near Sare and, discouraging inquiries about their past, had slowly been accepted in the district because they had plenty of money and entertained well. They said they were American, but with both of them their speech in English was accented more than in French, and they spoke German perfectly. Lottie Aspender, not shooting, loaded for her husband. In between shots, he reached for a brandy-filled flask which went wherever he went, though no one had ever seen him drunk. He was a big, fleshy man, powerfully built, dark-haired, blue-jowled and with the permanent look of someone who had been up all night. His wife was red-haired, thin-armed and legged, looking as though if she fell she would crumble into pieces, bloodlessly, with just a faint puff of dust like the collapse of some wood-worm-ridden piece of furniture. Franz Aspender shot and took brandy and from the corner of his eye watched Pierre come along the distant path.

Behind the Aspender hide, a little higher up the funnel, was the hide which held Bernice Longeau-du-Quercy's mother-in-law. It was unlike the other hides. A tall stone tower had been built up from the hillside, solid all the way up except for the compartment, roofed over, which surmounted it. A series of wooden steps led up the side of the tower to this compartment. It was the best position of all the hides and, quite rightly, belonged to the *comtesse douairière*, Estelle Longeau-du-Quercy. In the tower with her were three other people, two loaders, one of whom was her chauffeur, and her son – the husband of Bernice – the Comte Aristide Longeau-du-Quercy.

Both the dowager countess and her son shot with a silent, dedicated passion, as though the flights of pigeons were the massed, advancing hordes of some army and that they alone stood between them and the sack of some treasured city.

The dowager countess was a fine, though remarkable-looking woman. She was well over sixty, tall, her carriage erect as though she held an immense contempt for her age. Her face was paper-white, for she disapproved of the sun on her skin, and she had a fine, long face, with a beaked nose and dark, commanding eyes. She wore an old-fashioned grey coat and skirt. On her piled white hair was perched a tweed hat with one long pheasant's feather arching from it. A grey silk blouse was tight about her throat, closed with a brooch of garnets set in gold, and her feet were comfortable in black, elastic-sided boots. She might have stepped straight out of an Edwardian fashion plate, and the look in her eyes said that she didn't care a damn what anyone thought about it.

Catching sight of Pierre distantly on the path, and reaching back for a fresh gun, she said sharply, 'What the devil is that Salgazza oaf doing? Doesn't he know that nobody moves except the beaters when the shoot's on? Damn him!'

Her son Aristide fired both barrels quickly at three birds that turned suddenly as they came sweeping up the funnel, sliding sideways with the wind for escape, saw the featherbursts and the birds fall. Then, handing his gun back, said, 'What would you like me to do, Mama; order him to be stripped and beaten?'

He smiled as his mother, after a quick look at him said, 'I can think of some who would benefit by the treatment. Why do you allow Bernice to be in that Grandier's hide? Don't you care for appearances?'

Her son shrugged his shoulders. 'Why should I care for appearances, since it is the only thing left to care for. She has given me a son; that was the contract.'

He took a fresh gun, oblivious that the loaders had heard their conversation, and raising it, watched the pigeons coming up, holding his fire, waiting for the pleasure of the difficult shot. He was tall, lean and elegant-looking, wearing a thin suede jacket, very narrow whip-cord trousers and a brown silk shirt with a white hunting stock showing at the neck. He was in his forties. The dowager countess, watching him for a moment, studying the lazy, long-drawn face, the beaky family nose, and the dark, unrevealing eyes that flicked once at a person and then stared right through them, wondered how much he cared really. A man had to care, a man in his position, a man of their family could not escape care. . . .

And, away to the left of the valley, Pierre Salgazza came along the path towards these people, letter in his pocket, one thought only in his head, to deliver it and then perhaps have the luck to borrow a gun and get some shooting.

*

At half-past ten that morning Ludmilla Miachin had a message from the dispatch and receiving office for decoding. It was from Limbo:

Limbo to Agrip
Action taken as advised. No results yet. Insist escape no responsibility this handler. Confirm payment as arranged.

When Ludmilla had decoded the message she did something which she had never done before going into Oleg's room. She slipped open her handbag which lay on the desk and looked at herself in the mirror which was glued to the back of the flap. She studied her face for some moments and then gave a little nod of approval.

When she took the message into Oleg and he read it, she saw his face tighten with a brief spasm of anger. He wrote an answer and gave it to her. She went back and encoded it:

Agrip to Limbo
Responsibility S.S. Lupka. *Payment will be made. Insist fullest check coast sections also examination your own security. Vital this not prejudiced.*

At twelve o'clock, when she had just finished decoding a long report from S.S. *Lupka* about the escape, another message was handed to her from Limbo:

Limbo to Agrip
Nothing to report yet coast sections. No police bulletin drownings or rescues. Own security not in question. Request positive instructions if contact made.

Oleg answered this:

Agrip to Limbo
When and if contact made take no action. Maintain contact utmost precaution. Report immediately. S.S. Lupka *reports escape facilitated by pepper in eyes guards on board. Pepper from your chamber. Imperative review security future consignments.*

At one o'clock Limbo reported that there had still been no contact. No comment was made on the pepper. At two o'clock there was still no contact, and Limbo requested permission to stand by only at three-hourly intervals.

At five o'clock Limbo reported that there was still no trace of Manston and Tovskaya. When Ludmilla took this report through to Oleg, it was to find with him a man she had seen before only once and who, she knew, came from Taru.

From five until eight she was busy, catching up on her arrears of normal work. Just after eight another Limbo message came in. There was still nothing to report. When she took this into Oleg the other man had long been gone. Oleg read the message, shrugged his shoulders, and, as she turned to go from the room, said, 'Stay.'

He got up and went across to a cupboard and pulled out a bottle of vodka and two glasses. Solemnly he poured them both drinks. Without a word he handed a glass to her and then raised his own in salute.

They drank and then, surprisingly, in a conversational mood which until now he had always reserved for a different kind of room, he said, 'What do you think of Limbo?'

Ludmilla was silent for a moment, then she said, 'I only have their messages to go on. They are usually efficient. The pepper was their fault, but equally they never gave this man a chance to use it while he was with them.'

'He is an exceptional person.'

Ludmilla nodded agreement, and went on, 'They do this purely for money. They think of nothing but money. With us it is different.'

'That is true. But we have to use them. Abroad we have to use others. Organizations like Capa and Taru are easy to set up and easy to replace, but always the final link is difficult. Once established it must be protected. It took a year to establish Limbo and it has served us for more than three years. There is no reason why it should not serve us for another three years, or even six. In fact, it must. This is not an opinion of mine. It is an instruction I have been given. Limbo must go on.' He reached for her glass and refilled it and also his own. Handing the glass back to her, he smiled bleakly. 'Any failure of Limbo's becomes my failure. It is a prospect that calls for a few glasses of vodka to brighten it.'

Ludmilla drank and then went over to him. She stood close to him and, no surprise in her now, she felt his arm go round her waist and his hand come up and hold her breast through the cotton of her blouse. 'Those two,' she said evenly, 'will possibly be drowned?'

'Possibly.'

'But, if not, what is there they can know of Limbo?'

'Nothing.' He was silent for a while and then he added, 'You are surprised that I talk to you like this?'

Ludmilla shook her head. It was good to stand there feeling his hard, strong body close against her, feeling the rough, cupping grasp of his hand against her breast. 'No. I ask nothing, demand nothing. But I am here and you are talking to me like this. That is a good thing. Also it honours a woman. You will not fail.'

'If I should, I would be moved to some other capital and my time for returning to Moscow would be extended another three years. I wish to return to Moscow.'

'Also I.'

He turned her round as she finished speaking, his hands on her shoulders now, and looked unsmiling at her for a few moments. Then he turned away and she knew that the moment of need, which all men have and no bed settles, had been smothered. She went back to her room, smiling, filled with the delicious sensation that comes from the exultation of being a woman and knowing her power.

At eleven o'clock that night, and three o'clock the next morning the reports from Limbo were negative, and Limbo closed down until nine o'oclock the next morning. At quarter past three when Ludmilla delivered her last report from Limbo to Oleg, she did so in his bedroom. He made no comment on the report and in silence, like a long-married couple, they undressed and got into bed.

*

At ten o'clock the next morning Sutcliffe was over Biarritz

in a chartered D.H. Dove. It was a lovely morning, the undersides of the high clouds were rose-tinted with flamingo colour. The white sprawl of buildings and long yellow sands of Biarritz tilted below him as the Dove banked, turning for the landing at La Négresse.

A few minutes later, Sutcliffe, briefcase in hand, dark-suited, went through the *douane* alone. In the park at the front of the airport buildings Casalis waited for him at the side of a car.

They drove away, by-passing Biarritz, and were soon out on the main N.10 and heading for St Jean-de-Luz. It was now past the beginning of September and the main road was crowded with returning holiday traffic, going against them.

Casalis said, 'You want it from me, or from him?'

'From him. Where have you fixed them?'

'In a small villa, the other side of St Jean. Ciboure. Manston insisted on being tucked away.'

'Quite right.'

'I got this place through the British Consul. He knows the owner. She's abroad, lets it most of the summer. Happily it was free. It's secluded. Not overlooked. Ideal, in fact.'

'How is he?'

Casalis smiled. 'Just the same. Why'd he ever leave us?'

'It's an old question. You meet it in every profession. The chaps that could go right to the top don't want it. I seem to remember that Sherlock Holmes had a brother who could wipe the floor with him. The girl?'

'She was pretty done in when I picked them up. Since then she's slept. She'll be all right. My God, he left it to the last minute. By the way, I've got a Sûreté man down there. Not local, but he knows the district and some of the people. We're going to need liaison.'

'How's Barry?'

'Up and about.' Casalis pulled out around a long-distance

coach, and then said, 'Look at them. Every one going home, and a boat on top of every other car.'

Some time later they went down the hill into St Jean, over the bridge at the top end of the harbour, a blue-hulled and red-sailed medley of sardine and tunny boats ranked together alongside the fishing quay; and then turned right-handed after the bridge to run down the far side of the harbour on the Corniche road to Hendaye. The road rose and curled and suddenly the whole spread of the bay was before them, breakwatered at its mouth. To their left the ground rose steeply, studded with villas and their gardens. Casalis pulled up about two hundred yards along the Corniche road.

'The road up to the villa goes around the back. Quite a drag. I thought you might like to go up unobtrusively. A few yards along you'll see a green gate marked *Ixas-Atou*. That's the villa. Path leads up through the gardens to the house.'

Sutcliffe nodded and got out. The car drove off and he sat for a while on the pavement parapet, watching some children playing on the rocks below. Then he walked slowly along the road until he found the gate. He went through and began to climb a series of steps overhung with palms and unkempt oleander bushes. On the sunny patches of the steps there was the quick flirt of lizards. Looking up, he could see the villa above him, the green shutters drawn back. Along its front ran a terrace made of stone and covered with bright red and yellow Virginia creeper and bougainvillea. Below the terrace was a little lawn, rough and untidy, that ran back to the pillars supporting the terrace. As he came up level with the lawn he saw Manston sitting half in and half out of one of the alcoves at a table. There was writing material on the table and a collection of bottles and glasses.

Manston, seeing him, stood up, a tallish figure in a white shirt and blue linen trousers. As Sutcliffe approached he said, 'After that climb up you need either a gin and tonic or a beer.'

'Beer.'

Sutcliffe, hot in his dark suit, dropped to a canvas chair; then, as Manston moved round the table to fix the drinks, Sutcliffe said quietly, 'I'm glad to see you, Richard. Very glad.' For a moment his right hand came out and just touched Manston on the arm.

*

There was a little balcony outside her bedroom window. She came out on to it and, after the cool of her room, the sun broke over her bare arms, flooding her with a quick embrace. For a moment all she was aware of was the sea, running away almost from below her feet in a wide, silver-flecked sweep. It ran away, and away, to lose itself in a smoky haze far to the north.

Away to her left, a crowd of small sailing boats with coloured sails circled and tacked aimlessly under the lee of the Socoa breakwater. A French cruiser was anchored just inside the mouth of the bay and a flock of small motor-boats fussed around it, carrying sightseers. Two hundred feet below her, cars and coaches whined along the Hendaye road. Her eyes, moving from the sea, to the road, to the terrace below, caught the movement of Manston's white shirt. He was standing on the grass just below the terrace, talking to someone she could not see. Just for a moment he looked up, saw her and his hand went up in greeting. Then his attention was back to his visitor.

There was something about that moment, the quick flash of his gesturing arm, and the sudden return to whatever it was that really held his attention, that crystallized the thing which had been forming within her for a long time. It was almost as though it were something as hard, bright and absolute as a diamond, that she could take out, hold to the light and find a continuing joy in watching, in acknowledging as hers. No matter what had been or what would be, the thing existed and she was glad to have it exist. She was in love with him . . . and the very phrase was inadequate, because this thing was not at all a match for anything she had ever imagined. It was a fact within her as simple and yet as cabalistic as *water is wet*. She loved him. There was no need to go beyond that because the moment it was acknowledged it needed no explanation.

There was nothing incongruous, either, in knowing that something as definite, as right and true as a dance pattern perfectly timed, music and body co-ordination all one thing, should have emerged from the brown, rain-swept murk of a nightmare.

Together in the water they had seen the ship turn and come about in a great circle searching for them, and three times they had felt that they must be seen; but the sweeping rain squalls had saved them. The real agony began after that, after the first hour. All her instinct had been to strike out and swim towards the distant lights they could see but he had forbidden her to do this, once even shouted angrily at her. All they had to do, he insisted, was to relax and let the sea take them. How could he have known that the sea would take them to safety. . . ? She remembered thinking that in the water, thinking it furiously, arguing once against him and he had replied, 'Never fight the sea. . . .'

Afterwards she knew that they had been in the water four hours. She could not even now remember much of landing. The dawn was coming up and she was being helped ashore by him, conscious that the rain had stopped, that everything was a murky, miserable haze of brown, with wet, rolling gravel underfoot and cliffs slanting away above them, sharp, razor-edged with their crazy, tilted strata.

He had found a rock cleft for her to shelter in, and then explained that he must leave her for a while. They needed clothes and food; and, above all, he wanted no one to know that they were safe. Limbo was in this district somewhere and he wanted to keep them in the dark. He had gone away, up the cliffside. She rested in the rock cleft in her wet clothes until she was aware of the sun. Then, strength returning, she had stripped off and wrung her clothes dry, sobbing a little like a child at the wet and cold. Then, as though the strengthening sun had made it flower within her, she was abruptly aware that she was safe, that she was being weak, stupid and ungrateful.

When he had come back he had brought a dress and canvas shoes for her, both too large but wearable, and he himself wore dry trousers and a shirt. He had, too, a half-bottle of brandy, bread and some cold meat and, to her question, had answered simply, 'I stole them.'

They had gone up the cliff, over the coast road and along a track, heading south into the broken hill country until he had found what he wanted; a small farm with a telephone and a housewife who openly showed her suspicion of them yet did all he asked. Listening to him dealing with the woman, she had been aware then, even more than in the past, how charming he could be. So that, in the end the woman had changed her attitude and they had stayed there secure, resting, until Casalis had arrived at four in the afternoon.

There was a knock on the room door and Casalis came through and out to her.

'Lunch in about half an hour. Good sleep?'

'Thank you.'

Casalis looked at her and smiled. 'Clothes fit?'

'Yes. Did you —'

'Yes. Pretty good, eh?'

'What will they do with me?'

'Do?'

'Now. I mean, this isn't all over, is it?'

'Not by a long chalk. But I should think you'd go back to London. Don't you want that?'

For a moment she did not answer. Manston was coming up the terrace steps now with a short, pudgy man in a dark suit, a pipe stuck out of the corner of his mouth.

'I don't know,' she said. 'Will Richard be staying?'

Casalis grinned. 'If there's one thing certain, it's that.'

*

The lounge of the Villa Ixas-Atou was a long, high, narrow room with three windows that looked out over the terrace and to the sea. It was full of heavy Edwardian mahogany furniture, Chinese screens, brass Benares ornaments, and shabby, but comfortable, chairs. Sutcliffe sat with his back to the far window, a small table in front of him. The others sat in various chairs around the room, except Irina, who had perched herself sideways on the music stool by an upright piano that stood in a recess behind the entrance door.

Sutcliffe felt that the girl vaguely disliked him. He couldn't blame her after what she had been through. He had an idea, too, that she was gone on Manston. That didn't surprise him. Just for a moment, on hearing her and Manston's story, he had wondered if Manston had slept with her during their captivity. He had done no more than wonder; not even venturing an answer himself. Whether they had or not had no bearing on this case and was worth no more than a cursory curiosity.

Apart from himself and Irina, there were in the room Manston, Casalis, and the Sûreté man Casalis had co-opted, Jean Guyon. Guyon was in his thirties, a short, dark-haired man, sleek, dapper and with the still, concentrated air of a blackbird, ear cocked for the subterranean murmur of worm movement and, Sutcliffe guessed, as fast in striking. The only thing he could take exception to was his habit of smoking thin, almost black cheroots which smelled abominably.

Sutcliffe said, 'Let's get this thing straight and then let's get moving on it.' He pulled towards him the pages of notes he had made while talking to Manston before lunch and to Irina over lunch. 'I'll read what I've got and you can come in on each point as you want to. By the way, Miss Tovskaya, purely as a formality, anything said here is secret.'

'I understand.'

Sutcliffe smiled to himself at the slight edge in her voice. For a moment he wondered whether he should not show open sympathy for her; then knew he must not. This was a job of work, and there was plenty to come which could be done better if he remained an official.

'She understands,' said Manston. 'Who more than she, for God's sake?'

Sutcliffe ignored this and began to read his notes, expanding them now and then as he went along. In essence they were:

1. Capa and Taru were either expendable or movable. Capa had already been written off and would, no doubt, be replaced. Taru would probably be moved. They had a reasonable description of the house and the French police would probably locate it – to find it empty. Guyon could have a description of all the people who had been seen there, and some of them might be picked up, but it would be doubtful whether they would have been allowed to know anything germane about Limbo.

2. The journey from Taru to Limbo. Manston had put forward the supposition that this must have been done in some kind of tanker specially fitted out. It could have been a wine, milk, coal-tar or petrol tanker.

3. There were various factors that could help in the attempt to locate Limbo. It was about thirty-five minutes drive from a level-crossing. The actual unloading had been done in some kind of barn and there had followed a short walk through pine trees, over a stream bridge, down stone steps and across heather and bracken to what was probably a cave or some structure built into a hillside. The walls of the chamber were natural rock.

Here Guyon, who had a map, said, 'In the whole of this area from Bayonne and Biarritz down to the Spanish frontier there are only two railway lines and they form the two sides of a triangle from the Bayonne apex down – one along the coast to St Jean, and the other inland down to Cambo. It won't be difficult to check the level crossings and work from there.'

4. The personnel of Limbo. Miss Tovskaya has seen the face of one man. From her description we can work up an identikit for the police. All the evidence seems to point to some kind of establishment in the country. Manston has a sample of typing paper and type from the chamber instructions, and can recognize crockery, wine and cheese believed to be local.

Here Manston said, 'Don't forget the dog with the curly tail.' He grinned. 'We could circulate a description, "Dog Wanted".'

Sutcliffe frowned at this and went on:

> Apart from the dog, five men at the most had contact with Manston and Miss Tovskaya while they were at Limbo; the two men who drove them down, their warder and, possibly, two different men on the boat which took them out.

5. The journey from Limbo to the coast. This took three-quarters of an hour and a small van was probably used. Embarkation was preceded by the descent of some form of covered steps. Miss Tovskaya counted the steps and made them forty-nine. Manston made them forty-eight. The boat – which was a working craft rather than a pleasure craft – was lying alongside some kind of concrete structure. This would hardly be a public quay of any kind. From later detail established by Manston the point of departure would seem to be somewhere along the coast between Biarritz and Hendaye, but probably north of St Jean.

Here Casalis said, 'The whole stretch of coast Guyon tells me is riddled with the remains of German fortifications. Part of the Atlantic Wall. Most of the gun emplacements have covered steps either down to the ammunition stores or to the beaches. I can start checking these with police help.'

Manston said, 'Keep the police help unobtrusive. We want to hold our advantage as long as possible.'

'Sure.'

Sutcliffe, picking up his cold pipe and lighting it, said, between puffs, 'We'll come to that.'

He then went on.

6. The S.S. *Lupka.* Manston twice saw the name of this steamer while it searched for them. While he was in the cabin he established by his watch compass that it was on a westerly by south course. Guyon has already confirmed that this was a Rumanian boat that left Bordeaux that same day. No action can be taken with S.S. *Lupka* – the master will have no details of Limbo anyway. He will have had orders simply for a rendezvous. As certainly he will have reported the escape of Manston and Miss Tovskaya to AGRIP.

7. Manston and Miss Tovskaya —

Here, Manston broke in with a look at Irina, 'Don't mind him and this Miss Tovskaya business. He's known me for years and I only get called Richard about once every six months.'

Sutcliffe looked from Manston to Irina and for a moment said nothing, but he was telling himself that it went both ways. Manston had a thing for her. Maybe not so important as the thing she had for him, but he had it. It wasn't something that helped in this kind of affair.

Sutcliffe grunted and went on.

7. Manston and Irina came ashore just before dawn at a point three kilometres to the west of Socoa. Realizing the

necessity for keeping their survival a secret – since Limbo might already have a search party out for them – they struck inland away from the coast and found shelter in a farmhouse near Urrugne until Casalis picked them up.

8. The Limbo position. They are in it for money, clearly. As clearly, it is probably manned by local people. An organization like this takes time to establish and for their own reasons neither AGRIP nor Limbo will want to close it down. At the moment they do not know what has happened to Manston and Irina. It is doubtful that they know a man's face was seen by Irina. They must feel pretty safe about their own security.

Sutcliffe stopped reading and looked round the room. Through the open windows came the sound of cars along the Corniche road.

Then, in a pleasant tone, friendly, he said, 'We've got two advantages. One, a bundle of facts which we can get to work on. Two, for the time being we've got surprise. Limbo are in the dark. But I don't imagine that they will be for long. When that happens they may well be provoked into action; and that often opens up a short cut to the end. Agree?' He looked directly at Manston, and he knew that Manston understood perfectly what he meant, and Manston's reply showed it.

He said, 'Of course, I'm staying here.'

'I know . . .' Sutcliffe tapped the loose ash from his pipe into a tray. 'I've got to go back to London tonight. The plane's waiting for me at Biarritz. Miss Tovskaya – can you be ready to leave in an hour?'

Irina stood up, one hand smoothing along the run of the piano, and she looked down at the dark, polished wood as though it held some mirror-like fascination for her. Then her eyes came round to Sutcliffe.

In a firm voice, she said, 'You mean that while you are all

doing this work here there could be danger from Limbo? For Richard?'

Sutcliffe, noting the use of Manston's name, knew that common-sense was now going to be involved with emotion, a mixture that always made him impatient and suspicious, and he attacked it at once.

'I do. One never knows the extent of desperation on the other side. Never knows when their own fears may not push them into stupid violence. Frankly, they might try anything. Manston knows this – and he accepts it as a professional risk. But I can't allow you to share this. You've done more than anyone could ask already, willing or not. You must come back with me.'

'No. I'm not coming.' Her voice was clear, definite, and her head went up. 'How can you ask me to do that? If I stay here I can help. And I want to help. You took the responsibility of letting me be kidnapped. You risked me quite callously. That's past and I say no more about it. But I hate this traffic, hate the thought of others suffering and now' – she paused, her dark eyes unflinching on him, – 'I have a right to decide for myself what risks I should take.'

Sutcliffe showed no signs of the quick anger he felt. He said, 'You must return, I'm afraid. Please be reasonable.'

Irina shook her head. 'I'm staying here. And I'm being reasonable. Look, I've seen one of the men. No description or made-up drawing of him from that description could be very accurate. But if I'm here, moving around, I may see him. Also' – she put her points, not pleading, but with a bold, logical emphasis – 'I have my own memories of the place, of the steps down to the sea. I know almost as much as Richard. I can help in identifying places.'

'If you move around,' said Sutcliffe heavily, 'you could finish up with a bullet in your back.'

'You risked my going back once. That would have been

worse than any bullet. Now, I decide my own risks.' Her eyes flashed and her face was set firm, defiant. 'I have that right.'

For a while Sutcliffe said nothing. Although he was angry at her stand, he was also aware of the logic, human, emotional logic behind it. She could possibly give some help; but he had to carry the risk she took, explain it to a higher authority already flexing the rod for his back. But more than all this, he distrusted the intimacy which he could sense, no matter how far it had or had not gone, which rested between her and Manston. Manston was hard and competent, but with that kind of thing hanging around him he could, from a moment's anxiety for her, from the slightest hesitation that the thought of her safety could evoke at the wrong second, find his timing late, his hand slow . . . No man should have to carry that. Sutcliffe looked at Manston, counting on him for support, and said, 'What do you think, Richard?'

Manston uncrossed his legs, sat forward and stared at his bare toes sticking out at the end of his sandals.

'The lady wants to stay. She knows the risks. In my book – because of the way she's been used and what she's been through – she's got a perfect right to insist. Mind you, I'd advise her to go. But I don't think – short of getting out the red tape and the rubber stamp – that you can make her.'

Sutcliffe stood up, his anger open now, and stumped across the room to stand in front of Manston.

'I expected more sense from you, Richard. We've got a chance of pulling this thing off and they'll all cheer if we do – but not if Miss Tovskaya —'

'Irina . . .' Manston grinned.

'But not if Irina is killed or something. No —' Sutcliffe swung round and looked at Irina, 'I'm sorry. But, if necessary, I get out the red tape and the rubber stamp and the French can demand that you leave the country.'

Before Irina could say anything, Manston was on his feet.

'Don't wave the big stick. She can help, and she wants to

help. She's not a child. She knows the risks. Your back's strong enough to carry anything the people at home can load on to you. Now stop bullying.'

Sutcliffe said, surprise in his voice, 'You really want her here?'

Manston nodded. 'If she wants to stay. You forget that she was with me on the S.S. *Lupka.* She doesn't flunk in an emergency. I can't think of a woman on your staff who could have done as well as she did, and most of them are pretty tough characters. Let her stay; we'll always have someone with her, every moment. So stop fussing.'

Momentarily Sutcliffe wanted to go on, to force his will on them, but abruptly he decided not to do this. If Manston was ready to accept her, then he would agree.

He said, 'All right. But get this place sewn up for security. And I don't want her ever to be alone when she goes out and about.' He turned then and smiled at Irina; and, no real change in him because there was little in him that was not professional and dedicated, he said charmingly and with apparent sincerity, 'Forgive me; there is nothing at all personal in this. This is a sordid professional business and I did not feel I could allow you to take the kind of risks that Manston has to take. Personally, I think your attitude is admirable.'

He went out of the room, and when he had gone, Casalis said, 'Quite a speech for the old man.'

*

Going up to his room that night, after working most of the evening with Guyon and Casalis on the arrangements for their search, Manston saw a light under the door of Irina's room. He knocked and her voice called to him.

He went in. There was a small bedside light burning, but she stood by the open window, looking out over the balcony rail to the sea. She was dressed for bed, wearing a silk dressing-gown which had been part of the wardrobe that Casalis had supplied. She half-turned and smiled as he went over to her.

He stood by her and put his arm around her. She rested comfortably against him and he wondered where it was, along the line of their relationship, that the moment had come when they were not just two people maintaining still the small defences that ward off intimacies. Between them now, established, never spoken, though still waiting for some ultimate recognition, was this warm promise of a welcome surrender to come.

She said, 'I did right to stay, didn't I?'

He shook his head. 'No. I think you were unwise. You'd be much safer in London.'

'To hell with being safe. I want to be here with you.'

He smiled. 'It's an argument that would have sent Sutcliffe through the ceiling.'

'But I can help, too. I meant all I said.'

'I know. Don't think Sutcliffe doesn't understand that. He knows that you can pass a limit where you don't care so much about yourself – where you only want to get something ended, no matter what it costs. But get this; as long as you stay, you do exactly as you're told.'

'I will.'

The Socoa light winked far away to the left, and there was a blaze of lights on the deck of the anchored French cruiser and smaller lights from moored yachts. The air came in warm and full of scents, and over the bushes in the garden below there was an occasional flash from a firefly. Headlights seared the darkness along the road below.

She said, 'Before you came in, I was standing here, trying to make myself believe I was here. That all the rest was behind me . . . In a way, I had to make myself believe that, too. That it had happened. Do you know the hardest thing?'

'No.' Against his arm and his body he could feel the warmth of her moving into him and he was aware of a slow contentment, undemanding, which was new to him.

'It was about you. I couldn't believe that it had all really happened so quickly. Only a few days, really. Somehow I seem to have been with you . . . Oh, I don't know' – she laughed quietly – 'for ages. Perhaps that's not a good way of putting it. But do you know what I mean?'

'I think I do.'

She turned against him, facing him now. Her lips came up towards him and he kissed her, his arms gathering her close to him.

When he released her she said, 'You know what has happened to me, don't you?'

'Yes, I do.' He smiled. 'After all I've been trained to watch points.'

He put his arms around her and kissed her again. And now the pulse of their contact which had been even, slow and rich on the balcony, rose, and when she broke from his arms, breathlessly, her hands held out as he retained them, she leaned back from him, her eyes dark and light-flecked from the bed-lamp, and said, 'How could I have gone back to London . . . I want to be with you. . . .'

14

GUYON, WORKING ON the fact that the rock chamber was some thirty-five minutes driving time from a level-crossing, had been busy with the map the previous evening. By a complicated system of intersecting arcs from all the likely level-crossings in the great triangle, Bayonne–St. Jean-de-Luz–Cambo, he had established a series of possible localities. The St Jean-de-Luz police had been furnished with all the available information and they had taken over the search in the northern part of the triangle, ready to refer to Guyon and Manston if they found anything that looked like the barn.

Guyon and Manston that morning took over the search in the southern section, and Irina accompanied them. Both men were armed; and they used a *deux-chevaux* with the top rolled back and made themselves look as much like tourists as possible. Although Manston knew that eventually they must lose their anonymity, he was not anxious to hasten this moment. Both he and Irina wore dark glasses. Casalis, in the meantime, went off with help from the Biarritz and St Jean-de-Luz police to check on the coast steps.

Manston drove down into the town, over the harbour bridge, past the railway station and out to the level-crossing on the Ascain road. Guyon sat with the marked map on his lap beside him and Irina was in the back. It was a bright, clear day with the long line of mountains sharply etched against the sky to their left, the slopes running up from the river Nivelle to the crest of La Rhune. The river was tidal for some way up and the tide was out leaving bare, brown mud banks flecked here and there with the white movement of feeding egrets. They passed the golf course at Chantaco and, when they reached Ascain, began to work the side roads, following a plan which Guyon had devised.

Irina, sitting alone in the back, found it hard, after her recent experiences, to imagine that what they were doing was real and urgent. Tension had collapsed inside her and she was content for a while to sit back and enjoy the beauty of the morning. She was enchanted by the mountains, by the narrow roads that wound up into them alongside rushing streams, and by midday her mind was just a jumble of names of villages . . . Ascain (here, Guyon said, Pierre Loti had either lived or written a book), St Pée-sur-Nivelle, Souraide, Aïnhoa . . . no side turning was overlooked. Time and time again they got out and walked up farm cart-tracks, even found barns and out-buildings, but none that fitted the description they had both built into their memory. Somewhere close there had to be pine woods, a bridge over a stream, and the stone steps. Every time they left the car she noticed that the two men kept her between them. She could not believe that in this bright sunlight there could be danger for her, but from their actions she knew that they did not share her opinion. Both of them were used to the unexpected, both of them knew that in the moment of apparent safety there could be danger.

At half-past twelve, working their way back to St Jean-de-Luz, they drove into a small hill town called Sare. The street leading into the main square was narrow and crowded with people, and in the square itself there was an even bigger crowd. They decided to stop here and have a drink and find a place for lunch. They parked the car up a side turning which was crowded with other parked cars and went back to the square. As they walked towards it down a sloping street, lined with shops and tourist stalls, they did what they had done that morning in all the other places they had visited; they kept their eyes open for crockery stalls and shops that sold wine and cheese.

At her side Manston groaned humorously and said, 'I don't think I can face tasting any more cheese. We must have a couple of pounds of the stuff in the car already. I don't mind the wine side of it.'

Guyon said, 'Let's have a proper drink and some lunch first.'

Lower down the street they found a café-restaurant and took a seat at a table outside. They then saw the reason for the crowd. Facing the café, with a narrow road running up its right-hand side, was the open square. This road and the square immediately in front of the café were packed with people ing a pelota game.

Irina was always to remember their lunch for it seemed as though some fate had deliberately set out to humour and help them. They ordered a bottle of wine, a fresh sardine salad, and decided to eat outside where they were. The girl who took their order came back and began to lay the table. As she put the plates around Irina was conscious of shock. She looked down at the plate and then her eyes came up to Manston. He gave her a look and then said to the girl:

'This is interesting crockery. I like the design. Is it local?'

'Yes, monsieur. It's very nice, isn't it?' said the girl. 'It's made locally. Tourists buy a lot of it.'

'And I suppose the people here use it?'

'Yes, monsieur' – the girl smiled – 'but they don't pay the same price as the tourists.'

When the girl had gone, Manston said to Guyon, 'This is the stuff. I remember the design. Right, Irina?'

Irina nodded.

Guyon said, 'We'd better try the wine and cheese.'

They ordered a bottle of white as well as red wine and after their salad asked the girl to bring the cheese board, saying they wanted to try some local cheeses.

Curiously, after the first moment of shock at seeing the crockery, a moment which brought back vividly her memories of the rock chamber and awoke her to reality again, Irina found herself almost impervious to what followed. It was as though they had slipped into some planned sequence of events deliberately ordered for them. The wine, both red and white, they could not be entirely sure about; it could have been the same as they had had before. But about the cheese there was no mistake. It was the third one they tried from the board, strong and creamy under a hard crust, and the girl told them that it was a local goat's cheese made at three or four farms in the neighbourhood. Apparently it was a very popular cheese, being sent to the other villages around, and into St Jean-de-Luz.

The square was noisy with the shouts of the crowd watching the pelota game. Guyon, smoking a cheroot over his coffee, said, 'It's a fair assumption from the crockery and cheese that the place might not be far from here. The Limbo people would buy locally. But it would take us ages to get lists of customers for cheese and crockery – even if there were records. We can only say that the place isn't far from here.'

Manston, looking up from the map he was studying, said, 'This place is about twenty-five minutes from St Jean. That gives us another ten minutes anywhere to the east, north or south of it.'

'We've already covered that this morning.'

'Then we'll cover it again more carefully.'

'Not until I've finished my coffee,' said Guyon.

At this moment there was a stir and a shout from the crowd and a pelota ball, wildly slung, hit the top of the canvas awning outside the café and rolled to the ground. Someone at a nearby table retrieved it and flung it back, laughing, over the heads of the crowd.

Their bill paid, the three of them got up and moved for a moment into the crowd to watch the game. Irina noticed how in the crowd the two men flanked her. They looked a casual enough trio, but she knew that not for one moment was either of the men being casual.

At the far end of the square was a tall wall, built like the front of a church, but without doors or windows; and, in the open square running back from it, the pelota game was being played by two teams of men in white shirts and trousers, each man with the sickle-shaped basket-work *cistera* strapped to his right wrist. Guyon tried to explain the game to Irina, but it made little sense to her. A lot of men were hurling a small ball prodigious distances one to another, catching it expertly in the sweeping *cistera* and hurling it back. The far wall, Guyon explained, was called a *fronton* and the ball was served by one side against this and returned by the defending team. The score was kept by a scorer, called a *cantara*, who stood in a corner to the left of the *fronton*. Quite clearly his score-calling, embroidered with his own comments, was keeping the crowd laughing and shouting ribald responses. The ball went whizzing backwards and forwards and, now and again when a player failed to catch and return it, it would come shooting into the crowd; quite dangerously, Irina thought, though none of the spectators seemed to mind. It came bounding back and hit a dwarf-sized man a few yards in front of Irina on the chest, with a thud that, instead of making him shout with pain, caused him to roar with laughter and the crowd around him to pat him on the head and thump his shoulders. One of the players came running back to receive the ball from the dwarf. He stood a few yards in front of the crowd, his *cistera* hanging at his side, his chest heaving with his exertions, and called to the dwarf for the ball. The dwarf kissed the ball, rubbed it on his nose and shouted something that made the crowd rock, and then threw it to the man who caught it in his *cistera*.

Irina saw all the movement, heard all the noises as though in a dream. All she was really aware of was the man waiting for the ball. Could it be? She shut her eyes, memory taking her back to the rock chamber. She saw the thin beam of a torch and a man lying on the ground. The blurred lines of the man's face rose in her imagination. Surely it was . . . she opened her eyes. The man was laughing, tossing the ball now in his free hand and calling something to the dwarf. No . . . it wasn't, or was it? She tried hard to force memory to exactness. The man turned away to rejoin the game.

She gripped Manston's arm and said, 'Richard – the man who's just taken the ball. It may be him. The one I saw.'

Manston handed the bus conductor a five-franc note and said, 'All the way.' Where all the way was he did not know or care. All he knew was that if he had paid for all the way he could get off when the man standing a few people ahead of him did. The single-decker country bus was crowded with people going home from the pelota match, or their marketing. It was crowded to an extent that would have given the London Transport Executive heart-failure; and, brought out by the hot afternoon, was an astonishing selection of smells . . . garlic, sweat, Gauloise tobacco, dog, poultry and the Lord knew what else.

From the moment that Irina had said it might be the man, Manston had been very conscious of Sutcliffe. He realized that he was deeply concerned about Irina. Ultimately, she was Sutcliffe's responsibility. And he was responsible to Sutcliffe. It was his job to be so. That was why, after Irina had got another look at the man, and still thought she might be right, he, Manston, had thought first of all of her security. He had no idea what the other side might be doing. They might already know that he and Irina were about. The pelota player might be a deliberate decoy – if they had any idea Irina had seen him before – stuck up in public just on the chance that he would be seen, and with the hope of perhaps reducing Irina's bodyguard.

Guyon was competent and armed, but one man was not enough. The whole thing, too, was complicated by the fact that Irina was not sure. It was this finally that made Manston decide to play it cautiously on his own. He had made Guyon show his credentials at the Sare police station and arrange for a man to accompany Irina and him back to St Jean.

When they were safely off he had gone back to the square. At the end of the game the man had taken his jacket from the road wall and hurried out to the main street to catch a local bus, giving Manston time to get on behind him. The man was talking now to people seated near him and the bus was noisy with laughter and talk. The bus had threaded out of Sare and then turned south up a long valley road, following a small river. Now and again it stopped and people got off with their baskets and bundles.

The road began to rise through oak and chestnut woods and the man turned and started to work his way backwards. He passed Manston, squeezed by him, and there was no hint that he had given him any special notice. Manston watched him. He went to the exit and dropped down on to the lowest step without looking back. Manston began to move after him. The bus changed into a lower gear for a steep rise and the man suddenly dropped off as it slowed. He ran a few steps with his own momentum and then turned aside down a small path. Fifty yards farther on, as the bus ground up the steep slope, Manston dropped off. He walked back to the path and began to follow the man who was about a hundred yards ahead of him, climbing a rough track that led up through bracken and sporadic clumps of trees. The man had taken his jacket off against the afternoon heat and was carrying it over his shoulder. Manston made no effort to conceal himself. The man had gone about a quarter of a mile, climbing all the time, before he was aware that he was being followed. Manston saw him stop and look back. He watched Manston coming on and then he turned and went on himself, not quickening his step. Some time later the man disappeared through a belt of pine trees that fell away from a tall, grey outspur of craggy rock.

Manston went on through the trees to find on the other side a level, sheep-cropped stretch of grass and beyond it a small stone and slate-roofed cottage. Some hens picked about in front of the cottage and to one side of it were conical-shaped stacks of bracken built up around centre poles, fodder or bedding for the winter.

To Manston's surprise the man had halted a few yards out on the grass and was waiting for him, turned towards him, frowning slightly, his hands thrust into the top of his leather trouser-belt. He stood there, the sun beating down on his weather-hardened face, and watched Manston come up to him. Manston halted a yard away from him.

The man said, 'Are you following me, monsieur?' There was a touch of belligerency in his voice and his French was thick with the local accent.

'Yes, I am.'

'Why?'

'Because I think we've met before and I'd like to ask you some questions.'

'We've never met before, monsieur.'

The man stood there scowling and Manston began to wonder if Irina had been wrong. All she had seen was a face briefly . . . it was so easy to be wrong.

Manston reached up and took off his dark glasses.

'You don't recognize me?'

The man gave an impatient shake of his head.

'No, monsieur.'

'I think you do. A few nights ago we fought together. You and I. Don't you remember the fight? There was a girl there, too.'

'I don't know what you're talking about, monsieur.'

For a moment Manston hesitated. He could be on the wrong track altogether. Was this the man whom he had thrown over his shoulder, smacking him into the rock wall . . . ? The memory of that moment came back vividly to Manston and, with it, a sudden flash of inspiration. What a fool he'd been not to remember the crash of the man's back against the rock wall.

Manston slipped his hand into his pocket and brought out his automatic.

For the first time the man showed genuine surprise.

'What is that for, monsieur?'

'Turn round,' said Manston.

'Why should I?'

'Turn round.' Manston jerked the automatic forward.

'You're mad.' The man turned and when he faced the cottage, he shouted suddenly, 'André! André!'

Manston stepped forwards and jerked the shirt upwards, free of the man's trousers, ripping it partly. One glance was enough. The man's back was bruised and thinly lacerated in places.

At that moment the man began to run towards the cottage, shouting as he went, and Manston saw another man appear at the cottage doorway. The running man swerved sideways and Manston saw the swift glint of sun on a gun barrel. There was an explosion; and the grass and dirt a yard to his right suddenly spurted with the impact of shotgun pellets. He felt some of them bite into his right arm and leg.

He turned and ran for the pine trees, and another burst of shot hissed through the bracken to his left. The next moment he was in the shelter of the trees, then heading down the hill as fast as he could go. Nobody followed him. There was nothing he could do. An automatic was no good against a blast of shot the moment he tried to approach the cottage. All he needed now was a telephone as quickly as possible.

*

At eight o'clock that evening Ludmilla Miachin decoded the following message from Limbo:

Limbo to Agrip
Manston alive, active this area. No information where located or whether Tovskaya with him. Own security not in question, but situation serious since apparent Manston must have certain data pin-pointing this area. Request action to be taken.

Five minutes after she had taken it into Oleg, he had come through her room and told her briefly to stay on duty until his return. He was back within the hour and a few moments after his return he had handed her a message for encoding.

It was a warm September night and she had the lower part of the window open so that the noises from the Quai des Célestins drifted into the room. Ludmilla worked happily and with a deep content. The truth was well established. She had fallen in love with Oleg and, she was sure, he had with her. Love had been something she had never expected in her life, since she had so long been content with lovemaking, imagining that that was all she had capacity for. The softness of feeling in her which now merged with her passion made her feel as though she were a new and different woman.

The message to Limbo read:

Agrip to Limbo
Essential fullest check your security. Take no action. Repeat no action. Agrip representative with you tomorrow evening latest.

*

Guyon came back at ten o'clock. Manston had picked up a lift on the valley road very quickly and had returned to Sare from where he had telephoned through to Guyon at St Jean from the police station. Guyon had been out within the half-hour and had taken over with help from the Sare police. Manston had gone back to the villa, where Irina had been left with the house-guards who had been loaned by the St Jean police.

Guyon's report on his return was that the two men were well-known locally. They were Pierre and André Salgazza, brothers who lived alone in the cottage which they rented from a local farmer. They were French nationals but from a family on the other side of the border in the Spanish town of Echalar. Both were known smugglers, and they also worked intermittently for various farmers. Neither of them liked a regular job, though Pierre had for a long time been a gardener for a married couple called Aspender who lived near Sare. Neither of the men was in the cottage – no surprise to Manston – and no trace of them had been found, though a police call and check of all roads and frontier posts had been set up as unobtrusively as possible. As their cottage was only a couple of miles from the border and they both knew the mountains inside out, it could be assumed that they had gone over the frontier clandestinely.

There were moments, as Guyon gave his report, when Manston felt he ought to have taken a chance and tried to pin the two men down in their cottage, in the hope that eventually Guyon would have come out to look for him. But commonsense told him that the Salgazza brothers, knowing then who he was, would not have let themselves been pinned down. They would have come out with shotguns and he would have had no chance against them. They could have dropped his body in some gully or ravine where it might not have been found for weeks.

Guyon said, 'I've got some information on the Aspender couple and I'll check the area around their house tomorrow. They live in a largish villa off the road up to the Sare grottoes.'

'Grottoes?'

'Prehistoric caves. The Aspenders have been here about four years. They're on American passports, and they seem bona fide. Though there's a rumour locally that Franz Aspender is really a German. The usual Nazi-in-hiding story. The police here have back-checked on him and there's no proof.'

'We should have picked that bastard up in the square, you know. That needles me. We boobed.'

'I don't see why. If Irina was wrong, you would have had an innocent man on your hands, and a fine old fuss.'

'Not if I'd thought of his back. That was the mistake. I thought of it too late, blast it.'

Guyon smiled and lit a cigarette. 'You've got too high a standard. No one can think of everything.'

'Yes, but now Limbo must know we're after them. We've lost that advantage.'

At that moment Casalis came in. He poured himself a whisky and flopped into a cane chair.

He said, 'I've spent all the day between Hendaye and Biarritz going up and down steps – and what steps! You've no idea how the French – pardon Guyon – use the old German coastworks. A thoroughly unsanitary day.'

Guyon smiled. 'How else would you expect a Frenchman to use German steps?'

'What's the form?' asked Manston.

Casalis reported that with his police help they were pretty certain they had located the steps, about three miles away on the Biarritz side of St Jean-de-Luz, on private land. There was a holiday bungalow at the head of the steps which were protected by doors top and bottom. The top door had been locked, but fortunately the bottom door had been open, and since there was no one in the bungalow, they had been able to check them from the seaward side. On the rocks to one side of the private beach there had been a small concrete landing platform.

Through the St Jean police Casalis had learned who the owner was; a bachelor, one Amadeo Grandier, who lived near Sare and who used the bungalow for holiday purposes. So far as the police knew, he never let the bungalow to anyone. Amadeo Grandier had been in trouble once for smuggling, but because of a legal quibble the charge had failed. But down here smuggling was not regarded as a crime of much importance. Anyone living near the border had something to do with it some time or other, simply because it was regarded as an economical way of shopping for spirits and other necessities.

Amadeo Grandier was thirty-five and he had come to the area from Paris about three years ago. Before that, he was in the army in Algeria, but there had been some trouble there and he had been dismissed the service. So far as the police knew, he was of independent means, popular socially. He was known to be having an affair with the wife of the Comte Aristide Longeau-du-Quercy who also lived just outside Sare. The police were inclined to regard Amadeo as the type of man who, with luck, would remain straight, but would not hesitate to go over the line if he needed money.

Listening, Manston thought that described a lot of people. The thing which interested him was the way the name Sare came popping up all the time.

He said, 'Does this Amadeo own his house at Sare?'

Casalis shook his head. 'No – he rents it from a friend of his who lives near Sare.'

'What kind of a friend?' Manston asked the question, knowing that Casalis would have dug out all the information he could.

'An old family friend. Apparently the Grandiers used to live here when Amadeo was a boy. His parents are dead now. The friend's name is Louis Saint-Amand. I got some dope on him, too.'

Louis Saint-Amand was a man nearing his sixties with an only child, a daughter, Claudine, who was twenty-one. The Saint-Amand family had lived in the Sare district for generations. Louis Saint-Amand had independent means but was by no means wealthy. He was a scholar and occasionally published articles in obscure historical journals. In his young days he had been known as a skilled pot-holer and spelæographer, and had written a small brochure on the caves, pot-holes and underground rivers of the western Pyrénées.

'Caves . . .' Manston cocked an eye at Casalis.

Casalis shrugged his shoulders.

Manston went on, 'Tomorrow, Irina and I had better check the steps. If the bottom door is unlocked we can do it from the seaward side and you can have your boys up on the road by the bungalow . . . just in case.'

15

THE NEXT MORNING, the police put a motor-boat at the disposal of Manston and Irina. Guyon and Casalis, in case of trouble, took one of their French house-guards and arranged to meet them by car from the land as they checked the steps.

The tide was at half-flood as they left the beach below the villa and motored out into the St Jean-de-Luz bay. Behind them, they could see the massed cream, white and coloured buildings of St Jean ringing the great stretch of golden sands, gay with coloured umbrellas and quick with the movement of holiday-makers. Inland, big puffy white clouds were rolling slowly along the crests of the mountains, now and again blotting out the dominating peak of La Rhune.

There was a long, easy swell going as they cleared the breakwater and turned up the coast towards Bidart and Biarritz.

Manston looked across at Irina who sat opposite him, wearing red trousers and a white sweater which had been bought in St Jean. Catching her dark-eyed smile he told himself that it was really against all the odds that the two of them should be here. It was a smiling, sunlit world which forced the imagination to work hard to accept that behind it, somewhere close, lay the Limbo organization. Looking at Irina, remembering with a smile the way she had fussed the previous evening over the few shotgun pellets in his arm and leg, knowing clearly his feeling for her and hers for him, he found it hard to look back and see himself as an unattached Binky sort of man, no strings, no ties . . . complete freedom from any binding emotions. Now, the whole thing was different. The moment of truth, the moment of holding her in his arms in her bedroom, had passed between them with a quiet ecstasy and frankness. There was only one true aspect of himself now and he only hoped that he would be worthy of it.

Irina said suddenly, 'A penny for them?'

Manston shook his head. 'Not for sale.'

'Pig.'

He said, 'Your English is too good.'

They kept well out and, after some time, Manston picked out the bungalow on the cliff-top, which had been described to him by Casalis. He cut the motor down and they rose and fell gently on the swell.

They both looked towards the shore and for a time neither of them spoke. There was the red roof of the bungalow showing on the cliff-top and below it was a cliff-enclosed beach; but on the beach, either under coloured umbrellas or playing about at the water's edge, were a dozen or more people. Two speedboats were tied up alongside a concrete platform by some rocks, and the sound of laughter and voices came clearly across the water to them.

Manston lit a cigarette and looked at Irina. 'So much for our private little snoop around. I wonder . . .' he let his words trail away.

After a moment's pause Irina said, 'Why do you need to wonder?'

Almost to himself Manston said, 'These are pretty certainly the steps – and, almost as certainly, Amadeo Grandier is in there with a bunch of his friends. After that business at Sare yesterday with Pierre Salgazza, Limbo must know that at least I'm alive and kicking. Just that's enough to give them a headache. Also it means that I don't have to worry about being under cover any more.'

'Then why don't we do it?' said Irina firmly. 'We can make some excuse and go right in there. Nothing can happen to us in broad daylight and we might learn something.'

'You've got more faith in broad daylight than I have.'

'I've got faith in you. And don't look so hesitant. If you were by yourself you'd go in, wouldn't you?'

'Yes. Yes, I would. I think the time has arrived to bring something into the open.'

'Then stop thinking about me. I made Sutcliffe go back without me. I want this thing ended, and I'm prepared to take any chance that you are.'

And she was, he knew that. Perhaps more than he, she was determined to see an end to the inhuman Limbo traffic, because she and her people were concerned. She was emotionally involved whereas he was just a professional . . .

Suddenly he said, 'O.K. It'll give Casalis and Guyon heart failure watching from the cliff-top, but I think you're right. We'll go in. Listen, you stick close to me – and keep your eyes and ears open.' He pulled her to him and kissed her then, as he released her, added, 'But you behave yourself.'

She said, 'Do I have to do anything special?'

'No. Just be yourself. If you're asked your name, give it. Just be absolutely honest in reply to any normal question. You're on holiday, staying at the villa Ixas-Atou. But to get in' – he smiled – 'you're going to have to do a little work.'

Manston cut the engine dead. He bent down and fiddled about with the distributor head for a while. The boat drifted a little towards the beach with the tide. After a time Manston straightened up and got out the pair of spare oars. Without hurry, he and Irina rowed into the beach and came alongside the small jetty just beyond the speedboats. Manston calculated that at low tide there would still be a certain amount of water alongside.

From the party on the beach which had watched them row in a man now detached himself and came strolling down to the jetty. He was wearing beach trunks and a pair of canvas shoes. His fair hair was cropped short and there was a pleasant smile on his square, good-natured face.

'My apologies for disturbing you,' said Manston in English, 'but my distributor head's broken. I wondered if there were a telephone I could use?'

'Jump out,' said the man. 'There's one up in my bungalow.' He spoke English, slowly and deliberately, the process of translation creasing his forehead. 'I'm the owner here. Did you hire the boat?'

'Yes. From St Jean.'

'On holiday there?'

'Yes . . . I'm sorry —' Manston turned towards Irina. 'This is Miss Tovskaya, and I'm Manston – Richard Manston.'

The man showed no surprise at the mention of their names.

He said, 'Grandier. Amadeo Grandier. Come on.' He reached down a hand and helped Irina up on to the jetty.

As they walked back to the beach someone from the party shouted to him and he called back in French, explaining what had happened.

At the bottom of the steps he said, 'There is no need for Mademoiselle Tovskaya to climb all the way up.'

'I don't mind,' said Irina, 'I'm stiff from sitting in the boat. The exercise will do me good.'

Amadeo shrugged his shoulders and led the way up the steps.

There was a stout wooden door, open at the bottom, bolt and padlock showing. Amadeo led the way and the two of them followed, Manston counting to himself as he went and now and then shutting his eyes to get the feel of the place. By the time he was half-way up and they had come to a small level landing affair, there was little doubt in his mind. When he reached the top he was sure. There were forty-eight steps. As Amadeo went over to the bungalow ahead of them Manston looked at Irina. She nodded. The head of the steps was protected with a door similar to the one at the bottom.

In the little hallway of the bungalow was a telephone. Amadeo put his hand on the telephone and said, 'How's your French? Would you like me to do it?'

'No, I can manage, thank you.'

Manston called a garage, had a conversation, and then put the receiver down.

Amadeo said, 'You speak French as well as you speak English. What's the verdict?'

'They're sending a man out. He'll be here in half an hour.'

'That means an hour,' said Amadeo. 'You'd better come back to the beach. You've got plenty of time for a swim and a drink.'

After that it was easy. In fact, there were moments when Manston wondered whether the whole thing was not being made too easy by some turn of fate. There was no doubt about the steps, and on the beach were quite a few of the people in whom they were interested. There were about half a dozen young girls and young men and a handful of older people, who at once made them at ease; treated them, in fact, as though they had been invited to the beach party.

Under the umbrellas a table was laid with drinks, and these were being dispensed by Franz Aspender who poured them the largest gin and Campari Manston had seen for some time. Manston watched all these people as they were introduced; not one showed the slightest surprise at their names. Irina was taken off by the Comtesse Bernice, the one, Manston remembered, with whom Amadeo was having an affair. Her husband was apparently not there. But her mother-in-law was, the *comtesse douairière* Estelle Longeau-du-Quercy. The dowager countess sat in state under a red umbrella in a canvas beach chair, wearing a blue and white striped silk dress, white gloves and a large, flower-decorated hat. She was a commanding woman, and was not hesitant in issuing decrees which were instantly obeyed. Close to her sat a priest, a short, square, nondescript figure in a soutane and fried-egg black hat who – when she could give him her attention – was reading the paper aloud to her. But most of the time she was engaged in an argument with a Monsieur Louis Saint-Amand over some question of land ownership at the beginning of the century. Both of them were reeling off names and relationships which Manston could not follow. When they were introduced to her, she raised an eyebrow at Irina and said, 'You are Russian?'

'My family come from Russia.'

The *comtesse* smiled briefly, 'These days it is a good place to come from.'

Louis Saint-Amand said, 'You are staying in St Jean?'

Manston said, 'Yes. We've taken a villa. On the Ciboure side.'

The countess looked for a moment at him and then at Irina and then said primly, 'Just the two of you in this villa?'

Manston sensed the disapproval for young couples unchaperoned.

'No,' he said. 'There is a friend with us and more coming.'

'Oh, I see . . .' The *comtesse* relaxed her manner a little.

They spent an hour on the beach with the party, bathing and drinking. Manston, with all the people sorted out in his mind – the Aspenders, the countess and her daughter-in-law, Louis Saint-Amand and his daughter Claudine, the restless pack of young people, Amadeo Grandier who never seemed to be still . . . a bright, gay, animated beach party – found it hard to believe that a few yards away were the steps down which he and Irina had been led not so long ago, on a rainy night. There was no menace here, only friendliness and an eagerness to make them welcome. He did not even have to dig for the simple facts he wanted.

Amadeo said to him, 'The town beaches are crowded. Any time you want to come here, please do. I am staying here for the next two or three days. You are always welcome. But when I leave – then you will find the keys to the steps under the large geranium pot in the doorway of the bungalow. All I ask is that you lock up the doors when you go and put the keys back.'

And, thought Manston, if he made this offer to them, there was no doubt that he had made it among his friends. Any of Grandier's obviously large circle of acquaintances could use these steps with impunity. From Manston's point of view that did not make things easier.

When the mechanic arrived, Amadeo Grandier asked them if they would like to stay to lunch, but Manston refused, saying that they had already promised to go to lunch with friends at Ciboure.

As they went back along the coast, Manston said, 'What did you think of them?'

'They seemed a nice, normal lot of people.'

'The *comtesse* is a bit of a character. I wouldn't like to get on the wrong side of her.'

'I liked her daughter-in-law, Bernice. She's taking me to her hairdresser in St Jean tomorrow morning. Is that all right?'

'Fine – we've got to get to know them well.' He looked at her, smiling. 'What's wrong with your hair?'

Irina shook her head. 'It feels like a bird's nest.'

*

That afternoon there was a message from Paris from Barry Dymen, now recovered and working, to say that the French police had traced the house used by Taru. It was on the Loire, between Orleans and Blois. It was vacant and had been rented from its innocent owner two years before by a man called Lognard whose description tallied with that of the man who had given Manston the whisky flask. The occupants had pulled out without warning, owing three months' rent. Barry also sent a list of wine and other heavy tankers registered in the St Jean area. There were a great many of these and most of them were owned by public companies or wine co-operatives. Individual tankers showed no names as yet connected with Limbo.

Casalis, reporting this to Manston, went on, 'I'm worried about the way you've stuck your neck out with these people – particularly Irina. Watching you on the beach gave me the willies. If they got desperate they might try anything.'

Manston shook his head. 'They're nowhere near desperate yet. That's the object of cultivating them. Somewhere among Amadeo's friends – maybe Amadeo – is the person who's running the show. By the way, you and I are going to have a look around his house at Sare tonight. He's not living there at the moment.'

'I'm all for that – but what about Irina going to the hairdresser with . . . what's her name?'

'*Comtesse* Bernice. Why shouldn't she? They took quite a fancy to one another. Just put our two men and yourself on her tail. And if you still feel uneasy, get the St Jean police to have a discreet word with the hairdresser. We've got to get in with these people and hope for a break. What about their houses?'

'The police checked them this morning. None of them have any barn just off the main road near them.'

'There was a scruffy-looking priest reading to the dowager countess. Can you get a line on him?'

'Already have. He's an old friend of the family. Doesn't have a *cure* anywhere now – but he's a sort of unofficial chaplain to the old girl.'

Manston smiled. 'I'll bet she gives him hell, too. She doesn't stand any nonsense from anyone. Which is interesting; because why does she put up with Amadeo and the affair with her daughter-in-law? I should have thought she would have jumped on that one.'

'Don't ask me. Some strange things go on in these old families.'

Manston changed the subject. 'By the way, we've got a no-limit drawing account at the *Crédit-Lyonnais* in St. Jean, haven't we?'

'Yes. Why?'

'Oh, nothing. I just wanted to know.'

Casalis gave him an odd look, but said nothing.

That afternoon Manston went down to St Jean on his own. When he came back, he went upstairs to Irina's room. He found her resting on her bed in a dressing-gown.

He went across to her and sat down on the side of the bed. He leaned over her, put his arms round her and kissed her. For a while they were silent, lost in their embrace.

When finally he released her, Irina smiled up at him puzzled.

'Nice?'

She nodded, slowly sitting up. 'Very nice. But why? I mean without warning, without a word.'

'You want to be warned before I mean to kiss you?'

'No . . .' She laughed. 'Richard, what is it? You look very pleased with yourself.'

'I am. Here, I thought this would make it official.'

He took her hand and slipped a ring on to her engagement

finger. She looked down at it and her eyes widened with pleasure.

'Oh, Richard . . . it's wonderful. Wonderful!' She held up her hand to the light for a moment. The ring was in blue enamel, oval in shape, surrounded by small diamonds and with a large diamond in the centre. Then she turned to him and flung her arms round his neck kissing him and pulling him down on to the bed with her.

Lying there together, she said, 'I think you're very clever. It fits perfectly. How could you know?'

'Well . . .' he teased her, 'I'm always giving girls rings. I get to be able to guess the size from a look at their hands.'

She frowned with mock anger at him. 'You give nobody a ring but me. Is that understood? It is official – only me.'

'O.K. You really like it?'

'Of course.'

'The chap in the shop said it had belonged to some French *marquise*. I thought it was a bit ostentatious myself – but then, I said, anyone to do with the theatre would like that.'

'For that,' said Irina, 'I take my revenge some time.' She turned her face towards him and her lips came up to his.

That evening before dinner, over a bottle of champagne, Manston and Irina announced the news to Casalis and Guyon. Later, Casalis got Manston alone on the terrace.

'Sutcliffe won't like that, you know,' he said.

Manston shrugged his shoulders. 'He's not marrying her. He doesn't have to.'

'But you know what he's like if any of us gets involved on the job.' He fiddled with a cigarette. 'It sometimes takes the edge off a man at the wrong moment.'

Manston shook his head. 'This just makes me more than specially concerned to see that nothing goes wrong.'

'Well, there is that, I suppose.'

Manston laughed. 'For Pete's sake, don't be so gloomy. I'm happy about it. You should be, too.'

'I am. Or at least, I will be when this business is all wrapped up. Don't you think she ought to go back to London? It would be safer. You could persuade her.'

'I could try, but I wouldn't have any success. So I'm not trying.'

*

Oleg's orders had been quite specific. The Limbo organization as a clearing-station was admirable, it had taken a long time to establish and would be far from easy, for a variety of reasons, to replace. It must, therefore, be maintained. It might have to go out of action for a few months until things quietened down, but it must not be broken, either voluntarily, or by outside interference. The other links in the chain could be replaced, but not Limbo. The importance attached to it by his superiors was confirmed by the fact that he had been directed to come down and handle this affair on the spot. It was not often that he was sent out to do any actual field work, not in recent years, anyway, but he had seen quite clearly that the Limbo organization was not equipped to deal ruthlessly with outside opposition; nor was it safe for it to do so.

At first he had contemplated bringing Ludmilla with him, but a few moments' reflection had shown him that this was dangerous and merely an emotional desire that could contribute nothing to the solving of the problem. Even so, as he sat now, comfortable and relaxed, but his mind acutely aware of the problem ahead, he felt that it would have been pleasant to have had her here. He had left Paris early that morning, taking far more precautions than he had for his visit to Bordeaux; and by car and a devious route he had arrived at seven o'clock that evening to stay at the house of the man who had been known at the Hôtel Royal Gascogne as Monsieur Edouard Cadillet. Travelling by another route, two outside operators from AGRIP of the same nationality as himself, but fully documented and easily passing as Frenchmen, had gone to the town of Cambo, about twenty kilometres from Sare, and were staying at the Hôtel Saint Laurent. Oleg, himself, was staying with Edouard Cadillet.

Oleg sat now, comfortable in an armchair, a glass of brandy in his hand. Edouard Cadillet's cellar was as carefully chosen as his books; the books which lined this small study, their brown leather spines glowing in the soft light from the table lamp. The window was half open against the balmy September night, and now and again a moth came blundering through to whirr and flap about the crown of the lamp. Monsieur Cadillet, velvet jacket open, sat in another armchair, his slippered feet up on a stool.

Oleg, his voice mellower than usual, said, 'While I agree with you that it is extremely unlikely that anyone could find the rock chamber, the fact remains that this man Manston is no fool. He's a trained man, and there must be things he will have noted. Already he has identified the steps.'

'That means nothing. At least fifty people have the open use of them.'

'Pierre Salgazza?'

'That must have been during the fight in the cave. His mask came off. I imagine the girl saw him briefly in the torchlight. Manston took a chance on him and identified him by his back wounds. It was clever of him to remember that. As a man he is quite likeable, I find.'

Oleg stirred, his mouth tightening. Then, mellowness giving way to asperity, he said, 'It is dangerous to like that kind of man. It gives an advantage often without your knowing it. There could be other things he has noticed, things we know nothing about. These could be the things they are working on. That makes it imperative that we do something before they have time to develop them. One thing that I don't like is that they have kept the girl with them. Originally, I suppose, that was because she had seen Pierre Salgazza. But if she still stays with them, it could mean that she knows other things. The obvious solution is to deal with both of them quickly.'

'How?'

'We want the girl to go back to our country. We can still arrange that —'

'They won't give you a chance.'

'Chances can be made.'

'And Manston?'

'He's caused enough trouble. We can eliminate him.'

'Kill him?'

'Yes. But you will not be directly involved in that. We kill him and take the girl back.'

'I presume you will pay again for re-shipping the girl?'

For a moment Oleg said nothing. He raised his brandy glass and took a sip, deliberating. Money . . . always money.

'Yes,' he said briefly.

'Good. Then what do you want done?'

'Manston and this girl – they have a villa, you say?'

'The villa Ixas-Atou in Ciboure.'

'They have already met a good many people you know. Well, let them go on meeting them. Cultivate him and her, show them nothing but friendliness, and the moment will make itself. If it does not do so quickly – then we will make it.'

Edouard Cadillet stood up and moved across to a bookshelf. He put up a hand absently and touched one of the volumes, looking down at Oleg.

'Any violence towards Manston is your concern. Our business is quite different.'

Oleg nodded. 'That is understood. From you I just want information about them, everything they say, do, or are going to do.' He paused for a moment and then said, 'Is violence so distasteful to you?'

'Frankly, yes.'

Oleg gave a dry laugh. 'You surprise me. . . . However, I suppose you are entitled to make the distinction between murder and the thing you do now.'

'I think we are. These people become useful citizens again in your country.'

'Useful, but unreliable. We are not concerned with them, but with the reaction of the people who see them back again. That is important to us. For that we pay money.' Oleg drained his brandy and stood up. 'I think now that I shall go to bed.'

In his bedroom he stood at the open window with the light off, the room dark behind him. Only once before had he stayed here, when he was fixing up the Limbo organization arrangements. A thin night mist was drifting low beneath the chestnut trees beyond the garden, and the fat edge of a September moon was just beginning to show over the shoulder of the Pic Dassou. A brown owl called sharply from the trees and, distantly up the valley, he could hear a dog barking. He stood there, brooding, and was suddenly conscious of the loneliness in him. For a few moments he could admit to himself that he was tired of being away from his own country so long . . . the slow mist under the trees wakened nostalgia in him and he resented his loneliness. Maybe, when this affair was completed, they would send him back . . . give him a responsible job in an open organization. He could even get married to Ludmilla, settle somewhere. . . . He turned quickly from the window. It wasn't likely . . . no, it was not for him. The more successful he was the more certainly he would stay with AGRIP . . . Paris, Cairo, New York . . . maybe Africa somewhere, Ghana . . . there was no end to the possibilities.

Later, when he was in bed, he stayed awake for a long time, thinking to begin with of Ludmilla. But before long he came back to this affair, going over all he knew of Manston and Irina Tovskaya, his mind working away at the problem like a mouse gnawing at a cob nut.

*

Down below in his study, the man Edouard Cadillet was preparing to go out. Although he hadn't mentioned it to Oleg – it was such a small detail – there was one thing worrying him, one thing which that day had come to his attention. It might mean nothing; but with Oleg so insistent on their security, he felt that it would be unwise to disregard it.

16

AMADEO GRANDIER'S HOUSE lay at the head of a small lane which wound off to the right of the Ascain-Sare road a mile beyond the Col de Saint Ignace.

Just after midnight Manston and Casalis left their car some way short of the lane and made their way across a couple of fields to the back of the house. Casalis had checked that Amadeo had taken his only permanent servant with him to the bungalow. Manston was reasonably certain that the house would now be empty, but he took no chances. He left Casalis to keep a watch outside the house and made his way round to the front. It was a still, warm night with a blaze of stars above. A terrace in front of the house was overgrown with shrubs and he had plenty of cover.

He had no difficulty in getting inside. Amadeo was not a careful householder. A french window at the end of the terrace had been left unlocked and Manston went into a lounge which, in the pencil beam of his torch, was untidy with shabby furniture. Keeping the beam down, he made a rapid examination of the room and then moved out into the hall. To the right was a small door. He eased this open gently and went, torchless, into a darkness that smelt of cigar-smoke. There was no light from the stars outside and he guessed that the long window curtains had been drawn. He felt his way forward a few steps, then switched on his torch, keeping it low. It showed the bottom of a bookcase, full of paperbacks, a sporting gun leaning against the books, and a worn carpet. He swung the torch round and raised it slowly. It was a study, untidy like the other room . . . an old jacket lay across the arm of a chair.

The torch came up above the chair on to the wall and a moment of shock went over Manston like a cold draught. Pinpointed in the light a face glared down at him, grotesque, drunken and leering, made sinister by empty eye-sockets under thick brows. It was a carnival mask of the kind worn by their attendant in the rock chamber.

Manston moved the torch along and saw that there were a row of masks hanging on the wall. One of them was identical with the mask he had seen before.

Manston unhooked the mask. It was a heavy affair, made of papiermâché, and obviously not machine-manufactured. Someone had fashioned it by hand, a craftsman's job. A stout piece of elastic ran across the back to keep it on the face. The inside of the mask around the mouth was marked and slightly stained. Manston put the mask back and checked the others. They had all been worn at some time, all carrying stains around the mouth.

He turned away from the masks and, close to the drawn curtains of the window, saw a small desk. The top was a mass of loose papers and envelopes and there was a bill spike, so loaded with bills that it looked like a gigantic candy-floss cornet. Alongside it was a portable typewriter.

Manston went to the typewrier and slipped a blank envelope into it. He tapped away quickly along the lines of keys . . . qwertyuiop . . . asdfghjkl . . . jerked the envelope out and slipped it into his pocket.

As he did so, standing in the quiet of the room, he thought he heard a noise from the hallway. He snapped off his torch and froze.

Distinctly he heard the movement of the study door handle. He swung round, slipped behind the desk and pulled the long curtains aside, hiding behind them.

He stood there in the darkness waiting. There was no other sound for some time; and for some moments he wondered whether perhaps he had imagined the noise of the door handle.

Then, not more than a yard from him, he heard the sudden rustle of papers. Whoever it was at the desk had come into the room with a quietness which would have done credit to a professional thief. Manston caught the corner of the curtain and eased it aside. There was nothing but darkness. He heard a slight movement, the sound of a quiet breath, and then there was silence again.

Slowly Manston raised his torch. Whoever was in the room had no more right to be there than he had, but, at a guess, it was someone who knew the layout of the room well since no torch had been used.

Manston waited for the sound of movement, wanting it to focus his torch. Whoever it was, he told himself, would be someone he would like to talk to. . . .

He waited, listening, but there was no other sound. He snapped his torch on and the beam shot across the room. There was no one in the room. At the far end the door was half-open. But, even as the torchlight swept across the room, he noticed that the typewriter had gone from the desk in front of him.

Manston raced for the door. As he turned into the hall, he heard a noise from the far end. He ran through the house and found himself in a large kitchen. Ahead of him was a thick door and he was just in time to see it closing. He threw himself forward, grabbing at the handle; but as he did so, he heard a key turn in the lock outside. For a moment he tugged furiously at the handle of the stout door. Then he turned and ran back through the house and out on to the terrace by way of the open french window.

He raced around the terrace, calling for Casalis, and found him eventually on the far side. They searched through the garden that led away from the back door and into a small wood that bordered the garden, but without any success.

Driving back in the car Casalis said, 'Whoever it was had a key and knew the house. I came round to the front after you were in . . . Damn it.'

'And the typewriter has gone. But I beat them to it by a few seconds. . . . And it's not hard to think why the typewriter was wanted. Someone in Limbo has just got round to spotting that I tore off a piece of the directions. . . .'

Back at the villa Manston handed the sample of typing to Guyon. Guyon had spent most of the day doing a check on the neighbourhood of all the houses belonging to the people they had met who lived near Sare. Nowhere was there a turning off the road that led to a barn with pine woods and a wooden-bridged stream. Guyon went off to check the typing and Manston sat with a whisky nightcap, brooding.

The Sare set, innocently or not, had been very friendly. Why? Limbo was in this for money. Who wanted money? Amadeo to playboy around, maybe even to persuade Bernice to go off with him? Louis Saint-Amand? Devoted to his daughter. Enough money could make any man forget her plainness. The Longeau-du-Quercy family? Did they need money? It would hardly seem so – they owned half the country around their house. The Aspenders? They seemed well-heeled, but you never knew. A lot of people, their desks untidy with unpaid bills, seemed well-heeled. Somewhere among them, or on the fringes of their set, was someone who needed money so badly that they had been able to swallow – probably after a preliminary gulp or two of nausea – the bait put out by AGRIP for carrying out this inhuman traffic. Who was it?

Guyon came to him half an hour later with two pieces of information.

The typewriter in Amadeo's house was the one on which the instructions in the rock chamber had been typed. The only difference was that the ribbon had been changed. The chamber instructions were bluish type and the present ribbon was a black one. That fitted, because the instructions could have been typed a couple of years previously.

The other, less comforting, crumb came from Barry Dymen in Paris. Oleg was no longer at AGRIP headquarters. It was not known whether he had been transferred to some other post or had gone down to direct the fieldwork personally.

Guyon said he would get the police to check all the hotels in the neighbourhood, but neither he nor Manston felt that Oleg – after the Bordeaux incident – would have much faith in hotels.

'What do we do about Amadeo?' asked Guyon. 'Jump him? It might be a short cut.'

Manston considered this, then said, 'No. If we jump him and he's guilty he will just deny everything and we couldn't hold him. Anyone could have used his typewriter. I don't know . . . I get a feeling that things are beginning to simmer up, but not quite enough for us to do anything. If we get really stuck we'll jump him, but not until then.'

*

Coming back after her visit the next day to the hairdresser with Bernice – they had taken coffee together afterwards – Irina told Manston, 'Her marriage was purely one of arrangement between the old families. She has a son of eight, but I don't think he means much to her. The dowager countess and her husband have taken him over and – though she didn't say this – probably turned him against her. One thing is clear; she's madly in love with Amadeo, but she won't ever do anything definite about it. I mean, like going off with him. Even she has the family name complex. I should think that's why her mother-in-law and her husband tolerate it – they know she will stay with them. By the way, she thinks I'm terribly lucky to have a man like you. . . .' She smiled, arching one eyebrow.

'She's a sensible woman. You are.'

'We've been asked this afternoon to a tennis party at the Longeau-du-Quercy place. I said we would go.'

And they did go, with Casalis and one of their bodyguards left to hang discreetly about in the neighbourhood.

The château was about four kilometres from Sare and south of it in a long valley that ran up through beech and chestnut woods to the Spanish frontier. A driveway ran off the road through ornamental iron gates, supported by stone pillars topped with griffons holding the family coat of arms, three scallop shells on a plain shield. The drive was tarmacadamed, running through a small, well-kept park to a series of gardens that clothed a steep rise on the crest of which the château, flanked by terraces, stood. The drive curved round the back of the house into an open square which held a large fountain and stone basin. Beyond the square the drive ran on up the hill and, a kilometre away, came out on to the road again nearer the Spanish frontier. The château was an eighteenth-century building, the centre section mansard-roofed and the wings broken into a series of small towers, Gothic and rather grim-looking.

Irina did not play tennis, but Amadeo lent Manston a racquet and with Claudine Saint-Amand and another girl they made up a mixed doubles. Manston and Claudine just managed to win.

When they came back to the terrace, more people had arrived and were clustered round the shaded terrace tables.

One of them – a man Manston had never seen before – was Comte Aristide Longeau-du-Quercy; tall, lean and elegant-looking with a tight-drawn face and beaky nose. Manston knew at once that he was not the kind of man he was going to like and, equally certain, not the kind who was going to like him.

Wearing a bronze-coloured silk suit, cream shirt and a little yellow bow-tie, he stood by his mother as though he were on guard duty and bored to death by it. Amadeo introduced him and said how good he was at tennis.

Aristide, scarcely looking at Manston, said, 'Indeed? I can't understand this passion for ball games which the English have. Tennis, golf, football – it seems such a pointless waste of time. No?'

Manston said, 'No, I don't agree. But I don't think you'd really want to hear my defence of ball games.'

There was a chuckle from behind Manston and he turned to find Louis Saint-Amand. 'Don't be put out by Aristide, monsieur,' he said. 'A day for him is not pleasant unless he has succeeded in being offensive to at least twenty people. Isn't that right, Aristide?'

Aristide shrugged his shoulders. 'If you say so. But I assure you I am not aware of being offensive – and I apologize to Monsieur Manston if I gave that impression.'

The dowager countess from behind him said curtly, 'You did give that impression – and you were right to apologize. And let me say that when a man is not working he is entitled to occupy himself how he chooses. The important thing is that he should have legitimate pleasures and pursue them with passion.'

'As you say, mama.' Aristide turned and made a little bow to her.

Later Manston wandered off by himself into the house. At the far end of the inner hallway he came across a row of grotesque carnival masks hanging on the wall.

As he stood there a voice said pleasantly, 'You are interested in carnival masks, monsieur?'

He turned. Louis Saint-Amand was standing just behind him.

'Not really,' Manston replied. 'But I was attracted by the workmanship of these. They are very well made.'

'There is a man at Ascain who makes them. This is a great country for carnivals and fêtes, monsieur. Did you enjoy your tennis?'

'Very much. Your daughter plays a good game, monsieur.'

'She does?' Saint-Amand's face lit up. 'How good of you to say so.' He came over and stood under the masks looking up at them. 'I often wonder, you know, how much of a tragedy it is to a woman to be born ugly. Claudine is plain and appears not to mind. But underneath a woman must mind, mustn't she? The world is inclined to make quick, and no doubt harsh, judgements simply on appearance. And then, of course, there is the question of marriage. The beauty of a woman's soul doesn't mean much to a man in the early stages. What do you do for a living, monsieur?'

The question, flicked in unexpectedly, made Manston wonder if the preamble had been meant to throw him off his guard.

He said easily, 'I'm a partner in a firm of diamond merchants. Hatton Garden.'

'Ah . . . interesting. I was noticing your fiancée's ring. The diamonds are beautiful.'

'They had to be.' Manston smiled. 'A diamond merchant is called on for something special. They're blue-white diamonds from Oranjemund – the famous Diamond Coast operated by the Consolidated Diamond Mines of South-West Africa.'

They talked for a while about diamonds, and then Manston went back to the terrace.

Some time later he was cornered by the dowager countess's private priest who, having heard he was a diamond merchant, began a long monologue about the precious stones in the head-dress of a Madonna in one of the local churches and then, rather astonishingly, went on to discuss some new method being perfected in America for drilling holes in industrial diamonds with a high-energy beam of light.

'Just imagine it, monsieur; the surface of the diamond, exposed to the high-energy light, is vaporized instantaneously. That means the heat must be greater than 3,500 degrees Centigrade, which is the vaporizing point of diamonds. Such is the power of light, monsieur. You have heard of these experiments, of course. Tell me . . .'

For the next five minutes Manston, well briefed as he was on his cover occupation, had found himself having to box very cleverly and was relieved when Amadeo joined them and rescued him by saying, 'Claudine tells me that Mademoiselle Tovskaya says your real game is golf. It's mine, too. Why don't we have a round at Chantaco tomorrow? After lunch? What's your handicap?'

'Five,' said Manston and was relieved to see the priest walk away.

Half an hour later, the guests began to say good-bye to the dowager countess. When Irina and Manston made their *adieux* she said, 'You must come again when there are no other guests. I'd like to show you the château properly. We are very proud of it, aren't we, Aristide?' She turned to her son who stood behind her.

'Indeed we are,' said Aristide. 'We have a château and hectares and hectares of land, a family genealogy which takes up two pages in the *Almanac de Gotha*, now no longer printed. We are unique. Living museum pieces. Do please come and see us again soon.'

The dowager countess smiled. 'It is not one of Aristide's good days,' she said, and then added, 'But then it seldom is.'

Going down to their car, Manston said to Irina, 'He's one of the most unpleasant types I've ever met. I wonder why he dislikes everyone, and particularly his mother, so much.'

'He dislikes her?'

'It sticks out a mile. He'd like to screw her neck.'

Later, at the Villa Ixas-Atou, Manston could not shake off the feeling that somewhere something had gone wrong. Something should have happened by now and it hadn't. The fact that it hadn't made him edgy and, although they had two bodyguards in the house, he insisted that he, Casalis and Guyon should break the night into shifts and keep watch on Irina's room.

Manston, during his watch, sat at the foot of the stairs leading to Irina's room and did a crossword puzzle in an old *Times* which was in the house. Nothing happened that night. He went to bed, but was a long time getting to sleep, thinking about Louis Saint-Amand and Amadeo. It could be that they were working together.

What a dirty business it all was, thought Manston . . . and suddenly he longed for the farm-house in Kent, for the bright splash of water into the swimming pool and the cool evening smell of rising summer mist.

*

At nine o'clock that evening Oleg put through a call to the Hôtel Saint Laurent at Cambo. Half an hour later a car drove up to the house of the man who called himself Edouard Cadillet. A man got out and a few moments later was closeted with Cadillet and Oleg in the study. The study table was covered with a large-scale map of the district. Standing over this, using a silver pencil as a pointer, Oleg gave his instructions. The man listened, nodding occasionally and only once asking a question.

Oleg finished by saying, 'Tomorrow morning I want you to go over the whole route. Make yourself and the others absolutely familiar with it. You understand – no mistake is going to be tolerated.'

The man nodded, rising to go.

Cadillet said, 'A glass of brandy before you go?'

The man shook his head.

When he had gone Oleg sat down and wrote a message to AGRIP for Cadillet to send off. Although Cadillet would normally have encoded it, Oleg – a competent code clerk once – did it himself. The message read:

Limbo to Agrip
Miachin. Arrangements here completed tomorrow. Shall leave tomorrow evening. Change-over car to meet at Limoges, same procedure as outward journey. No objection your being with it. Love

It had been some time before Oleg had decided to add the last word. But a sudden, warm mental picture of Ludmilla had eventually decided him.

17

At twelve o'clock the next day Manston drove down into St Jean. He stopped, and bought himself a pair of rubber-soled shoes; and then drove on, past the railway station and over the level-crossing, taking the Ascain and Sare road up the Nivelle valley to the Chantaco golf course. Irina, with Casalis and Guyon, was going to join him at one o'clock for lunch. Manston had decided that Casalis and Guyon could no longer be kept in the background. He would introduce them as friends of his paying a brief visit and they could walk round together. As time ran on, anxiety for Irina was strong in him and he was determined to take no chances. In fact as he drove he was debating with himself the wisdom of stalling any longer. Maybe the time had come to jump Amadeo about the typewriter. There was always a critical moment when nothing moved that demanded force, brutal ham-handed methods. The moment, he knew, was approaching.

The club-house was a large stucco building, Venetian red in colour and overhung with Virginia creeper. Manston parked his car under the acacia trees by the club-house, paid his dues at the secretary's office, then changed and hired a set of clubs from the professional. He walked across the road to the practice ground, which cut at right angles into part of the sixteenth fairway, towards the river. From a small kiosk he bought himself a full bucket of yellow practice balls and went to one of the practice tees. There were three or four other people practising. It was some time since Manston had played golf and, although his mind was on other things, he gradually succumbed to the magic of feeling the leather grips in his hands again, listening to the sudden vicious swish of the club-head through the ball as he loosened up. Maybe because his mind was not entirely on golf, he found himself swinging easily, the sweetness of true impact running up to his hands from the club-head. He worked up from his seven iron to his spoon, banging the balls away, while out ahead of him the ball boy cycled about on a machine protected by wire netting, picking up the balls.

After a while he sat down on a bench and lit a cigarette, taking a breather. As he sat there he saw Claudine come along to the row of tees, a boy following her with her clubs and a basket of balls. Seeing him, she stopped and said, smiling, 'What are you doing here?'

'I'm having a game with Amadeo after lunch. Just loosening up.'

'Amadeo —' She made a quick face. 'What's your handicap?'

'Five – the same as his.'

Her plain face moved again and there was a slight roll of her eyes. 'Don't you believe it; he's nearer scratch. Good luck, but don't have too much money on it.'

She moved away to a tee and he watched her as she began to punch balls away with an iron, smacking into them solidly like a man.

Manston did another fifteen minutes' stint and went back to the club-house and bought himself a beer. A little later Amadeo arrived, bringing Bernice with him; and shortly afterwards

Casalis and Guyon appeared with Irina. Manston introduced the two men as friends of his from Paris. For a moment he thought Amadeo gave them an odd look, as though he had seen them before, or as though something about them stirred some memory, but he welcomed them amiably, and they all had lunch together.

By the time they had played four holes, Manston realized that Amadeo took his game seriously, and was, as Claudine had said, nearer scratch than five handicap. Manston won the fourth hole, after losing the first three.

As they walked to the fifth tee, their two girl caddies close behind them, Amadeo looked back for a moment. Bernice and Irina were together and Casalis and Guyon stood a little apart from them, waiting for Manston and Amadeo to drive. It was a clear day, the heat baking up from the ground. Away in the distance the peak of La Rhune stood sharply out against the cloudless sky. There was a warm smell of pine needles in the air. A perfect afternoon for golf.

Amadeo said, 'She is charming, your fiancée. You don't know how lucky you are to have things so plain sailing.' As he spoke Manston could see that he was looking at Bernice.

'We have our problems, you know,' said Manston.

'Not like mine,' said Amadeo. Then, with a change of manner, he went on, 'Your honour. This is a dog-leg hole to the right. Three eighty-five metres. Keep your drive well up to the left. With a good second shot you can get the green. If you're too much right it becomes difficult.'

Manston teed up and took his driver. The fairway ran uphill, the green out of sight beyond the rise. There were pine trees on the left. To the right the ground sloped sharply away into thick woods. He swung and hit a long low shot, slightly hooked, which disappeared over the rise and which, he thought, might have caught the trees on the left. Amadeo hit a screamer, dead straight and slightly left of the middle of the fairway, to open up the green.

Manston found his ball, short of Amaedo's and just on the left edge of the fairway. From the top of the rise now he could see the green ahead. It was a flat plateau, flanked on the left with an open forest track. To the right the ground sloped down into a deep cut, bordered by thick woods. From his position it was all he could give it with a spoon. Amadeo, ahead of him and much better placed, had an easy three iron to the green.

Manston, in the moment of addressing his ball, was suddenly struck with the thought that all this business had begun with him playing golf at Rye with Sutcliffe. It would be odd, some needling voice of anxiety within him prompted, if it all ended with him playing golf here at Chantaco. He swung, half concentrating, and cut his ball. It soared out towards the green and then began to fade quickly. It hit the right-hand edge of the mound slope below the green and bounced down towards the trees, coming to rest about half-way down.

Amadeo hit a crisp three iron to the green and the ball rolled to rest a few yards to the right of the pin.

Manston waited for Irina and Bernice and walked with them to the green. His girl caddy came with them and they stood on the edge of the road. He took his nine iron and walked across the green and down the slope. Amadeo stood on the edge of the green to give him a line to the green. Manston played a pitch from a tricky lie and saw Amadeo nod down to him, approving a good shot. He began to clamber up the slope to the green. This, he thought, was a hole he was going to lose. Amadeo was too damned good. Amadeo, on the edge of the green, watched him climb up. Then, when he was only a few feet from Amadeo, Manston saw the man's eyes suddenly looking past him. In that moment Amadeo leapt for him, driving his shoulder against him and both of them went to the ground. As he fell, Manston heard the sound of a rifle-shot; and, as he rolled, there came another shot and the ground a foot away from him burst into a plume of dust. Manston rolled away, got his hand into his back pocket and pulled out his automatic. In those few seconds his mind worked sharply and quickly. The shots had come from the wood below and Amadeo must have seen something, the flash of a barrel which had given him a split second's grace to save, as far as he knew, himself or Manston. Manston flattened himself and pumped three shots into the edge of the wood. Over their noise he heard Casalis and Guyon shouting and then some way in the wood glimpsed briefly the figure of a man running. The next moment Casalis and Guyon were past him, running down the slope. Amadeo pulled himself to his feet, gave Manston a quick look to see that he was all right, and then followed the other two.

Manston got to his feet and instinctively began to run after them; but before he had gone ten yards he heard a noise behind him, and the sound bit into his brain, waking his imagination. He checked himself and turned and began to go up the slope as fast as he could. . . . As he came level with the green he saw that he was too late.

On the far side of the green Bernice was picking herself up from the rough track. A haze of dust rose from the roadway and Manston saw a car moving away into the pine trees that bordered the track, its engine racing. There was no sign of Irina. The two girl caddies stood stupefied, immobile, at the edge of the green.

*

The next hour was something which Manston was never to forget. From the moment of seeing the car disappearing between the trees he reverted, thoroughly and completely and ruthlessly, to the kind of man he had been when work in the service had claimed him entirely. Whatever qualities he had brought back to this job when Sutcliffe had persuaded him to rejoin them temporarily, were nothing compared with the hard, dedicated venom which prompted him now. Casalis, maybe, was the only one who realized fully what had happened to him. Outwardly he was crisp, competent, taking no evasion from anyone. Inwardly he was a volcano, ready to blow his top.

The man who had fired the rifle-shots from the woods was not caught. Casalis and Guyon had soon given that up, their instinct working more tardily than Manston's, and had returned with Amadeo to the fifth green.

Bernice explained what had happened. As the shots had been fired and Casalis and Guyon had disappeared over the edge of the green, the car – which she could only describe as a sort of van, black she was sure – had come out of the pine trees along the track behind them. Two men, their lower faces masked, had jumped out. Irina had been taken by one of them and the other had pushed Bernice brutally to the ground and then gone back to help his friend. Irina had been forced into the back of the van with one man, and the other had driven it away.

The moment she had explained this Manston had ordered Guyon to go as fast as he could back to the club-house and get out a police call and road blocks to try and pick up the van. From the fifth green it would take Guyon ten minutes, at least, to reach the club, and then maybe another half an hour to have the police net operating. Forty minutes, Manston thought. It was a lifetime too long. He shut from his mind the image of Irina. Cursing himself now would help no one. She just had to be found.

From Amadeo, who knew the course well, he learned – waving aside for the moment any attempt at explanation to him – that the track diverged beyond the pine trees. One branch led back to Chantaco, to the villas to the north of the club and so to the main St Jean-Ascain road. The other went northwards on to a road that led to St Pée-sur-Nivelle. Leaving the party, Manston ran down the track to the junction, but it was impossible to tell which way the van had gone. The track was used frequently by the golf-course tractors and grasscutters, and the ground was hard, marked in places with smooth layers of rock.

Eventually he rejoined the party and they hurried back to the club-house. Here, Guyon had already put the secretary into the picture, as much as he felt wise, and had commandeered a room with a telephone. The police were already moving into position.

Manston took charge. The girl caddies could add nothing to Bernice's descriptions and were dismissed. Amadeo and Bernice were held and Manston had Amadeo brought in alone.

Amadeo explained why he had taken the action he did. He was shaken and confused and Manston gave him enough details to impress on him the urgency of the affair.

'I saw the sun on a rifle barrel . . . what I did then was instinctive. I thought it was for me really. I've been in trouble with the O.A.S. and had threatening letters. You see —'

'Never mind that. You jumped to save my life.'

'Yes.'

'All right. Now – the typewriter in your house. Who uses it beside yourself?'

'The typewriter, but what has that —'

'Just answer. Who uses it?'

'Well, I don't very often. Friends do. I mean, anyone can walk into my place. Saint-Amand types some articles on it occasionally and —'

'Casalis,' Manston turned to him. 'Get the police to pick up Saint-Amand and Claudine. We're going to crash this bloody thing through. It's the only way.' He turned back to Amadeo. 'You know nothing about kidnapping, grabbing people who've left Russia for Europe and shipping them back from somewhere around here? Nothing about a secret rock chamber where they're held?' He flung it at Amadeo, watching him.

'Good God, no.'

'You're a liar!'

Amadeo's face reddened and he made a move towards

Manston. Manston, who had watched him closely, suddenly shook his head.

'I apologize. I don't think you are. Now then – how many people knew you were going to play golf with me today? This thing was organized beforehand. Kill me, make a diversion and grab Irina. Who knew?'

'No one except Bernice. I asked her to come along.'

'Get her in, Casalis.'

Bernice was brought in. The question was put to her. Had she told anyone that she was coming to Chantaco?

'No . . . Amadeo telephoned me, inviting me. I came without saying anything to anyone at the château. They were all going out on a pigeon shoot. Oh, wait a minute. . . . Yes, as I was coming through Sare I saw Lottie Aspender in the square. I pulled up to talk to her and I said that I was going to watch Amadeo and you play golf.'

'What time was that?'

'About half-past twelve. Just before I went to Amadeo's house to meet him.'

'I want the Aspenders,' said Manston to Casalis, but while he could not ignore them he felt that it was unlikely that they could have organized this since just after mid-day. Claudine, too, had seen him on the practice-ground and now was no longer at the club . . . she could have had time to tell her father, just time for this to be organized.

Within the hour the police brought in the Aspenders and the Saint-Amands. Guyon had the St Jean *commissaire de police* out to join Manston and the two groups were questioned. Saint-Amand admitted that he had used Amadeo's typewriter now and then. Claudine had come home but had not mentioned anything about golf. With the Aspenders it was the same. Lottie Aspender had not mentioned her meeting with Bernice to her husband.

Listening to them, watching their faces, Manston realized that they all looked confused, not seeming to understand what all this was about . . . and realized, too, that if any one of them was guilty the same reaction would be assumed for protection. There was nothing that could be pinned on these people. But somebody had known that he was going to play golf with Amadeo, somebody had had time to organize this. Who had known that he was going to play golf . . . ?

Suddenly he stood up. There was somebody else.

He called to Casalis to follow him. Leaving Guyon and the *commissaire* in charge of Amadeo and the others, Manston went out to the car park.

Getting in the car he said, 'There's one other person who could have known I was going to play golf. The dowager countess's priest was talking to me when Amadeo came up. He could have heard. Where does he live?'

'In a small house near the château,' said Casalis. 'I came across it when we were checking for the barn.'

'What's his name?'

'Dorat. Father Dorat.'

'Well, we're going to have a chat with him.'

*

There had been nothing Irina could do. There had not even been time for her to cry out. She had seen Amadeo lurch forward and had thought he had slipped. The following rifle-shots had just been a confusion to her for at this moment she had heard the sound of the van behind her. After almost knocking her over, it had pulled to a stop and a man had jumped from the cab and caught her, clamping his hand over her mouth and swinging her up in his arms. Briefly she had seen the other man attack Bernice, and then she was being bundled into the back of the van with the man pushing her flat and holding her down as the van drove off. He had held her like that, while the van had jolted at high speed along the rough track. Eventually, she had felt the van strike smooth roadway and then the man had released her. As she had sat up she had seen that they were on the Ascain road, just passing the golf club-house and moving towards Sare. A scarf was wrapped around her eyes and tightened, and then her hands were jerked behind her and bound together.

From then on she had been in the dark with only the van's motion to give her any idea of where they were going. The van slowed once and the horn was blown in three short blasts. From somewhere ahead another car answered with three blasts. Then the van put on speed.

Neither of the men spoke. She sat there, too concerned with what might have happened to Richard to be frightened for herself, the memory of those moments by the fifth green coming back clearly to her. The rifle-shots must have been fired at Richard as he came up the slope. Two shots. She had been unable to see him. There was an agony in her at the thought that he might have been killed. She shut her eyes against the thought. Oh, God, no . . . please not that! For half an hour she was in the van. She had a good idea where they might be taking her, and, as she thought about it, she remembered how she and Richard had made this trip together . . . Suddenly she felt the van swing away and begin to bump and jolt over rough ground as it left the main road. Where was this place, she wondered . . . this turning off the main road which led to the rock chamber? The whole area had been searched by Richard and his colleagues without success.

The van halted and the whole programme was gone through again. In darkness she was lifted out of the back of the van. On either side of her a man took her arms and she was hurried along between them. The wooden bridge . . . the stone steps . . . the path across bracken . . . the feeling of hard stones under her feet and the sudden chill of losing the sunlight.

A few moments later her blindfold was taken off and her wrists freed, and she was facing the open door of the rock chamber grille. The men pushed her through, the door was slammed and locked and the two men left her.

From the high roof the light blazed down. She went over

to one of the camp beds and sat down, her face in her hands, a black misery possessing her, dispelling all thought, all feeling, except the anguish of not knowing what had happened to Richard.

*

Half an hour later, in the roof attic of the house owned by the man who called himself Edouard Cadillet, Oleg sat by the transmitter enciphering a message to send to AGRIP. The message read:

Limbo to Agrip
Consignment for re-dispatch recovered. Second consignment still giving trouble. Cancel change-over car arrangements until further notice. Give soonest date for first consignment pick-up.

And, he was thinking, the sooner the date the better. He had no doubts in his mind about the security of the rock chamber, but it would be wise to have the Tovskaya girl away as soon as possible. They would have to use one of the alternative coast pick-up points . . . the steps at Amadeo Grandier's place were out for good. Thinking of Grandier, he cursed him, his face set hard at the memory of Manston, an easy target over his rifle sights. Grandier had spoiled that for him. Now he had to stay on and complete the job. His superiors would not be interested in why he had failed. Success was the only report they would want from him. If Grandier had not acted so quickly, he could now have been on his way to Limoges to meet Ludmilla. His two men – the van, which had been stolen from Cambo, had been abandoned in a quarry – were already on their way out of the district in his own car. He needed no further help from them. To kill a man was not difficult. His mouth firmed angrily as he thought how his neat, original scheme to complete the affair in one swift operation had only half-succeeded.

*

It was five o'lock as they went through Sare. People were sitting in the sun at the café tables and a few boys were playing a pick-up game of pelota against the *fronton* at the top of the square. Manston, sitting alongside Casalis who was driving, was deep in black thought. There was a ferment of impatience in him which he held down firmly. They had got together a handful of people and a handful of clues, but, except for the vanished Pierre Salgazza and his brother, they had no one on whom a shred of exact evidence could be laid. Whoever was at the head of Limbo amongst these people could sit tight and deny everything. It seemed that only the discovery of the rock chamber could bring any positive result. Meanwhile, Irina almost certainly would be hidden away in the rock chamber, waiting to be shipped from some new point on the coast. Limbo might do that quickly and then lie low for a while, or they might decide to keep her there for a long time . . . content to wait until the hue and cry died down.

And it would die down, Manston knew that. He had been within a hand's grasp of success in many cases before and had then been baulked. You persisted in the face of defeat, you kept the police on their toes, you tried new lines . . . but in the end you had to give up. The thought that this might happen here sickened him.

They were through Sare now and moving up the valley road towards the Château Longeau-du-Quercy. A mile after they passed the upper drive gate, Casalis turned the car into a side road. The road dipped through woods, crossed a small river by a stone bridge and there on the rising far bank was the house of Father Dorat, a small stone-built place with a slate roof weighted with boulders against the winter gales and snow. It looked like two or three farm cottages that had been converted into one house. There was a small garden, badly kept, in front of it and a lawn at the side dominated by a storm-riven cedar tree. Casalis pulled the car up by the garden gate and a few moments later the two of them were with

Father Dorat in his study. Father Dorat stood by the study window, a square, black figure in his soutane, a friendly, curious smile on his face.

'May I offer you a liqueur. . . . ?' His hand gestured towards a small table which held decanter and glasses.

'We've no time for that, thank you, father,' said Manston. 'Our business is urgent, more urgent than I have time to explain. All we want from you are the answers to some questions.'

Casalis, seeing the blank look on Father Dorat's face, added, 'I am working with the Sûreté, father, and Monsieur Manston is from the English police. Please be absolutely frank in your answers.'

'But, of course . . . any help that I can give, messieurs.'

Manston said, 'Have you ever used the typewriter in Amadeo Grandier's house?'

Father Dorat nodded. 'I have. Some years ago, though. I stayed with him for a while when alterations were being made to these cottages. Sometimes I used the typewriter for sermons and lectures. Why?'

'Never mind the why, father. Now tell me, the other evening when you were talking to me on the terrace of the Château —'

'Ah, yes – about diamonds.' He smiled. 'You are not a diamond merchant, then?'

'Listen,' said Manston curtly, 'while I was talking to you, Amadeo came up and spoke to me and you went away. Did you hear what he said to me?'

Father Dorat frowned briefly, the moment of concentration as a man thinks back, and Manston, watching him, thought how impossible it was to tell anything from a man's face. Innocence was a guard and so was guilt. Just for a moment his hands trembled with impatience.

'Yes, yes, I do,' said Father Dorat. 'He asked you to play golf with him.'

'Good. Now – did you mention that fact to anyone else?'

Father Dorat without hesitation said, 'Yes, yes, I did.'

'To whom?'

'Well, let me think . . . Now, who? I talked to the doctor, and I mentioned it to him. We were talking about you – you understand, since you were a stranger, you and Mademoiselle Tovskaya, you were objects, or persons rather, of interest —'

'Yes, yes, the doctor and who else?'

'I told the doctor and his wife, that's right. She plays a little golf – for her health. Yes, I remember I told them because the doctor had mentioned something about asking Amadeo to go with him to the pigeon shoot today, and I said he would not be free.'

'Could anyone have overheard this talk?'

'No. We were quite alone.'

Manston looked at Casalis. 'You know the doctor?'

'Yes, a Doctor Sellart – we can check on him.'

'Did you mention it to anyone else?' Manston asked the priest. 'Then or later?'

'No . . . no, I'm quite sure I didn't. The fact went right out of my head until you reminded me just now. May I ask why all this is so important?'

'I'm sorry,' Manston shook his head. 'I can't explain that now. But thank you for your help.' He turned to Casalis. 'We've got to follow this. It's the only way. When we know all the people who knew I was going to play golf, then we can get to work on them. We've got to have the whole field to work on.' Manston moved towards the door of the study and Father Dorat slipped ahead of him courteously to open it for the party.

As he pulled the door open a dog came into the room from the small hallway outside. It was a small white mongrel dog, with an elegantly curled tail and a large black patch on its side shaped roughly like the map of Australia. It leaped at Father Dorat, placing its front paws on the folds of his loose soutane. The priest bent and fondled its head absently with one hand.

Manston, ahead of Casalis, stopped dead. For a moment he was back in the barn just after being taken out of the tanker. He could remember the moment vividly, his hands going up to his blindfold, jerking it partly upwards, the instant of shadowed daylight, the earth-packed barn floor and, for a second or two before a pair of hands clamped on his stopping the half-completed movement, the dog standing on the ground, looking upwards . . . the same curly tail and colouring, and the black patch which, in that fraction of time, had registered itself as shaped like the map of Australia.

Suddenly, coldly, the tension in Manston hardened, and he was emotionless, his brain ice-clear, a string of consequences and deductions striking his mind like plangent anvil strokes.

Slowly he put his hand over Father Dorat's and closed the door. With his other hand he pressed the priest back into the room.

'Casalis,' he said, 'stand by the window.'

Casalis did as he was told and Father Dorat watched them, puzzled, and then said, 'Monsieur Manston?'

'Stay exactly where you are, Father Dorat,' said Manston evenly.

The dog sat at the priest's feet and looked up at him, whining gently.

Manston said, 'That is your dog?'

Father Dorat nodded. 'Ratoutou? Yes. I have had her for some years. She goes everywhere with me. Is something wrong, monsieur?'

Manston nodded. 'Something is very wrong, Father Dorat.'

'I'm sorry to hear it, my son. Maybe I can help further?'

'Yes, you can, father. You can answer some more questions.'

Manston paused, watching the man's face, and the priest met his eyes frankly, standing with the dog at his feet, his hands slipped into the wide side pockets of his gown.

Casalis said, 'What is this?'

Coldly, his eyes on Father Dorat, Manston said, 'It's a simple matter of this dog.'

'Ratoutou?' Father Dorat looked down at his dog.

For a moment Manston said nothing. He'd been given a break. The first real break and, momentarily, he was debating how to handle it; with finesse or brutality. The thought of Irina alone, scared, in the rock chamber decided him.

Sharply, Manston said, 'Father Dorat – have you ever heard of AGRIP?'

'AGRIP? What is that, my son?'

'I think you know, father.'

'I'm sorry. It means nothing to me.'

'You're lying.'

Father Dorat's face stiffened.

'You're lying, father,' Manston repeated. 'You know all about AGRIP, and the man called Oleg who runs it.'

He was watching the priest's face but now only confusion showed there. He went on, hammering at him; 'An organization that kidnaps Russian citizens abroad and takes them back to Russia. You know about that, don't you?'

'No, my son.'

'You do!' Manston cracked the words at him. 'Miss Tovskaya was kidnapped by them and so was I. Somewhere around here is a subsidiary organization called Limbo which ships these people off. You know all about this, father!'

Father Dorat shook his head, but Manston fancied he caught the small grey shadow of anxiety in his eyes. He plugged on.

'Yes, you do, father. I've seen your dog before. The night we were brought down here. We were taken into a rock chamber where you keep these people. You're the go-between here for Limbo and AGRIP.'

'This is nonsense!' For the first time indignation marked the priest's voice.

'No, it's not.' Manston moved close up to the priest looking him hard in the eyes. He had to batter him now, break him down. 'No protesting will help you. We're going to search this house. Somewhere we'll find your means of communication with AGRIP. In the roof? But before we even bother to do that, you're going to talk. Listen —' Manston gripped the priest's arm, his face taut, no pity in him – 'you're mixed up in a filthy business, and we're under no obligation to be any more particular in our methods than you. We're going to make you talk. It's easy, you know. The two of us – and just you. Now – think! AGRIP, Oleg, the S.S. *Lupka*, Capa, Taru . . .' Manston flung the words at him. 'Think. Do you talk? Or do we make you talk?'

'I protest. This is —'

Manston grabbed the front of the priest's soutane and forced him back against the book-lined wall.

'Don't protest – talk! The rock chamber? Meetings with Oleg when he stays at the Royal Gascogne in Bordeaux. I'll bet you don't wear priest's clothes when you go to meet him there. Talk fast, because you're one wearer of this cloth that I don't have to respect. Talk!'

He shook the man hard. His head thudded against the books behind him and Manston saw the quick movement of panic darken the priest's eyes. As it did so, he felt the man's right arm move, the hand deep in the pocket of his soutane. Manston grabbed at the lower part of the man's arm and twisted him violently sideways, flinging him to the floor. Before Father Dorat could make any move Manston was on him, jerking the right hand from the soutane pocket. He stood back, a small automatic in his hand.

Manston tossed it to Casalis and pulled out his own automatic, covering the priest.

'A priest with an automatic instead of a prayer book. But you're going to need prayers now, Father Dorat. Unless you talk.'

From the floor Father Dorat looked up at him and suddenly

the resistance went from him. He pulled himself to his feet ponderously, his head dropped forward and his body seemed to collapse slowly, to shrink up inside his soutane. His head came up and then he said, 'All right . . . I will show you . . .' Then, his voice thick with dejection as he accepted his defeat, he said, 'You need never have had any qualms about striking me, monsieur. Though no one else knows this, I was rejected by the priesthood more years ago than I care to remember. . . .' He put a hand across his eyes and, almost to himself, he said, 'It is that which my lady will never forgive . . . that I have performed the rites without authority. . . .'

He walked across the room and opened a pigeon-hole in his desk. Before he could put his hand in, Manston was at his side, grasping his wrist.

Father Dorat smiled ironically. 'Take it yourself then. It is the main key to the rock chamber.'

Manston reached into the pigeon-hole and brought out the key. It was a heavy, antique-looking affair about eight inches long, the terminal decorated with a wrought-iron design.

Manston moved back and looked across at Casalis. Through the open window behind Casalis came the sound of bird song and the distant echoes of shot-guns firing at the pigeon shoot.

Manston said, 'Watch him, Casalis, as we go. I don't trust him.' He turned to Father Dorat. 'How far is it from here?'

Father Dorat gave a shrug of his shoulders and said, 'We can be there —'

He never completed the sentence. Behind Casalis the open window was darkened suddenly by the bulk of a man's head and shoulders. The swift change in light in the room made Manston swing round. He saw the man's face for a moment, shadowed, vivid, striking into his memory; and then a hand came up. The room burst with the thunder of a shot.

Father Dorat jerked forward, cried out, and then dropped to the floor with a crash. Another shot followed as Manston whipped up his automatic and crashed into the books behind him. Casalis's body reeled across his line of fire and Manston had to jump to one side to get a clear field. He fired as the man at the window ducked and disappeared.

Manston ran to the window, each detail of the room burnt into his mind . . . Father Dorat lying face down on the carpet with half of the back of his head blown away and Casalis struggling to his feet, one hand clamped over his right arm that hung limply at his side.

Casalis shouted, 'Get him ! It's Oleg.'

Manston wriggled through the window and dropped to the ground outside. As he did so he saw Oleg pause near a belt of trees twenty yards away, turn and then fire. The bullet smacked into the stones of the house wall a foot from him. Manston fired back, dived for the run of the garden hedge and saw Oleg disappear into the trees. He went swiftly down the far side of the hedge for cover and then was in the trees. The ground sloped upwards and he could hear Oleg about a hundred yards ahead of him, crashing without regard for caution through the undergrowth. Oleg . . . of course. Oleg. That was why the face had been familiar to him. He remembered the times he had sat with the Limbo file in front of him, studying that face. And Oleg, at the moment when Father Dorat would have shown them all, had killed him and blocked the path to the rock chamber. Only Oleg could now open the way.

Manston went after him, cold with fury. The ground steepened, lost its shrub growth and the chestnut trees, and became pine-studded. Away ahead of him he could catch an occasional glimpse of Oleg. Then the pines disappeared and they were out on the open hillside, smooth turf, boned with grey thrusting rock shoulders, and wide sweeps of bracken and juniper bushes. An icy passion in him, Manston forced himself hard, gradually eating up the distance between them, determined now to stop for nothing, but to go in, risk shot for shot and get his hands on the man . . . to make him talk, to beat from him what he wanted to know.

After a mile there was less than eighty yards between them and Oleg was still going strong, racing up the great bluff. He halted twice, waited a few seconds for Manston and pumped shots back at him, but they went wide and Manston held his own fire. But it was a good sign; the hint of desperation in Oleg. A moment's thought would have shown a cooler man that he could not turn from frantic running and hope to fire accurately.

Ahead of him the ridge of the bluff was dark against the bright sky, boulders throwing long shadows across the turf from the lowering sun.

Oleg disappeared over the crest and a few moments later Manston topped it himself. As he came free of the ridge he checked himself and dived sideways into the cover of a long slab of rock. A bullet shattered the rock face a foot from him, the shards of stone singing away viciously.

Oleg was standing fifteen yards from him, his body blocked by the slanting, misshapen trunk of a stunted oak tree. Behind him the scarp face of the bluff went down steeply through a fall of loose scree and stones. Another bullet thudded into the turf a yard behind him as he crawled along the rock slab to deeper cover.

Neither of them was going any further. He knew that. And for the moment he was at a disadvantage. He did not want to kill Oleg. But Oleg had no such inhibitions.

Oleg had dropped to a crouch now behind the bole of the tree. Manston crawled farther along and found a break in the rock through which he could safely see the man. He lay for a moment getting his breath back, letting his pumping lungs ease down and his muscles settle.

There was no doubt in his mind what he was going to do. This was no time for finesse, any more than it had been with Father Dorat. He was going to go in hard at Oleg, firing as he went, keeping Oleg down and – he had known it work before – flustering him. He gave himself a minute to steady down. Oleg fired twice more and Manston nodded to himself approvingly. Go on, he told him silently, waste your fire. It couldn't be unlimited. In a few moments he was going to have his hands on him . . . he felt the hot temper of desire for that moment blaze through him. Deliberately he checked the rounds left in the magazine of the 9 mm. parabellum Browning pistol which Casalis had provided for him at the Villa Ixas-Atou. He had fired three shots on the golf-course and two at Father Dorat's. He had eight shots left in the thirteen-round magazine.

He counted ten slowly to himself . . . it was good to feel the moment of *Go* coming up. . . . Then he was on his feet and charging towards the tree, firing as he went, firing, not at Oleg, but pumping his rounds into the ground a foot in front of the tree bole, the dust and earth and small stones bursting up in a wild fan which he knew must put Oleg off. Oleg fired back. Something tugged at the looseness of his jacket. A bullet whipped past his head, but he kept on, charging across the open space, the pistol barking as he went.

He saw Oleg stand, jump wide of the tree, stumble a little on the uneven ground; and then the man's firing hand came up. In that moment Manston dived for him. For a few seconds there was no consciousness in him except the shock of their meeting bodies. Oleg reeled backwards and Manston went with him, the pistol dropping from his hand, his fingers searching for a hold on Oleg's throat.

The impetus of Manston's dive took them both to the ground and they rolled over together, their legs thrashing against the turf and bracken. Manston got a grip on Oleg's throat and felt the great body jerk and twist beneath him. A knee came up and drove hard into his stomach and then Oleg's hands were about his throat and the hard bite of fingers fired Manston to fury. He rammed his head forward and crashed his skull into Oleg's face, felt the fingers slacken their hold and then Oleg's body arch and roll under him in tremendous effort.

They both slid sideways and suddenly they were falling, the movement of loose scree and stones roaring in Manston's ears. There was nothing he could do to stop the fall. They went over the steep side together and he hung on to Oleg, feeling now the other man's body take the shock of their rolling, plunging fall; and then his, battered and smashed, as Oleg's weight rammed down upon him. Their momentum increased until a great jolt tore him away from Oleg and he felt himself falling, saw the sudden swift wheeling of the sky above him and then a grey, mottled slide of earth and stones pouring over him like a great water-fall. He fell free through air and thudded hard into the ground, his head jerking backwards and cracking violently against rock. Darkness came clanging down like a steel shutter falling.

Then, he had no idea how much later, the world came reluctantly back to him. He sat up slowly, stiff and dazed, and looked stupidly round. For a moment he struggled to remember what had happened. Why was he here? Away to the south he could see the peaks of Dassoa and Ormantelli, and the air was full of intermittent shotgun fire. To the west, the sun was almost down to the saddle of the Col de Marietta. He put his hand to his face and found blood on it. He reached into his pocket for his handkerchief and felt something hard and cold. With his handkerchief he drew out a large iron key. The sight of the key suddenly brought everything back.

He stood up, wiping his face, and saw Oleg lying a few yards away, his body very still. He looked back and a hundred and fifty feet above could just see the overhanging branches of the oak tree. The fall was steep and, for the last twenty feet, absolutely sheer. He moved slowly towards Oleg, feeling the aching protest of his battered body.

Oleg's face looked up at him, the eyes shut, and one arm was twisted back underneath him in an unnatural way.

Manston dropped to the man's side. He turned the man's face and the big head rolled over like a great weight as though it were no part of the body. Behind his left ear the skull was smashed. Oleg was dead.

Slowly, still fighting to orientate himself, he went through the man's clothes. There was nothing on him of any importance.

As Manston straightened up from the man, a wave of nausea hit him and he sat down on a rock, leaning his head forward on his elbows. The spasm passed but he still sat there. What now? Father Dorat was dead. Oleg was dead. And Irina was locked away in the rock chamber somewhere. Where? All he had was the key. It was in his hand still and he looked down at it. If only the damn thing could speak, he thought stupidly.

Distantly there was a staccato burst of shotgun fire. Then, his eyes on the key, he saw that the wrought-iron decorated terminal was of familiar design. His head was still not entirely clear and he searched for the memory. . . . Hard and sharp, it came to him suddenly. The ironwork was shaped into a winged griffon holding a shield before it, and on the shield were the three scallop shells of the Longeau-du-Quercy arms. . . . He had seen similar devices on top of the pillars of the drive gates . . . Longeau-du-Quercy. . . ? Father Dorat was the dowager countess's priest. Something hammered in his brain for attention. What was it the priest had said. . . ? Slowly the words came back, little noticed at the time, but clamouring for attention now. What had he said about not being a priest? *It is that which my lady will never forgive . . . that I have performed the rites without authority*. My lady! And he had thought then that Dorat was referring to Our Lady – but he wasn't. It was to his mistress, his lady, the dowager countess. It must be. Dorat was her right-hand man. Dorat ran Limbo for her. It must be. And the countess was now the only one who could show him the rock chamber.

He stood up. There was a whirr of wings above him and

a handful of pigeons went slanting down the scarp face to the wooded valley below. Southwards, the shotguns spoke. The pigeon shoot. In another hour the sun would be gone and the shoot finished. But now, the countess was there. He put the key in his pocket and began to work his way southwards along the skirt of the loose scree.

18

IT WAS GONE six o'clock and the sun was dipping rapidly behind the hills. Long shadows were beginning to mould the lower sweeps and hollows of the valleys. Close ahead of him now he could hear loud and clear the noise of the guns, and as he neared the top of the valley he merged with the beaters who were almost at the end of their last sweep. Beyond the trees he could see the hides and the platforms from which the slate-throwers threw their slates out over the valley as the last of the driven birds came upwards. An occasional slate crashed through the trees behind him.

He came out into the open. A hundred yards ahead of him was the tall stone tower of the dowager countess Estelle Longeau-du-Quercy. He went up through the browning bracken, some of it already cut in places and stacked for winter bedding, and behind the tower the sun gilded the chestnut and beech trees.

Nobody took any notice of him as he came to the foot of the run of wooden ladders that led to the top of the tower. He climbed up stiffly, his face set hard, no mercy in him, only one cold, imperious resolution. He had to take Irina from the rock chamber.

He came out on to the rear of the open wooden platform.

The countess was there and close behind her were two loaders. One of the loaders turned and saw him but said nothing. The countess in her long-skirted suit, the pheasant tail in her hat touched by the late breeze, picked off a couple of birds that came drifting over, side-slipping away from the main valley. She handed her gun back and took another from her loader; and she did not see Manston. A handful of birds, close-crowded, dipping in panic, came over the trees from the left. The countess fired one barrel and then the other, quickly. Manston saw the evening sky go grey and white with the featherbursts. The birds fell, plunging a hundred feet below to the foot of the tower where the ground fell away sharply, studded with rocks that showed through the brown bracken.

The countess turned with her gun, and this time she saw Manston. For a moment she looked at him without speaking. Then she stood up slowly and faced him, her old hands caressing the smooth wood of the gun stock.

'Monsieur?' Her voice was full of cold authority.

Manston, his voice harsh, hiding none of the loathing he felt for her, said, 'Father Dorat is dead. Killed by Oleg from AGRIP. Oleg, too, is dead. Before Father Dorat died he confessed.' He held up the key. 'Limbo is finished. You must come with me.'

She said nothing. She looked at him without any emotion and behind her the last of the birds went over. The two loaders moved awkwardly to one side of the platform. Then, her voice hardly audible, she said, 'Father Dorat is dead?'

'Yes, dead.'

She raised a hand and crossed herself, her head dropping for a moment and then coming up quickly. She looked at him now, autocratic, fearless.

'And I am to come with you?' There was contempt in her voice.

'It is the only thing you can do.'

She shook her head. 'No.' She half turned her head and

looked down the valley. Then, more to herself than to Manston, she said, 'These lands have been in my family for generations. Despite our growing impoverishment I have always refused to sell even one hectare. Our land, our name . . . these I had to preserve, and for this I would have done anything.'

Manston, moving impatiently, said, 'You will have plenty of time to explain. Come.'

She gave him an angry look then, and said quickly, 'Do you imagine that I intend to involve myself in tedious explanations? What I have done, I have done. Father Dorat and I between us. Nobody else knows . . . not even that fool of a son of mine or his loose wife. God help them both now.' She looked at her two loaders and, ignoring Manston, said to them, 'No matter what this man says later, remember you are my servants and you will speak the truth that I give you. I do not want any trouble with the Church, no vulgar talk of suicide —' She reached out and took a loaded gun from one of them and swung it round on Manston. Looking at him, but still speaking to the men, she went on, 'You will say that in standing up to make a difficult shot, I slipped and fell.'

Before Manston could move, she turned swiftly, raised the gun blindly and fired it into the air; and then she stepped off the platform.

Manston rushed to the edge of the platform. He was just in time to see her body hit the ground far below, jerk upwards, roll and fall, and then lie still, half-hidden by the bracken.

*

For the next half-hour, as the dusk fell, Manston lived in a cold fury of frustration. He was hard, callous, unaccommodating. His mind held room only for Irina; Irina, towards whom his every step had been blocked. He cursed himself for giving the countess a chance to kill herself. He'd been a fool . . . a thousand times a bloody fool. And, while the turmoil beat within him, he went icily through the things that had to be done. He sent the two loaders down for the body of the countess, and he cut sharply, disregardingly, through the questions of the rest of the shooting party, brushing them aside, taking command; grim, brooking no interference.

The men made a stretcher for the body and it was carried along the mountain path back to the frontier post at the Col de Marietta. Here, at the café-restaurant, it was put into the countess's car, blanketed in the back seat.

And now one of the loaders drove the car and Manston, silent, shrouded in his own black thoughts, sat alongside him as they made their way back to the château. And all the way down the two-mile stretch of road to the top drive entrance Manston hammered at the problem. Where was Irina?

Surely, if Dorat and the dowager countess had run Limbo between them, with the Salgazza brothers and maybe a couple more of her men or tenants to help, the rock chamber must be on her estate? So it might be, but it was an old and large estate. It might be some hiding-place that was a secret known only to her and the priest. She had said that Aristide knew nothing of Limbo. Irina might remain locked up for ever, lost . . . the days going by, hope withering. . . . He shut his eyes at the thought.

At the bend in the road ahead the drive gates appeared, the stone pillars topped by their shield-bearing griffons. He looked up at them as they swung smoothly in off the main road. Sharply, piercing through his concern a small bell began to ring in his mind. Why? Why? Then, dragged up by the fury of his desire to find Irina it came. . . . There had been no break in their progress. *No break in their progress* . . . the phrase hammered into his mind. He sat forward, tersely, watching the sides of the drive as they moved towards the house. Of course . . . fool again, fool, fool, it could be that! They'd searched everywhere for a rutted track off a main road. They'd never thought of a rutted track off a driveway on to which they could have turned without being aware that they had left the main road. It could be . . . it could be. He watched the drive side, but it was fringed all the way up to the house with shrubs and trees, no break, no track leading from it.

Then, as they entered the broad courtyard and the driver began to slow down, Manston said fiercely, 'Go straight on down the lower drive.'

'But, monsieur. . . .'

'Do as I say, damn you! Straight on!'

The man swung the wheel and the car swept on down the lower drive. It was the longer of the two sections of drive and a quarter of a mile down it Manston said sharply, 'Stop here!'

As the man pulled up he jumped out and there was a sudden lifting of hope in his heart. To the left, off the driveway, a track led away through a field. He began to run up it and, as he turned the corner of a coppice, he saw the barn ahead of him. He ran now, pelting along. Yes, there it was to the right of the barn, a rising path through pine trees. He tore along the path and now, clear for him to see, were all the things which he remembered from his blindfold walk. The small wooden bridge over a stream, the stone steps and then a path over bracken and heather. In front of him was the steep slope of a wooded hill and against the foot of the hill was a small chapel, built back into the rock which showed in grey crags through the trees. The path he was on led away from the main door. Another path to his left snaked away up to the hidden château. He followed this rough path across the chapel yard and there, in the side of the building, was a low, squat door with a great lock on it. He pulled the key from his pocket and in a few seconds was inside. He was in a pillared and stone-vaulted crypt. The walls were solid all around him. But at the far end stood a tall, old-fashioned cupboard, its open shelves untidy with dusty altar vases and ornaments. Manston grabbed at the side of the cupboard and pulled it towards him. It had to be this. The cupboard refused to move. Then he got to one side of it and pushed it and, to his relief, it slowly slid along the wall revealing a dark passage-way, about six yards long. Just inside the passage-way a bunch of keys hung on a wooden board. He grabbed them and rushed forward. The end of the passage-way was blocked by a door. He unlocked it and slammed it back. . . .

A blaze of light from the rock chamber burst into his eyes.

'Irina!' he shouted.

He saw her sitting on one of the camp-beds. She turned, and the reflection of the roof light slid over her hair. The next moment she was on her feet, running towards the grille and he was reaching through to her, his hands on her face, her shoulders, her lips against his through the wide bars. Then, as he started to fumble with the keys, working at the grille lock, she sobbed and laughed and called to him.

The grille door opened and she was in his arms.

*

The last message which Ludmilla Miachin ever sent from AGRIP was five days later. It was a straight, uncoded message to Moscow and read:

Body of former AGRIP member, Oleg, will be dispatched tomorrow, Le Bourget, Tupolev Flight Ten. Inform relatives death due to hunting accident.

It was the last message of the day and, when it was done, she began to clear out her desk before going up to her room to pack. The next day, while Oleg went back to Moscow, Moscow which had always been in his heart, she would go back to the Embassy. She moved mechanically, not allowing herself too much thought, for thought was only misery. What happened now had no significance. It did not matter what she did, or where she was sent, because for her there did not seem anywhere to go, or anything to do, that would ever lighten the darkness which had settled over her.

*

That was two years ago. Irina Tovskaya never danced again

at Covent Garden. In Kent, one of the farmhouse rooms has been turned into a nursery and soon the swimming pool will have to be fenced to prevent a small child falling into it. The young hopbines snake up their supports each spring, there is golf at Rye, people to dinner and bridge parties; and, sometimes, on a warm summer's evening the mist-draped surface of the pool is shattered as they dive together. The marauding moorhens at the far end half-run, half-wing their way back to the stream and Manston turns on his back and sees the dark, wet hair of Irina and the pale oval of her face close to him.

IN THE UNIFORM EDITION BY

VICTOR CANNING

BLACK FLAMINGO

DELAY ON TURTLE

A DELIVERY OF FURIES

THE DRAGON TREE

THE HOUSE OF THE SEVEN FLIES

MR. FINCHLEY DISCOVERS HIS ENGLAND

MR. FINCHLEY GOES TO PARIS

MR. FINCHLEY TAKES THE ROAD

PANTHERS' MOON

THE SCORPIO LETTERS

THE WHIP HAND

YOUNG MAN ON A BICYCLE

"Victor Canning is one of the world's finest story-tellers." James Gordon, *Good Housekeeping*

"as a thriller-writer Canning seems to be getting better and better."

The Times Literary Supplement

Also by

VICTOR CANNING

THE MELTING MAN

"A long, complicated, exciting and brightly written thriller by a master of the art with an international setting and a whole gallery of good characters."
Guardian

QUEEN'S PAWN

"Mr. Canning has created a thoughtful, engrossing, splendidly effective thriller, with a remarkable climax when a ton of gold bullion is stolen from the *QE2's* Specie Room during her maiden voyage."
Sunday Times

THE GREAT AFFAIR

"As a thriller-writer Canning seems to be getting better and better, and *The Great Affair* is a stunningly enjoyable and original job . . . enjoyability of top order."
The Times Literary Supplement

FIRECREST

THE RUNAWAYS